BECAUSE I WANT YOU

A ROMANTIC SUSPENSE NOVEL

CLAIRE

NEW YORK TIMES BESTSELLING AUTHOR

CONTRERAS

Copyright © 2022 by Claire Contreras

All rights reserved.

ISBN: 978-0-9995844-0-8

No part of this book may be reproduced in any form or by any electronic or mechanical means, including information storage and retrieval systems, without written permission from the author, except for the use of brief quotations in a book review.

Edited by: Liza Tice
Proofread by: Gina Licciardi
Formatted by: Champagne Book Design
Cover Design: Hang Le

to the rulebreakers

PREFACE

Dear reader,

This book contains dark themes. While they're not explicit (de-tailed) scenes, they may be triggering for you. The characters in the book are victims of an armed home invasion/shooting. While it is mostly talked about in the story and not shown, if you've been involved in a shooting or robbery, please take care reading this.

Much love,

Claire

BECAUSE I WANT YOU

A ROMANTIC SUSPENSE NOVEL

CHAPTER ONE

THE MASSACRE HAPPENED ON A TUESDAY.

Seven days later, we were all burying loved ones. Shortly after that, we fled the scene of the crime and let new families build dreams where ours had shattered. Before that fateful Tuesday, our cul-de-sac had been tight-knit, families sharing meals, kids riding bikes and walking to school together. If a complete outsider dropped by during dinner, they would have seen a beautiful mix of cultures blending at the table. It was us (the Vegas), the Marchettis, the De Lucas, the Patels, and the Patriarchas. We'd always felt fortunate to share a block with those names. After all, they practically owned Providence, which ensured no one fucked with us. Until they did, in the worst imaginable way.

Dad ripped us out of there with such force that it took a couple of years for our roots to attach to new land. Since the move, he'd preached so much about wrongdoings that I thought he had cleaner hands than a surgeon about to walk into the O.R., but of course, I'd been wrong. I wasn't sure if all of the warnings he'd given were for my brother's and my sake, or his own. Maybe to talk himself out of whatever he was thinking about getting into. The reason didn't matter anymore, since his own warning didn't resonate enough in himself. They say children shouldn't have to pay for their parents' sins, but all of us who grew up in that cul-de-sac knew better. We knew it was only a matter of time before someone knocked on the door to collect some kind of favor, or in Dad's case, money he'd borrowed.

I hadn't seen Gabriel De Luca in ten years before he waltzed into the club where I was currently paying my father's dues. Time had done him well, at least physically. He looked like he'd walked right off the pages of *GQ Magazine: Wall Street Edition*. He'd been my first boyfriend and first kiss, but our relationship was cut short prematurely. When we reconnected a few weeks ago, it was as if no time had passed at all. Not in a fairy tale, love at first sight sort of way. Sparks didn't fly, and butterflies didn't flutter, but there was a bond, a kinship. The kind only a person who'd survived the same trauma could understand. Some would say it was kismet that he ended up working as the accountant for the man who owned the club where I was bartending, but because Tommy Costello was the owner, and Gabe De Luca was, well, a *De Luca*, I'd call it inevitable. It wouldn't have mattered, us sharing this boss, if not for the fact that I'd poured my heart out to Gabe about everything from how I'd ended up working for Tommy in order to clear my dad's debt to him, to some of the personal things I'd overheard Tommy talk about in his office. Gabe hadn't stepped foot here since that night, and while some may call that a coincidence, I knew better. I'd seen the way the bouncers practically dragged him out of here and put him in the back of an Uber. To make matters worse, he wasn't answering my calls or texts, and I had no idea who to turn to about this. The only person who could possibly know his whereabouts was his brother, but I'd been careful not to ask about *that* De Luca. Besides, Gabe told me they'd moved to Italy to be with their father when they left Providence. I was sure his brother had managed to take over the entire boot by now.

"Your hands are shaky today." Ruth's voice cut through my thoughts over the music. She was the best mixologist in here, so of course, she'd notice everything about the way my untrained self made shitty drinks.

"I know." I wiped my hands on the rag hanging in front of me.

"Nervous?"

"No." My eyes swept the entire VIP area. "I don't know."

"Because of you know who?" she asked, shooting me a concerned look.

"No." I shook my head and picked up the bottle of champagne to deliver to one of the tables in VIP.

That was the thing about working a bar; the people mixing and pouring the drinks paid attention to everything. *Everything.* On my way to the section, I spotted Reid, the man Gabe was always accompanied by. Reid had been here all of their usual nights sans Gabe, drinking his overly expensive bourbon that I swore he only ordered to show off that he could afford it. As I walked over, I noticed that Gabe was nowhere in sight again. The smile he was directing at the woman in front of him grew when he saw me and let his eyes trail up and down my body. I held my head high as I stood in front of him.

"What's up, Rosie?" he asked, shouting over the music.

"Work, as usual." I smiled. "Where's Gabriel? I haven't seen him in a while."

"I should be asking you that question." His brows rose.

My smile slipped. "What do you mean?"

"He hasn't been in the office all week. I figured maybe you knew why." He gave a wink. I stared at him. His eyes were all shifty, the way they got after he'd just done a line. I clenched my fists at my sides.

"How would I know why?" I shouted, and it had nothing to do with the loud music. "You're his friend!"

"Aren't you two . . . you know." He winked.

Of course he thought that. Because I paid extra attention to Gabe, everyone thought we were fucking. I hadn't bothered to correct them or tell them that we'd known each other since we were kids. This was a temporary job, so I really didn't care if they thought I was screwing the regulars. My real job, the one I had before this mess, was as a soloist dancer at the city ballet. I was on the cusp of getting a promotion to principal dancer when this went down. Besides, letting people think I was screwing Gabe was better than the reality, which was that the owner's sleazy brother, Anthony Costello, was the last one who had the privilege and the one who was constantly sexually harassing me just because he knew he could.

"He hasn't been in touch," I shouted.

"Oh. Well, then he's probably just out of town on business," he said, leaning in closer. "Sometimes he goes out of town to visit clients and forgets to tell us."

"Oh." I frowned. *Wouldn't he have access to his phone, though?* "Yeah, that could explain it."

"I'll let him know you asked about him."

I nodded and waved as I walked back to the bar. Normally, because it was so loud and fast-paced, it was easy for me to tune out thoughts I could easily obsess over. It wasn't working tonight. I tried to recount every single conversation I'd had with Gabriel since he started coming in here. I'd said too much. I shouldn't have told him about Tommy's accounts or about Dad owing him money. I definitely wished he hadn't seen the way Anthony manhandled and groped me in the hall last week. Gabe didn't ask about it though. He'd just offered me a sad, sympathetic smile, and that might've been worse than asking because, behind the smile, I saw the pity.

I had no idea what his brother was up to, but Gabe became a hot-shot accountant and was obviously rolling in money, so he probably saw me working here as a step down from the life he led. It was bullshit and unwarranted. Bartending was a demanding job, a necessary job. I hated the way people looked at us as if they were superior because it was their credit cards we were swiping. I added calling him out on his superiority complex to the list of things I was going to address when I saw him again.

"Yo, Rosie," Ruth called out above the music. I looked over as she nodded at the dance floor. "Your lover boy is here."

My head whipped in that direction and sure enough, Gabe was walking up the stairs. I studied him as closely as I could from a distance and the poor lighting of the club. He had a light beard he never had before that made him look rugged. It wasn't just the beard, though. His hair was shorter and the way he walked just exuded confidence. It was unlike him. Normally, his steps were fast-paced, as if he were in a hurry to do something. This gait made heads turn in his direction and the crowd part for him to walk through. I wondered if he was high or something. *He had to be, right? How else could I explain this?* The thought made me fume.

"Is it me or does he look hot with facial hair?" Ruth asked next to me.

"It's not you." I threw down the towel in my hand and whipped around the bar at record speed.

Before I could stop myself, I marched over to him, grabbed the lapels of his suit in my fist, and pulled him into the hallway behind the bar. His eyes widened as if he was surprised by my reaction to seeing him after he'd ghosted me all week, and my already boiling blood seemed to reach a tipping point. Before I could stop myself, I lifted a hand and slapped him across the face as hard as I could muster.

"What the fuck was that for?" He set a hand on his face, nostrils flaring.

"Where the fuck have you been?"

"Where do you think I've been?" He eyed me suspiciously, as if I'd been the one to up and disappear and not answer my freaking phone.

"How would I know? You haven't answered my texts or my calls. If you wanted to ghost me, fine, but at least respond when I ask if you're alive!" I growled, then looked away to regain my composure. Each breath I drew brought clarity and made me feel horrible for hitting him. With a deep sigh, I met his gaze again, taken aback at the intensity in it, but I managed to push on. "After everything I told you I just thought, I don't know what I thought. The worst, obviously."

He studied me for what felt like hours before saying, "I've been busy."

"Yeah, I got that part." I laughed shakily, looking away again. "A simple text would have sufficed."

"Hey, what could I have possibly gotten into?" He reached for my hand and that was when the butterflies hit, the spark, the skipping heart. My eyes snapped back to his. If he felt anything, he didn't let it show, but I could've sworn his expression had grown darker. "Rosie. What did you think happened?"

"I don't know." I pulled my arm from his hold and took a step back. "Are you wearing a different cologne?"

"Um, yeah."

"It smells nice."

"Thanks." His smile was fleeting. "What happened last time I was here? I don't remember much of it."

"I wouldn't expect you to, as high out of your freaking mind as you were. That's why I've been so damn worried. They escorted you out and put you in the back of an Uber and then . . ." I shrugged exaggeratedly. "You could've at least answered your phone."

"I lost it that night." He stepped away. "As you can see, I'm here."

"Look." I signaled between the two of us. "I don't know what this is tonight, this sudden shift of energy or whatever, but I'm telling you right now, I won't be with someone who does those kinds of drugs. I draw the line at marijuana. If you want to dabble in other things, fine, but I won't be here, not even as a friend. I can't." I swallowed once I finished my speech.

"Noted." He kept looking at me like he was trying to solve a freaking Rubik's cube. After a second, he took another step back and started turning to leave. "I'll see you around."

"What?" I set my hand on his arm to stop him from leaving. "That's it?"

He arched an eyebrow, eyes dancing. "You have something else in mind?"

"No." I scowled, dropping my hand quickly and crossing my arms.

"Hey." He tilted my chin to meet his eyes. *Was he taller tonight?* "You don't have to worry about me, Rosie."

With that, he left, and I was left frozen, looking at the expanse of his back as he went downstairs and disappeared into the sea of people dancing. That was weird all around, but at least he was safe.

CHAPTER TWO

Dominic

THERE'S A CODE BETWEEN BROTHERS. I SHOULD KNOW, I HAVE A lot of them.

Don't lie.

Don't steal from each other.

Don't fuck each other's women (without permission).

This particular situation made that last one a little less black and white since my brother, the one who shared a womb with me, failed to tell me that the bartender he'd been visiting there was Roselyn Vega. Of course, the motherfucker wouldn't tell me that. Why would he, when he knew exactly what I would do had I known she was in the same city as us? It had been ten years, but we both knew if we ever saw her again and she was single, she was fair game. We hadn't said that, but it was another unwritten understanding between us.

I'd never been jealous of Gabe about anything. Not his good grades, not his ability to juggle school and sports easily, not even the way Mom laughed extra loud at his lame jokes. The only thing he'd ever had that I'd ever been jealous of was Rosie. I wasn't a selfish asshole, I didn't go around lusting after any of my brothers' girlfriends or wives, but Rosie was the exception to the rule. We'd known her since we were kids, but something happened between the ages of fourteen and sixteen that made me really start to notice her. When I told my brother about the crush I had, his response was, *"She's saving herself for marriage. Leave her alone."*

Because I hadn't yet gotten laid but knew I wasn't going to

wait until marriage, and I respected Rosie, I decided not to pursue her. Not even two weeks later, she was Gabriel's girlfriend. Even after all these years, my jaw clenched just thinking about all of it. I never outright told him I held that against him, but he knew. It didn't help that I acted like a total asshole whenever Rosie came over for dinner or to watch a movie with him. That was ten years ago, though, and his hiding Rosie from me was just one more thing to add to the list I was pissed off at him about. First, he led me into Costello territory, then, he led me to Rosie, and lastly, *he was doing hard drugs*? I couldn't even choose which of those made me more upset.

"Is that all?" Gio prompted from across the table after hearing everything I had to say, from my brother's voice message, which I'd played twice now, to the club, to Rosie.

The guys in this room were my brothers. My ride-or-die family. The ones I didn't share a parent with, but would lie, steal, and cheat for me if I asked them to. People called us criminals, gangsters, but somehow the men in this room were more trustworthy than anyone else I'd ever met. Including my twin brother.

"What else do you want?" I asked.

"Do you think it's wise for you to look after this woman, considering she's involved with Costello?" Loren asked.

"You heard what he said. He told me to 'find her and look after her'," I said, mimicking my brother's voice, with air quotes. "What the hell am I supposed to do, ignore him?"

"I can't believe he didn't tell you about her," Rocco said, smirking. I shot him a look in hopes to make him shut up, but I knew he wouldn't.

"Why would he tell him about her?" Lorenzo asked.

"What are we missing?" Gio added, frowning.

"Rosie is his brother's girlfriend," Rocco said, sounding entertained by all of this.

"She's not his girlfriend." I hit the table with my fist because despite myself, the fact that she had ever been pissed me off to this day. Rocco knew that, too, which was why he kept chiding. Besides, I was almost certain she wasn't involved with my brother in any way. Not like that, anyway. Maybe they were acquaintances. Or, maybe I was just reading the situation like that since that was all I wanted them to be. I looked at every guy in the room and added, "It's complicated."

"It's not that complicated." Rocco chuckled. The rest of the guys turned their attention to him. I closed my eyes and counted to ten because even though I loved my best friend and took an oath to protect him, right now, I was liable to kill him. "She was Gabe's high school girlfriend that Dom had a massive fucking hard-on for."

"Good to hear you know how massive my hard-on is, Marchetti." I reached for my drink and took a sip, smirking at him.

"It's a saying, asshole."

"Never heard it." I shrugged a shoulder, enjoying his sudden annoyance, then turned to Dean. "Can you get access to the cameras in his building?"

"I can." Dean nodded.

"You want me to track the last place he used his phone and get the outgoing and incoming calls?" Rocco asked, finally getting back to the issue at hand.

"How?" I finished the last of my drink and set the glass down on the table.

"Use a fucking coaster," Gio muttered, tossing me one from the other side of the table. I caught it with a glare and set my glass over it.

"I know a guy."

"What guy?" Dean leaned back in his seat.

"Just a guy." Rocco took his phone out and started typing something.

"What did the Rosie chick have to say about Gabe's absence?" Dean asked, lighting a cigarette.

We weren't even supposed to smoke at The Place, which is what we called out hang-out spot, but Dean never seemed to bother abiding by that rule. I took a moment, trying to figure out how to explain what happened without looking like a complete asshole, first for wanting my brother's high school girlfriend and now for not telling her who I was.

"Dom." Rocco lowered his phone slowly. "Tell me you didn't."

"Didn't what?" Loren asked.

"He pretended he was Gabriel," Rocco said.

I kept my eyes on the deep scratch running down the round wood table that Gio deemed worthy of coasters. Sometimes I hated that Rocco and I could read each other as well as we did. It made it impossible to keep secrets. Dean and Gio started laughing at the same time, and Loren soon followed. I rolled my eyes, still not looking at any of them.

"I'm going to tell her," I said finally. "I was just focused on finding out what happened to Gabe."

"What do you think happened?" Dean asked.

"I don't know. That's why I went there."

"In a three-piece suit?" Loren eyed me suspiciously.

"I wanted to get a real reaction out of the people who were used to seeing him."

"How'd that work out for you?" Rocco asked.

I sat back in my chair with a scowl. What was I supposed to say? That Rosie slapped me and I stood there and took it—when in reality I wanted to grab her by the wrist, turn her around, and push her tits against that wall so I could play out all of my teenage fantasies? *Fuck.* I ran a hand over my face. Everything in my life was finally coming together. Even if Gabe was safe, an appearance from Roselyn Vega was the last thing I needed right now. The last nine months had been a whirlwind for all of us with all of the changes that transpired. The men in this room were now *the* bosses of organized crime. At the top of the food chain, which was something we'd all wanted, but now we had to do the work to make sure things continued going according to plan. I couldn't afford any distractions right now, and Rosie was the ultimate distraction.

"Maybe he's on a trip and lost his phone," Gio said.

"If that's the case, why would he leave that voice message?" I pointed at my phone, sitting at the center of the table.

"I'll get the camera feed," Dean said, putting out his cigarette in the ashtray as he stood. He paused and looked at Rocco. "Was the issue with the Colombians taken care of?"

"I think so. Ferreira didn't specify who he's getting his cargo from, but he doesn't seem to be a threat."

Dean looked at Gio. "What do your cousins say about Ferreira?"

"They say he's a businessman. Fair." He shrugged. "It may not be a terrible idea to build a relationship there if we'd have more access to Colombia. For the coffee, not the coke," he specified.

"Got it." Rocco gave a nod. My mind drifted back to my brother, to Rosie, to the incredibly weird situation I was finding myself in right now.

"You good, Dom?" The question came from Loren.

"Yeah." *No, I fucking wasn't.*

"Who else does Gabe do accounting for?" Loren asked.

"A lot of people, including the Costellos."

"Tommy's the brains behind that operation," Gio said. "Does he know you're Gabe's brother?"

"I mean . . ." I let out a short laugh. There were a lot of differences between me and my brother. I was an inch taller, full of tattoos, and had about twenty pounds of muscle on him, but to someone who didn't really pay attention, we looked identical. "Unless he's a complete moron, he'd put two and two together."

Gio shot Dean and Loren a look and I knew what they were thinking. After Gio killed Silvio Costello, Tommy, who was next in line, had risen to the head of the family, and word on the street was that he was out for blood, specifically ours. Tommy himself never lifted a finger, but like Gio said, he was the brains of the operation. If anyone got their hands dirty, it would be Anthony Costello, the youngest brother, and we'd ramped up security just in case. If they wanted to get to me, though, all they had to do was fuck with my brother. Gabe could take care of himself, but he'd been coddled by all of us, myself included, and didn't know how to handle people like the Costellos.

"We fucked up their businesses, took over all the seats," Gio said. "And Tommy hates Angelo Costello."

"Tommy doesn't like Angelo?" My brows shot up.

Angelo Costello was the boss of all bosses, the head honcho if you will. He also happened to be Lorenzo's father and related to Tommy and Anthony. Technically, Lorenzo having a seat meant that the Costello family in the U.S. was headed by him. They'd worked out some kind of deal with Tommy since Silvio had the seat originally. Technically, Tommy was next in line, but he wasn't Angelo Costello's son. Lorenzo was. That made him more important than just about anyone in the western hemisphere. If we were going based off of our last names and our families back in Italy, Dean would be number one, Lorenzo would be second, I'd be third, Rocco would be fourth and Gio would be last. Because we followed Italian-American rules, that wasn't the case. We also had too much respect for each other to count anyone out and didn't want to step on each other's toes. Our fathers may have said they were brothers, but that was all talk. The five of us were brothers despite hierarchy and last names. We wanted to make this an organization that we could be proud of, that our kids could hold on to after we were gone. This wasn't just business to us. It was family. Legacy.

"My father has a certain way of conducting business," Loren explained. "He's let Tommy think he has control, but it's only a matter of time before he takes it from him, and Tommy knows it."

"I figured he'd be fine with it seeing as Tommy sends a percentage of his earnings to Angelo."

"Tommy's a ticking time bomb." Loren finished his whiskey and set his glass down on the coaster in front of him. "He wants to take him out but hasn't found a way to do it without making a mess."

"Smart man," Dean said.

"I think the word you're looking for is cunning," I said.

Lorenzo smiled as if that was the ultimate compliment. Angelo Costello and my father, Giuseppe De Luca, reaped everyone's benefits without lifting a finger, but no one was going to go against them because of who they were. Those two especially had the ability to ruin your life with the snap of a finger. As far as I knew, Angelo didn't exercise that as often as my father did. Where my father liked to play twisted games, Angelo liked things done in a way that couldn't be traced back to him. That didn't make him any less ruthless, though.

Gio's phone vibrated on the table. He glanced at it, was about to put it down, but decided to answer it at the last minute. He held it to his ear. I wasn't sure if it was Petra or Nadia on the other end of the call, but it had to be one of them, as serious as he looked.

"Give me a moment, P," Gio said, looking directly at me. I waited, stomach clenching, even though I couldn't imagine what his right-hand woman could possibly tell him that involved me. "Tommy's out of the country."

Could Gabe be with him? "Do we still have eyes on him?"

"We do." Gio hung up with Petra and set the phone down. "She says there's talk about him wanting to sell the club." Gio looked around. "Isn't this the place he remodeled to look like Devil's Lair?"

"Oh shit." I frowned, realizing that Tommy's club did

actually remind me of Gio's renowned nightclub, Devil's Lair. "I see it. I mean, it looks like the Walmart version of Devil's Lair, but I see what he tried to do."

"Why would he be selling if he just remodeled?" Gio frowned and picked his phone back up.

"Maybe he remodeled it so that he could sell it," I said.

"Dom, my guy is going to forward you the last few texts that came through before it was shut off," Rocco said, interrupting.

"Thanks." I looked at Gio again as a thought occurred to me. "If someone was interested in buying the club, what would they have to do?"

"Speak to Tommy and have his people send a profit and loss report for the last year."

"So you'd essentially have to speak to Gabriel," I said.

"Yeah. If he's the one who does that, it would be easier to just talk to him."

I would bet money my brother was definitely in charge of that. Tommy would have to be an idiot to not have Gabe do anything and everything involving numbers for him. I looked at my phone again. The camera feed file hadn't finished downloading, but a text did. At first, it was just a phone number, but then a name appeared in the place of the number.

Rosie: I need to talk to you. Come to my place tonight. Make sure you're not followed.

She followed it up with her address, which made me think my brother hadn't gone to her place yet. Yeah, they definitely weren't fucking. Something wasn't adding up and I fully intended to find out what it was.

CHAPTER THREE

"I WISH YOU'D LISTEN TO ME AND GO TALK TO JOHN," YARI SAID across from me. "You know he'd treat you much better than Tommy and Anthony do."

When we moved here, I'd been completely unwilling to open up to anyone, but Yaritza was persistent and stuck around, so I had no choice but to be her friend. She'd tried talking me out of working at Tempt, even after I told her that Tommy was going to ignore the interest rate and just let me pay him back the rest of the money my father owed with the money I made at his club. The entire time I'd been working here, she'd been trying to convince me to work as an escort at the company where she worked, since it promised much higher pay and would help me pay the loan back faster. It sounded great, but according to Dad, Tommy's interest rates were worse than Bank of America's in the eighties.

"You know my schedule sucks." I wiped the glass in my hand before moving on to the next one. "And it's going to get worse as soon as *The Nutcracker* starts."

"Which is why going to see John would benefit you. He'd get you in the company and work around your schedule. You even get to pick who you say yes and no to. There's a whole damn questionnaire you fill out. Trust me, it's better than being here and having to deal with Anthony's slimy hands." She shuddered. "Is *The Nutcracker* still a definite yes?"

"Yep." I tried to fight a smile, but it was impossible. I'd be playing the part of the Sugar Plum Fairy and was nailing every single rehearsal.

"You need to text me the dates so I can come watch you. Maybe I'll convince one of my clients to take me." She winked. I laughed. She grew serious quickly. "Meet with John."

"Doesn't Giovanni Masseria own that club?" I asked, shooting her a pointed look. "You know he's fucked half the ballet company."

"Maybe a few years ago, but not anymore," she said. "He's happily married. Besides, he's never mixed business with pleasure." She shot me a look. She didn't need to add *"unlike Anthony Costello"* but she might as well have.

"Fine." I took a breath. "I'll meet with John, but I'm not promising you I'll quit here. I'm so, so, so close to finishing paying this back, Yari."

"I know, and if you want to keep bartending to come up with the money faster, at least do it at one of their clubs," she said. "John's always looking to hire new people, and it bears repeating that he's not going to try to fuck you just because you're an employee."

I set down the final glass. As long as I was able to get another job quickly, it shouldn't affect my ability to pay the debt or my rent. My father, on the other hand, I wasn't sure about. Anthony threatened to hurt him in the past if I tried to quit, but I wasn't sure how serious he was. What I did know was that I hated who I'd become since this started. I hated looking over my shoulder and living in a constant state of anxiety.

"When can you meet with him?" she asked, typing away on her phone. "Tonight?"

"I can be there after rehearsal."

"Ros." She glanced up. "Are you not going to sleep?"

"I don't work tomorrow, so I'll sleep then."

"You're crazy." She shook her head and went back to her phone, surely texting John. "Can you go tonight at seven?"

"Seven should be fine."

She beamed. "I promise you won't regret getting the fuck out of here."

I smiled back at her, wishing I had half her excitement. In her eyes, my getting out of here would fix all my problems, but I knew better.

I was downing the last of my water when I reached the door to Devil's Lair, where I was meeting John. I opened it and found a man, definitely security, standing on the other side. He glanced up from his phone when he saw me.

"Hi." I smiled. "I'm here to see John Spellman."

"You're Roselyn Vega?"

"Yep."

He gave a nod, his eyes traveling down my body. My shoulders were already rounded back. Otherwise, that was exactly what I would have done now, to show that even though I was half his size, I wasn't afraid of him. His lip twisted into a smile, seemingly reading me correctly.

"This way." He pushed off the wall, set his phone in his pocket, and led me into the club.

I wasn't sure what it looked like on nights that it was actually open, but I could picture it. There were stages similar to the ones at Tempt, which didn't surprise me since I'd been present when Tommy and Anthony had discussed installing them after someone sent them pictures from inside of this club. Apparently, they'd tried to copy everything, yet this club felt different. It felt luxurious. Tempt felt . . . well, like it was trying to be luxurious and failing. When we reached the second floor, the security guy opened a set of double doors and led me through them. Inside was a waiting area that looked like one I'd expect in a lawyer's office, not a nightclub.

"You can take a seat here. John will be right with you." He pointed at one of the chairs and walked out.

I took a seat. There were two sets of doors, one to the left and one to the right, and because I wasn't sure which ones John would come out of, I remained on high alert, my eyes bouncing between both. The doors to the left opened and I was about to stand up when I saw Giovanni Masseria himself walk out. I sat up a little straighter. I'd never seen him in person, not this close anyway. When his sister, Catalina, danced for the company, he'd go watch her, but I was one of the youngest dancers at the time and wasn't privy to the private parties they held for the donors. He was absolutely as handsome as they said. Behind him, a woman walked out, a huge smile on her face. She seemed to light up the room as she stepped into it, and instantly set me at ease. He turned around to look at her and grabbed her hand in his as he led her out of the office. I wasn't sure any man had ever looked at me the way he looked at her, but seeing it with my own two eyes gave me hope that one day I'd find someone who would. It wasn't until they were halfway to me that they seemed to notice someone else was in the room.

"Are you here for John?" Giovanni asked, finally turning his attention to me.

"Yes."

"Have you been out here long?" the woman asked. "Did you try knocking?"

"The man who walked me up just told me to sit here and wait."

She rolled her eyes, let go of Giovanni's hand, and walked to the doors across from us. She knocked loudly. "John, someone's here to see you."

"My wife is a problem solver," Giovanni said with a proud smile, looking at her. She smiled at him as she turned around. "Just open the door, babe."

"No, thanks," she said, "I never know what I'll find behind these doors. I'd rather knock and not take my chances."

"You never have to worry about my door." He winked at her and she blushed lightly.

The door opened behind her and a tall Black man, who I assumed was John, walked out. He was wearing a navy suit that was either custom-made for him or had been tailored to perfection. I wondered if being hot was a requirement to be employed by or married to Giovanni Masseria, because they were all hot as hell. John looked at the three of us as he held the door open, his gaze landing on Giovanni's wife.

"If you're here to steal my red pens, the answer is no, Isabel," he said.

"Don't worry, Gio got me three boxes." Isabel laughed. "She's waiting to see you." She pointed at me, smiled, and waved goodbye as she started to walk toward the doors, her husband hot on her heels.

"Remember, we won't be back until next week, and you may not be able to reach me while I'm gone." Giovanni reached for Isabel's hand, bringing it up to his mouth and dropping a kiss on the back of it. "I'm taking my wife on a honeymoon."

"Didn't you take her on a honeymoon nine months ago?" John asked. "This is called a vacation."

"It's called whatever I want to call it." Giovanni grinned at the look on John's face. "I'll bring you back some rum."

I waited until they were gone before I stood.

"So you're the famous Roselyn," John said, holding the door to his office and stepping back. "Come on in."

"I'm not sure if that's good or bad." I smiled shakily as I walked over and stepped into his office.

Every man I'd ever had to speak to on a business level always treated me like an object. I thought that was a ballet thing, where men and women alike were treated like pawns the companies played with. When we did things on behalf of the companies, we were told where to go, what to do, what to wear, and how to act. With Tommy, it had been more of the same. With Anthony, even worse. So far, John hadn't looked at me like a piece of meat, and when we walked into his office, he didn't close the door behind him. He left it ajar and invited me to sit as he headed to his chair. Once settled, he clasped his hands together on the desk. His actions were already ten times better than that of the men who came before him. Obviously, the bar was set in hell.

"Yari speaks very highly of you, so it's a good thing." He smiled at me from across the desk.

"She speaks highly of you as well and has been hounding me to meet with you."

"She says you currently work at Tempt."

"Yes."

"I heard they pay pretty well. Why are you leaving?"

"I feel like I need a change."

"So you want to go from one nightclub to another?" he raised an eyebrow.

"I . . ." I took a breath and decided to go with the truth. "I hate the people I work for."

"Can't say I'm surprised." He looked at his computer screen. "And you're a dancer for the city ballet."

"Yep."

"That must be time-consuming," he said.

"That's another reason I'm here. Yari said you may be able to give me a flexible schedule since that will be taking up a lot of my time." I paused again, unsure how much information to divulge, but Yari trusted him so I would as well. "I had to put a pause on my ballet career for a while, but I'm hoping I can start making my way back there."

"She mentioned that. She also said she spoke to you about escorting and you didn't like the idea," he said. "But it would be the best option, given your schedule."

"I'm not sure I can do the small talk and whatever else it entails."

"It's a small price to pay." He shrugged. "You could make as much as you would bartending in two nights."

"It just sounds so . . . I don't know. Intimate?"

"It's not." He laughed. "It's not all sex, drugs, and rock and roll. Most of the clients just want companionship, someone to have dinner with, go watch a movie, and yes, sometimes they'll need a date to a fancy event, while others prefer a little more, but again, you pick. You'd be your own boss in that regard."

"My own boss," I breathed. "That sounds ideal."

"I think it is."

"Okay, you sold me on it." I smiled. "What do I need to do?"

"Perfect. As of eight months ago, Oui is no longer a Masseria-owned company, so I would only be able to send you over there with high recommendations."

"Oh. I thought you were the one I needed to speak to about it."

"I used to be. I facilitated it for Yari and now she keeps sending people my way. If you're interested, I can send you over there right now."

I sat back a little. I hadn't expected it to happen so quickly, but I was already dressed in business attire, so I might as well. "Sure. I'm available right now."

"Good." He tapped his desk with his knuckle. "I'll make the call and you can head over to Oui now. It's not far from here."

I thanked him again. I was definitely nervous about this and despite the things he'd said to ease my mind, I still felt like I was in over my head, but I was running low on options right now.

CHAPTER FOUR

THE LAST TRACKABLE LOCATION ON MY BROTHER'S PHONE WAS IN or around La Guardia Airport. I wasn't in the habit of making assumptions, but all signs were pointing to him taking a flight somewhere. I watched the surveillance video that Dean acquired for me on loop. It showed my brother nonchalantly walking out of his building. His phone was pressed to his ear, and he had a bag in his hand. He didn't look scared at all, which didn't align with the urgent voicemail he'd left me, but it did put me at ease.

"Maybe he really did take a vacation," Rocco said next to me. He'd also watched it on loop at least twelve times.

"Why leave that message though? Why even tell me to go find Rosie?"

"He wouldn't tell you to look for Rosie if it wasn't important." He set his drink down. "He'd probably keep her a secret until he impregnated her or some shit."

I felt myself scowl. "Rosie doesn't even want kids."

"Sixteen-year-old Rosie didn't want kids. You don't know how twenty-six-year-old Rosie feels about it. They would make cute kids, don't you think? Little Dominican-Italian babies."

"Are you trying to piss me off?"

"Is it working?"

He knew it was fucking working. I looked at my phone again. "He didn't look like he was in a rush either. Gabe usually walks like his ass is on fire."

"You should ask Rosie what the fuck is happening. She has to know something." He finished his drink and stood up.

As if on cue, my phone vibrated in my lap.

Rosie: I took your advice and quit Tempt

Rosie: I'm FREAKING OUT!

Rosie: tell me it wasn't a mistake

Rosie: SERIOUSLY, GABRIEL!?!?

"His texts are coming in," I said. "New ones."

"Today's the last day you'll get the messages," he said. "So hopefully, there's something you can use there."

I stood up and headed out, calling Dean to see what else he was able to find out about her for me. I had one of my guys tailing her now, so I knew the moment she left Tempt after quitting her job. Well, now I knew what her celebration outside of the building meant. According to the guy watching her, she was smiling and jumping up and down with her phone in hand. Having her followed did nothing to subdue my curiosity. I wanted to know every fucking thing about her. Why she had that job, why she was leaving it, why she was so happy to leave it, and why she was so desperately looking for a new position as soon as possible. I'd already gone to her apartment looking for any sign that would lead to Gabe but found nothing. The next step was confessing my identity and asking her myself. If she slapped me the other night thinking I was my docile brother, I couldn't even begin to imagine what she'd do once she found out about me.

CHAPTER FIVE

Rosie

> **Santi: I think I'm gonna drop math**

> **Me: again?**

> **Santi: my professor sucks**

> **Me: you said that last semester, and the one before that. Just suck it up and take the damn class**

> **Santi: easy for you to say**

> **Me: don't drop the class**

> **Santi: the bodega has been poppin' lately**

> **Santi: not that it matters**

My heart stopped. The *one* condition my father had given me and my brother from prison was that neither of us step foot in the bodegas he owned. It was for our own good, he'd said, since Tommy Costello had taken over the business the moment dad was sent to prison for thirty months on a bogus racketeering charge. Taking charge of the bodegas was yet another thing Tommy and Anthony Costello held over our heads. *Bodegas D'Vega* were our family business. They were the only thing in the last ten years that had brought some sense of normalcy. Of course, Dad turned it into a nightmare the day he started borrowing money from Tommy, who had gambling rings in the back rooms of the bodegas. *Never get high on your own supply* seemed like a simple, logical concept, yet Dad had somehow broken every single one of the Ten Crack Commandments. For a man who claimed to love Biggie Smalls, he sure as hell did a poor job following instructions. But I guess greed defies logic.

Me: you went?

Santi: of course not. Jochy told me

Me: stay away from there. There's a reason you're living in the NYU dorms

Santi: *eye roll emoji*

Me: *eye roll emoji* right back

Santi: remember I'm going to Cabo for Thanksgiving

Santi: wish you'd come

Me: with a bunch of college students? No, thanks

Santi: you act like you're soooo much older than us

I was trying to think of a witty response when someone suddenly grabbed my arm and yanked me into the alley. I was slammed against the brick wall and before I got a chance to react, there was a hand around my throat blocking my airflow. I was met with icy blue eyes and started flailing to push him off, but it was no use. This was how things were with Anthony. If he wanted to back you into a corner, he would. Literally and figuratively, which was precisely why I didn't like to fuck with him and why I knew quitting Tempt would be challenging.

"I heard you think you're going to work for the enemy." He pushed me further against the wall as if he was trying to make me disappear into it. "That's not gonna happen."

The enemy? What the hell was he talking about? I knew Dad's bodegas were in Costello territory, which was the reason Anthony waltzed into them every Thursday like clockwork to collect their dues, but that was the extent of what I knew. I had no idea he had problems with Giovanni Masseria. Then again, how would I know? I kept my head down and my mouth shut. The last thing I needed was to be sucked back into all of that. When I was a kid, I had no idea how dangerous these men were, but I knew better now.

"What? No." I was getting lightheaded. I reached up and grabbed his arm, pulling it, scratching it, looking for some form of release from his grip. I scratched again, eyes wide, trying to get a grasp around his hand. If he'd just let me go, I could ask him what he was talking about and explain that I'd pay the money back faster this way. Of course, Anthony only squeezed harder. My eyes started to water. "Please."

"What were you doing at Devil's Lair?" He pushed himself onto me, nudging a knee between my legs and pushing me further into the wall. My already high anxiety went through the roof as I waited, expecting the worst. Even though there were people walking by just a few steps away, none of them would help unless I screamed, and I couldn't scream. I could barely breathe. Tears streamed down my face.

"Nothing," I whispered. "Anthony, please."

"Nothing?" He pushed his knee further up and I was instantly grateful for the barrier my jeans created. "That's funny. Lauralee told me you quit. Didn't even go in or give a two-week notice."

"Please. I ca-ca-can't breathe," I gasped loudly, taking in air when he loosened his grip around my throat.

"I can make your life hell. I can easily have Madame Costello make a call and pull you from your little Nutcracker show. Is that what you want? You want to force my hand and use my connections?"

"Please." My chest shook with barely contained sobs, with fear. I knew he'd make good on his promise. The minute he loosened his grip again, I rushed to explain. "I can pay back the money he's owes sooner."

"This isn't about the money." He brought his mouth to my ear. "Besides, you wouldn't want your daddy to get an unexpected visit when he's so close to getting out, would you?"

"Please." I was openly crying now, my voice hoarse. "Don't do this."

He let go of my throat suddenly and took a step back. I instantly fell to my knees, my hands finding my throat as I took a large gulp of air. Through my tears, I could see his boots as he walked away, leaving me in the alley without another word. I managed to pick myself up and ran the rest of the way to my apartment. I knew that for Anthony, it wasn't about the money. It was about the power he held over me. He got off on that kind of high. He loved to remind us that he owned us, and I wasn't even part of the group of girls they actually owned. A hard shiver raked through me at the thought, but it was too late. I'd already left Tempt and now I had to suck up whatever consequences that brought on. I just hoped he left my father out of this.

Something woke me up. A sound, I realized. I froze. Someone was in my apartment. *In my room.* If you'd told me a year ago that I'd be sleeping with a loaded gun under my spare pillow, I would've laughed in your face, but that was then, and right now I was glad I'd had the foresight to do so. I reached underneath the pillow and grabbed the gun quickly, holding it with both hands as I turned and pointed it at the darkness. If it was Anthony, I'd shoot him. I decided after what happened in the alley, that if he ever dared to waltz into my apartment, I'd shoot him on sight. I'd already run through every potential scenario that could come from it. Maybe they'd arrest me, but it would be self-defense. I'd probably have to give up ballet for good. I'd be depressed for the rest of my life because of it, but at least I'd feel safe. Would it have been worth taking a life? I wasn't sure, but right now in this instant, I had to choose myself.

I tried to stay quiet, heart pounding hard at the sound of the next movement. Fear gripped my belly, but I wasn't going down without a fight this time. At least, that was what I thought before he set his arms on the bed, making the mattress dip, and leaned in. The moment the scent of cologne hit me, I took the safety off, squeezed my eyes shut, and pulled the trigger.

Click.

I tried again.

Click.

"You didn't think I'd actually let you keep bullets in your gun, did you?" He chuckled a deep, dark sound that vibrated onto the mattress and through me. "My God. What has sweet, innocent, little Rosie gotten herself into that she sleeps with a gun underneath her pillow?"

That voice. Fuck. I couldn't place it, but something about it felt familiar. I lunged at him with the gun, ready to bash it against his face. I wasn't prepared for the force I was hit with. Strong arms pushed me back onto the mattress. A hard body pressed against me, chest to chest. He was huge and this felt way too intimate. Too scary. Too similar to the nightmares I had. I thrashed and screamed. One of his hands came down hard over my mouth. I bit his fingers.

He hissed. "I suggest you stop doing that while I'm on top of you like this. I may get other ideas."

"Get off me." My scream was muffled by his hand.

"I'm not here to hurt you," he gritted. "Stop screaming and I'll get off."

I screamed again. He brought his face down and I took in a sharp breath, inhaling his scent. It was eerily familiar. It wasn't a cologne, I realized. It wasn't an aftershave. It was *him*. I racked my brain. Someone from the club? From the ballet company?

Someone Anthony sent? None of it made sense. Unless this was about Gabe. That made my breath catch.

"You were always smart, so you may want to think about this." He set his mouth near my ear. "If I wanted to kill you, you'd already be dead."

Another muffled scream from me. More thrashing. I kicked upwards. Finally, I stopped moving altogether. I cleared my head and shut my eyes, trying to think of what I'd been taught during the many self-defense courses I'd taken over the years. I flipped my leg beneath him and turned him so that he was on his back, and I was on top of him. I punched him as hard as I could, not caring where my fist landed as I got off him. I ran, not out of the room like I should have, but to the light switch. He didn't move from the bed, I noticed belatedly. If he wanted to hurt me, he probably wouldn't have let me get this far.

Maybe he wasn't lying about hurting me, but accosting me while I slept was creepy as fuck, no matter how you spun it. Finally, I flipped the light switch, and he came into view. I blinked and blinked again, not quite understanding what I was seeing. Or rather *who*, because even though he looked like Gabe, I knew it wasn't. I purposely hadn't asked Gabe anything about his brother, so I didn't know what had become of him. The only thing I knew was what I'd always known. This was the De Luca I should stay far away from.

His grin was slow, wide, and wolfish. "Hey, Tiny Dancer."

Three little words were all he'd said, and the rage was back.

CHAPTER SIX

"**W**HAT THE *FUCK* ARE YOU DOING HERE, DOMINIC?" SHE emphasized each word as she asked the question, brown eyes flaring with barely controlled anger.

"I need to speak to you."

"So you show up in my apartment in the middle of the night and . . . Oh my God." Her dainty hands flew to her mouth. "It was you at the club the other night."

"Disappointed?"

Her eyes narrowed. "You cunning, lying, scheming, sneaky son of a bitch."

"Did you memorize the entire thesaurus?"

"Just that section, in case I ever saw you again."

At that, I laughed. God, I'd been such an asshole to her back then. I really couldn't blame her for having this reaction, and yet, I couldn't take my eyes off her. Even when she was angry, she was fucking beautiful. Always had been. I gave myself the opportunity to *really* look at her. She hadn't changed much. She still had the same banging dancer body, dark brown eyes, and caramel skin. Her brown hair used to be so curly you could pull a strand down and it would spring right back up. I'd done it enough times to get a rise out of her. Now her hair was longer than I'd ever seen it, down to her elbows, and pin straight. She looked beautiful no matter how she wore it and even more beautiful than I remembered, which seemed impossible. My eyes fell to her neck, which was clearly bruised, and my amusement faded. I stepped forward. She shrunk back slightly as if expecting the worst, and suddenly I regretted the way I came at her—pushing her into the bed like a fucking animal. It was a shit move on my part, especially with everything she'd—we'd—been through.

"Who did that?" I moved my eyes from her neck and met her gaze.

"That's none of your business." She crossed her arms, shifting from one foot to the other. "What the hell are you doing in my apartment?"

"Was it Gabriel?"

I wasn't sure what I'd do to my brother if he'd done this to her. I didn't know him to be violent, but then again, I didn't know him to do drugs either, and I definitely wasn't sure what he was capable of when he was on them.

"No." She frowned, dropping her arms at her sides. "Wait, where is he?"

"That's exactly what I'm here to talk about."

"You think I know?" She pointed at herself, eyes widening. "I have no idea where he is. He ghosted me."

"You were one of the last people to see him."

"I . . ." Her jaw dropped momentarily. "So he really has been missing since last weekend?"

"It appears so."

"And you just started looking now?" she asked.

"I was out of the country," I said, a little harsher than I wanted to, but the way she was questioning me as if I was the bad guy pissed me off. "Besides, I'm not my brother's keeper. I didn't know about the drugs. I didn't know about *you*."

"He didn't tell you about me?" Her brows pulled in a little more.

God, I hated my brother right now. Part of me even hated that he had another opportunity with her and fucked it up, but the selfish part of me was grateful for the opportunity.

"He left me a voice message," I explained. "He told me to go to that club and to look after you."

"Look after me?"

"He told me to '*look for her in the VIP bar.*' It took me a split second to realize it was you he meant."

"Why would–" She stopped speaking suddenly, eyes widening even more, if that was even possible, as she brought a hand over her mouth. "Oh my God."

"What?"

"Could he have gone to the police?" she asked, but she wasn't really asking me. She was talking to herself now. "Or maybe Tommy found out I told him. Oh, fuck." She paced again. "No, that can't be right. If he'd found out, I'd be dead, but then Anthony . . . oh shit. I don't know."

"Care to explain it to me?" I said after watching her talk to herself for a while.

"He could've gone to the feds and skipped town." She kept pacing. "They're going to kill me. They're going to piece it together and know I told him things and then they're going to kill me." She stopped walking and faced me. "He ran. He must have."

I let that sink in for a moment. "What did you tell him? Why would he run?"

"Oh God. Oh God. Oh God." She put her arms on her head and took deep breaths. "I have to get to Santi. Fuck. I have to call Dad. Oh God. I'm going to be sick." She ran into the bathroom.

I gave her space. I needed to think this over. Why the fuck would my brother go to the feds? What could she have possibly told him? He couldn't have been on the run. I saw him leaving his building calmly and knew my brother well enough to know that if he was in danger, he would have looked like he was. When Rosie stepped back into the room, she'd washed her face and picked up her hair in a neat bun but didn't look any less panicked.

"Pack a bag. You're staying with me." I took my phone out to text the two drivers I had waiting downstairs and told them to go home in one car and leave mine.

"What? I can't just go and stay with you."

"You have to." I glanced up at her. "We don't know what you're dealing with and if I leave you here, Tommy may get to you before I have a chance to stop him." I looked at her neck. Those bruises were fucking me up. "Was he the one who did that to you?"

"No." She set a hand there as if to cover it up, but it was impossible. As if realizing this just now, tears welled in her eyes. "How am I supposed to dance tomorrow night?"

"You still dance?"

She nodded. "At the city ballet. I'm . . ." she paused, shaking slightly. "I'm in *The Nutcracker*."

"I'm sure they can cover that up." I tried smiling, but my concern overrode my pride. She nodded, still in the same spot. I waved a hand around impatiently. "Pack a bag."

"I'm not going to pack a bag, Dominic."

"Either you pack a bag, or I do it for you, but I'm not leaving here without you."

"You're just going to, what, kidnap me?" she snapped.

"If that's what it takes."

"You can't be serious."

I took a step forward. "Do I look like I'm fucking joking?"

Her brows pulled, her eyes taking me in from head to toe. I watched her expression jump from one emotion to another as she studied me. It was as if her shock was just wearing off, and she was finally realizing that the person standing in front of her wasn't the one she used to know. She swallowed as she continued to size me up. I wondered if she was trying to figure out ways to get out of this. She had to know she couldn't.

"What the hell happened to you?" she whispered.

"What the hell happened to me?" I scoffed. "You're the one sleeping with a gun under your pillow."

"I'm . . ." she let out a single laugh. "You don't know anything about me."

"Yeah, well, you don't know shit about me either, Roselyn. Pack a fucking bag."

Finally, she started moving. I watched her every move as I tried to rein in my anger. The sadness in her eyes and the judgment in her tone made me go from curious to pissed off in a matter of seconds. She was right, though. I really didn't know her anymore but I intended to, because the Rosie I knew wouldn't have even looked at a gun, let alone owned one, and definitely would never have slept with one under her pillow. That was a stupid fucking move, but I'd have to save the gun safety conversation for another day. Was she sleeping with it because of what happened ten years ago? That would actually make sense.

"I have to call my brother," she said, "And I don't know how to get ahold of my dad, but he's in prison upstate and . . . what if he gets hurt because of this?" She stopped packing and looked up at me. The tears filling her eyes hit me right in the gut. "He gets out next month. He can't get hurt now."

"I'll handle it. Don't worry about him," I said.

She nodded and I knew she believed me. Trusted me. It was a wild concept, all things considered, but I'd take it and prove to her that she could. I'd have to find out more information on her dad. He used to launder money for some of the old timers back home, but despite that, he'd always been a good man, a devout Catholic. I wondered what the hell landed him behind bars and how long he'd been there. I wondered what the fuck that meant for Rosie and Santi. I didn't like it. I also didn't like knowing that she'd lived in the same city as me and I didn't know it until my brother pulled this idiotic shit.

I cleared my throat. "Where's your little brother?"

"NYU. He stays in the dorms."

"He should be safe there," I said. "What did you tell Gabe? Why would he be running?"

"I told him a lot of things." She bit her lip as if trying to remember what may have caused this. "He mentioned that he was doing some accounting for Tommy Costello and found some discrepancies in his account. He must've been drunk or high when he said it, but that led to me asking about the shell company I knew they had. Gabe asked me what I was talking about, so I told him what I knew—that Tommy shares a company with some other guys. Russians, Mexicans, some Colombians, Turks."

"Sounds like a trip to fucking Epcot," I said. "Aren't you a bartender there? How would you know all of this?"

"Because I heard them discussing it."

"Again, how?"

"They meet on Tuesdays when the club is closed to the public." She lowered her gaze and focused on her task again. "Sometimes Tommy asks me to come in on those days."

"To do what?" I asked, not intending my question to come out as harshly as it did, but there was no use in taking it back now.

"Make drinks during the meeting, sometimes dance." She averted her eyes when she said that last part. I didn't like it. "It's just a way to pick up an extra shift and make more money."

"Dancing," I repeated, searching her face. There was something she was leaving out and the way she was still avoiding looking at me rubbed me the wrong way. If she was stripping for him and his friends, she was probably also fucking him. I'd heard enough stories about Tommy and Anthony Costello to know that nothing good came to women who were around them. "Are you fucking Tommy?"

"No." Her eyes snapped up.

"Are you fucking Anthony?" I asked. She looked away again, swallowing hard, which further fueled my anger. "Does my brother know?"

"What difference does it make whether or not your brother knows?" Her eyes narrowed on mine for a moment.

Now my brother's message was becoming clearer. He wanted me to keep an eye on her because of Anthony Costello. I wondered what he'd seen, what he'd heard, why the fuck he'd be dumb enough to leave this woman behind. He must've been desperate to leave her in my care. This conversation was yet another sign that they weren't together though. Maybe Gabe wasn't into her anymore. Who even knows if Gabe was into her to begin with or if he was just with her because he knew I wanted her. That thought left a sour taste in my mouth. I shook it away and focused on the subject at hand.

"Is that the only thing you told my brother?"

"Yeah. Well, the only thing he'd be in trouble for, anyway." She zipped up her duffel bag and put the strap around her shoulder. "In *confidence*, but obviously he's an idiot and didn't keep it confidential."

"Yeah." I reached out and took her bag, putting it over my shoulder. "Let's go."

CHAPTER SEVEN

OF ALL THE PEOPLE IN THE WORLD TO BE STUCK IN A CAR WITH, Dominic De Luca would be my last pick. He used to go into the ice cream shop I had a part-time job at and blatantly flirt with me in front of whatever girl he'd taken there on a date. It was morbidly embarrassing, since of course, instead of being mad at him for being an asshole, the girls would get mad at me. When I started dating Gabe, the flirting stopped and the assholeness started. It was like dating his brother automatically put me in enemy territory. After that, whenever Dominic visited the ice cream shop, he ignored me. Once, another employee told me to give him the family discount since he was practically my brother, so I did, thinking it would earn me at least a simple thank you, but no. Instead, Dominic shoved cash into my hand and practically screamed, "I'm not your fucking brother." I stopped trying after that. He and Gabe may have shared a womb and some facial features, but they might as well have been from different planets.

Unlike his brother, who was all kind smiles and expensive suits, Dominic was pushy, broody, and full of muscles and tattoos. He was just the right amount of rugged, the type modeling companies salivated over. I knew I'd noticed differences the other night, but I chalked it up to poor lighting. With his large hand engulfing the stick shift, and his forearm twitching when he switched gears, it was impossible not to notice them now. Each time he glanced over at me, with those dark eyes that held a confidence few men carried, my heart sped up. I tried hard not to dwell on the fact that his brother hadn't made me feel this way, not ever. It wasn't like it mattered to Dominic anyway. He clearly still had it out for me and was only doing this as a favor to Gabe. He hadn't let me listen to the voice message, but I wondered if, in it, Gabe made it sound like we were together or something. It would make sense, seeing as he asked me if Gabe knew I was fucking another man. I wondered how long I could let him believe that was the case, and why it mattered to me that he didn't know I was available.

"So what have you been up to besides eavesdropping, dancing, and trying to whore yourself out?"

"Fuck you," I said between my teeth. "I do not whore myself out."

"Sounds like you do."

"I don't." My fists clenched on my lap.

"So you're telling me you didn't get a job at Oui a couple of days ago?"

My jaw dropped. "How do you know about that?"

"I've learned a lot of things about you these last couple of days." He looked at me fully when we stopped at a red light. My pulse quickened.

"You went through my things," I said, "when you took the bullets out of my gun."

"Naturally." He looked at the road again and started driving.

"Naturally? That's illegal."

"Do I look like a person who gives a fuck what's legal and what's not?" He raised an eyebrow.

I sighed. For some reason, that filled me with disappointment. "Let me guess, you followed in your father's footsteps."

"And if I did?" He spared me a quick glance.

"And if you did, then I guess I'd say congratulations on becoming your mother's worst nightmare."

"Don't talk about my mother." His hands clenched around the steering wheel and stick shift.

"Your mother was a good woman." I looked out the window. "She tried so hard to get you two away from that life."

"Shut up, Roselyn."

"I'm just saying, she wouldn't be proud."

"Shut the fuck up, Roselyn." He slammed a hand against the steering wheel, punctuating each word. I jumped in my seat. "You're in over your head, got your boyfriend mixed up in your shit, and you want to lecture me about what my mother would think about me? What would Tesalia say about her sweet, innocent daughter cheating on her boyfriend with Anthony Costello, of all people? What would she say about you being mixed up with those kinds of people in the first place?"

I swallowed back the tears that threatened and looked out the window. They say you shouldn't dish out what you can't take, and in this case, I'd done just that. I could've made the argument that I wasn't cheating on anyone, least of all his brother, but I couldn't do that without confirming the Anthony bit and that made me feel sick. Both our mothers died that night and there was no use in pretending—the loss still affected us deeply. Sometimes I thought maybe if I'd lost my mother to an illness or some kind of freak accident, it might have been okay, but I knew better. It doesn't really matter how you lose someone. The fact is, they're gone forever and you're always left missing them and wondering what could have been. What happened to us was unfair and traumatizing, though. Armed men walked into our homes, tied us up, and shot them point-blank. They didn't even bother taking anything to make it look like a robbery.

I never even understood why they tied us up at all. They just aimed, shot, and left. Whenever I thought about the unfairness of it all, a hole opened up in the pit of my stomach. When I was having a particularly shitty day, I thought about who I would have become if my mother hadn't been murdered. It was a stupid mental exercise, but I couldn't keep myself from doing it. At least I was still dancing. She'd be proud of that. Everything else, not so much. I looked at Dominic, who was still pissed off. Who would he have become if his father hadn't sunk his claws into him?

"I'm sorry," I said after a moment. "I shouldn't have said that."

"No, you shouldn't have."

I wasn't surprised that he didn't apologize back. Dom always meant what he said, and that bothered me even more. He turned into an alley and pushed a button on his car that opened a garage. He pushed it again as soon as we were inside, looking around as if to make sure no one had snuck inside.I followed him out, taking in the bare walls except for one that had tools. He opened the door that led inside the house and took his shoes off. I did the same. It smelled like he'd just cleaned. I'd never really imagined what his house would look like, but even if I'd tried, this wasn't what I would have come up with. It was modern, everything very sleek, including stairs that had clear sides and pieces of wood that looked like they were floating. The kitchen was immaculate as if he never really used it.

"I'm not gonna lie, I pictured you in a high rise," I said, looking around. The art that hung on the walls looked expensive.

He turned to me with a raised eyebrow and a smirk. "I'm surprised you thought about me at all."

"I thought about everyone," I said quickly.

"Sure you did."

I'd stopped getting taller when I was sixteen, so the last time we saw each other I was already five foot five. Dom must have been double that. The only way I could describe him was *imposing*. The kind of guy you wouldn't want to fight in a bar, or anywhere, ever. His brother was just a couple of inches shorter and was much leaner and definitely not covered in tattoos—not that I'd seen him naked, despite what Dominic believed, but I would never correct him. If he wanted to rub in the fact that I'd slept with Anthony—out of sheer terror of what would happen if I didn't—I wouldn't correct that either. In recent years, I'd stopped caring what people thought about me. You can show people exactly who you are, and they're still going to put you in whatever category they deemed right for you.

He led me upstairs where he said there were three rooms and a loft that he'd set up as a game room with a pool table, a foosball table, and a huge television that looked like it belonged at a bar. It felt cozy, the opposite of the man it belonged to. He walked me to the second to last bedroom and set my bag down by the door. The room had a queen size bed, a matching dresser, and a Jack-and-Jill bathroom that it shared with the other guest room, which he'd turned into a gym.

"My room is there." He pointed to the bedroom at the end of the hall, right next to this one. "I've had a long day, so I'm going to bed. You're welcome to anything. I don't cook, so I just have a lot of frozen shit and fruit. And beer. And whiskey."

"Thanks." I felt myself smile a little. "Really, thanks."

"Don't mention it." He turned around and walked into his room, shutting the door with such force, it made me flinch.

I walked back into the guest room and closed the door softly. I took out my phone and texted my brother to make sure he was okay and to tell him not to talk to strangers, like he was five and not twenty-one.

> **Santi: lol what strangers? did you forget I'm leaving for Mexico with Victoria?**

> **Santi: Snowbirds and all that**

> **Me: for two weeks, right?**

> **Santi: YEP. I'm sad you'll be alone for thanksgiving tho**

> **Me: don't be. Have fun and be careful**

> **Me: and don't drink too much**

Santi: yes master

Me: lol love you

I set my phone on the nightstand with a sigh and tried to find sleep.

I hear the screams first. My parents rarely argued, and when they did, Mom never screamed the way she was screaming now. It was what made me throw my covers off and run out of my bedroom door. Before I reached the stairs, I heard a gunshot, followed by Dad yelling. He sounded like he had something in his mouth. I stood frozen for a long time before rushing down the stairs. There were a lot of things I should have done before I rushed down there, but I couldn't seem to make one smart decision after hearing the sound of the gun. By the time I reached the first floor, I saw two men wearing black things on their faces, the holes poked out where their eyes were. The one guy I saw had brown eyes. They weren't dressed all in black like I thought they'd be. It wasn't until they shut the door behind them that I sprang into action and ran into the kitchen. That was where I found Mom lying on the floor and Dad all beat up with his hands and ankles tied to one of the dining chairs. Then it repeated: the scream, the gunshot.

At 4:13 on the dot, I sat up with a gasp, hand on my chest to settle my rapidly beating heart. Despite years of therapy and working on myself, I always had the same nightmare and woke up at the same damn time. Sometimes I went back to sleep. Today, I wasn't sure I would, but I settled back into my pillow and tried. A few minutes later, I heard a door shut, and not long after that, the sound of a treadmill coming from the other room. I sat up. Was he seriously working out at this time? I got out of bed and stopped at the bathroom to brush my teeth and pull my hair back up into a ponytail before exiting the opposite door. On the treadmill, running at a super-fast speed, was a shirtless

Dominic, and the only thing I could think was: *holyyyy shit.* His body was truly a work of art.

"You enjoying the view from back there?" he asked, still running, talking like he wasn't out of breath at all.

"How'd you even know I was here?" I walked over and stood near the front of the treadmill. Big mistake. This angle gave me a full view of his chest, abs, and arms, the combination rendering me speechless.

"You can look. I won't tell my brother." He winked with a lazy grin. I felt myself go hot all over.

I crossed my arms and looked away. "Do you always work out this early?"

"I can never sleep past four." He lowered the speed until he was at a walking pace.

My eyes snapped back to his. "Four?"

"Yeah."

"Every day?"

"Basically."

"Does that happen to Gabe as well?"

He scoffed. "You'd know better than I would."

I bit my lip and looked down. "I wake up every day at 4:13, without fail."

"Huh."

"I can't remember what time it all happened," I said quietly. "But I assume it had to be around that time."

He didn't say anything as he stopped the tread and hopped off, wiping his face and chest with the grey shirt in his hand. I was trying really hard not to look. I wouldn't. From my peripheral vision, I saw a large hand reaching for me and I froze, my gaze snapping to his. He didn't touch my face but reached behind my head and pulled the hair tie from my hair. It fell and covered my shoulders, my back, and my breasts. Back then, I still wore it curly most of the time, and sometimes when he wanted to call my attention, he'd tug on individual curls. It was meant to piss me off, but the only purpose it served was to make my stomach flip, like it was doing right now. I wanted to ask what the hell he was doing, but I couldn't find the words to speak. I dropped my gaze to his full mouth momentarily, and for a split second, I wondered what it would be like to kiss him. That was what made my eyes snap back to his. He licked his lips, gaze darkening. I had to be imagining the hunger in them. There was no way he wanted me, right? It didn't matter. It really didn't. That couldn't happen.

"I always loved your hair. It looks good like this too," he said, and I thought for a moment he might touch it. "It always smelled like flowers."

"Herbal Essence," I whispered, heart in my throat.

"I'll make sure to get you some."

"You don't have to do that."

"But I will." He brought his hand to my clavicle and ever so gently ran his knuckle along it, moving up to my neck. I shut my eyes, lips parting, and gasped when I heard him make a sound in the back of his throat that sounded like a mix between a groan and a growl. Whatever it was hit me right between my legs. I didn't want to know what I would find in his eyes, so I kept my eyes closed, but I felt a shiver roll through me when he switched from his knuckle to the pads of his fingers. He moved them softly over the marks Anthony had left there, as if to erase them. "Who did this to you?"

My eyes popped open. "It's none of your business."

"I have two names in mind," he said, bringing his hand up to my throat and covering it almost entirely.

It seemed like he was trying to measure the size of the hand that had been there. He just set it there, not squeezing in the least, but I felt like I couldn't breathe as his thumb moved over my pulse in a slow caress. Of its own accord, my neck rolled back a little more, as if to give him more access. His eyes burned into me. He was looking at me like he could devour me, like he would if I just said the word, and damn it, I didn't know what was wrong with me, but I really wanted to. I wanted to lean in so that he could press his lips to mine. I wanted to climb on top of him and wrap my legs around his waist. I couldn't though and it had absolutely nothing to do with Gabe. That relationship, if you could even call a six-month relationship that, was buried way in the past. I had no one tying me down and was free to do what I pleased, but I couldn't get involved with someone like Dominic. I would *not* get involved with anyone who did the very things I'd tried to stay away from. I'd already lost too much.

"Tell me who did it," he said, voice dropping as he inched forward. My heart skipped another beat. I shook my head. "Roselyn."

"I can't," I whispered.

"I'll find out. I always find out."

"Please don't." I swallowed hard and if possible, his gaze seemed to darken even more.

I watched his jaw work, a multitude of unspoken promises in his eyes that made me want things I shouldn't. His protection, his mouth, his touch. It felt like an entire breathless minute went by before he finally dropped his hand and took a step back. He spared me one last glance before leaving the room and it was then that I took a breath. This was the complete opposite of when Anthony had me up against that brick wall.

That had been scary, but this scared me in an entirely different way.

CHAPTER EIGHT

WHEN I FINISHED GETTING DRESSED, I GRABBED MY BAG AND headed downstairs. I wanted to leave as soon as possible. I wasn't sure I could look him in the eye after what happened upstairs. I was about to walk past the kitchen when I saw Dominic standing there, sipping on something and scrolling through his phone. He was wearing a black t-shirt and matching jeans. He used to wear his hair longer, in a messy way that looked like hands were always running through it. Sometimes I'd dreamed those hands were mine. Now, he had it cut short and let a layer of scruff grow on his face. Not quite a beard, though I could tell he definitely lined it as such. All of it suited him. Everything about him made my mouth water. Everything about him also made alarm bells go off in my head that told me to run the opposite way.

"If you keep staring at me like that, I'm going to get the wrong idea," he said, still looking at his phone.

"I'm just, I was just trying to figure out whether I liked your hair longer or shorter," I said quickly, as if I hadn't been standing there for at least a full minute and couldn't have gathered that kind of intel in under five seconds.

"Really." He glanced up with his eyes. How the hell did he even make that look hot? *Jesus.*

"Yes, really." I stepped into the kitchen.

"And? What's the verdict?"

"I like it long." I tore my gaze from the twinkle in his. "I like it short too though. Jesus Christ. I don't care about your hair." I turned around and walked out of the kitchen because what the fuck? I wasn't even an awkward person, but this guy, who'd been such a jerk to me when we were kids, had me all tongue-tied? Ugh. I hiked my bag higher on my shoulder and spared him one last glance. "I guess I'll see you later? I have to be at rehearsal in an hour, so I figured I'd head that way."

"You figured, huh?" He set his phone on the counter and gave me his full attention now. "You should eat."

"I will once I get over there. It's going to take me thirty-five minutes." I looked at the time on my phone. "Forty, maybe, depending on how fast I can get to the train."

"The train."

"Yeah, you know, the form of transportation that over four million people in this city use."

His mouth twitched. "You're not going on the train for the foreseeable future."

"But—"

"You're not riding the train." He tilted his head back as if asking for patience, and I decided that if he was mine, which he would never be, I would hop on top of the counter and lick from his Adam's Apple to his jaw. I pushed the thought away quickly. When he looked at me again, he seemed a little more relaxed. "Look, this is temporary. As soon as all of this is handled, you can go back to your regular life and ride the smelly train, but for now, you're not doing that. Don't fight me on this. You won't win."

"Oh, I won't win?" I blinked. He almost had me agreeing, but he just had to throw that in there.

"No, you won't."

"Try me." I turned and headed to the door.

"Jesus Christ. Are you going to make me tie you up and carry you? Because I will."

That made me freeze on the spot. He'd already charged at me last night when he snuck into my apartment, and now he was talking about tying me up? I turned around slowly. "You'd really tie me up?"

"Rosie." He sighed heavily, shutting his eyes briefly.

"After what they did, you'd do that to me?"

"Rosie."

"No. I want to know." I swallowed back tears that threatened. I had nightmares of being tied up. He must have had them too. "I want to know what it is you're capable of, so I know what I'm dealing with. Who I'm dealing with."

"I would never tie you up, Rosie," he said softly, searching my eyes. "I wouldn't."

I stayed quiet because I couldn't trust myself to speak yet. He took it as an invitation to continue talking.

"I need you to cooperate just for now, okay? I promised to keep you safe, and this is the only way I know how."

"I have to go to rehearsal," I whispered.

"I'll take you."

I breathed in shakily and nodded in agreement.

He had a driver. I should've seen that one coming, but since he'd driven last night, I figured he didn't. Back home, all the old guys in organized crime had drivers. They also had shooters. I wondered if Dom had those as well. The one thing I'd always found interesting about all of it is how the side they showed us was different from the rumors we heard on the street. Seeing the way Dominic opened my door and carried my bag for me, like we were going from math to gym class or something, made me think about that. If he had really gone into the "family business," he was definitely involved in some serious shit, but despite that, he had a sense of humor and acted like a gentleman in some situations. I turned to him when we reached the studio door.

"You can't come in here."

"Why not?" he frowned, looking over my head.

"You'll make the dancers nervous, and we don't have time for that right now."

He searched my eyes. "By dancers, do you mean you?"

"No." I looked down as if that would help me hide my blush. The sound of his laughter, which seemed to spread through me, was what made me look up at him again. "What?"

"Nothing. I just think it's cute."

"You think it's cute that you make me nervous?" I asked. "It's not. This is my career, not some joke."

"I know it's not a joke."

"You're acting like it's all a joke."

"Rosie." He sighed heavily, shaking his head like he was trying not to say all of the things he wanted to say. "I'll wait outside the room, okay?"

I turned around and walked into the studio.

When we finished and I looked at the time, three and a half hours had gone by. I wondered if Dominic had left. I knew he wouldn't leave me alone, but for some reason, the thought of him not being outside when I finished didn't sit well with me. I groaned inwardly. This was the last thing in the world I needed right now. I'd had boyfriends. It wasn't like I'd been crying into my pillow, but I couldn't remember the last time I had this *"I'm so nervous about seeing them that the butterflies in my stomach are making me feel like I might throw up"* feeling, and he was the last person I should feel this way about.

"Hey." Joshua reached out and set his hands on my shoulders, turning me to look at him. "You did great. We did great."

"I know." I smiled.

"Why do you look worried?"

"It's not about the performance. You know I don't worry when I dance with you."

"The feeling's mutual." He threw an arm around me and held the door with the other as one of the other dancers walked out.

The hall was empty. I wasn't sure whether to be relieved or worried, but Josh kept talking about his last performance partner, who was brilliant, and I tried to focus on that. Not only did I have the pressure of doing my best so that I could show the company that I was worthy of taking back my spot as a regular, but I also had to live up to the many brilliant partners Josh had danced with lately. I knew I could do it though, so I was using all of it as fuel to keep my head in the game. When we reached the end of the hall, he turned me to face him and grabbed my shoulders again.

"We are going to nail this every night. You know why?"

"Why?" I smiled at his certainty.

"Because our chemistry is through the roof, off the charts, and we're fucking amazing."

At that, I laughed, shaking my head. "Always so cocky."

"You know it." He winked, kissed my cheek, and walked away.

I was still somewhat laughing when I turned to see Dominic watching me and nearly jumped out of my skin.

I set a hand on my heart. "Jesus, Dom. How long have you been standing there?"

"Long enough." He looked angry again.

"Ugh. What now?" I asked, walking over to him.

He grabbed the bag out of my hand. "I'm just trying to figure you out."

"Good luck." I laughed and walked to the door.

He reached up from behind and pushed it open, his chest pressing slightly against my back with the motion, and I felt a shiver roll through me. *What the hell was going on with me? Why was I feeling this way around him?* If he felt anything, he didn't let it show. In the car, he sat in the backseat with me as Nico drove back to his place. Dominic was telling Nico the list of things he had to do the rest of the day. Finally, when he finished speaking, Dominic relaxed beside me.

"You look comfortable with that ballerina guy."

"Ballerina guy?"

"What should I say? Ballerino?"

"Actually, yeah." I laughed at the expression on his face. "Or danseur, or just a dancer. In Josh's case, he's a principal dancer though, which is a big deal, so I'd refer to him as such."

"Hm." His eyes didn't leave my face, my mouth, my eyes, my neck. "What did Josh say about your bruises?"

"Nothing." I looked out the window briefly and back at him. "Not everyone scrutinizes me the way you do."

He didn't say anything at all to that, but the way he stared at me made heat spread through my body.

CHAPTER NINE

Dominic

I DECIDED THAT I WOULDN'T JOIN ROSIE ON ANY OF HER LITTLE BALLET adventures anymore. It was best to have Marco drive her around and watch her. Having her sitting next to me was too tempting. Even covered in sweat, she was fucking gorgeous. I hadn't expected her to walk out of the rehearsal room with that *principal dancer's* arm around her shoulder. For a long second, I envisioned all the ways I'd break his limbs and that was before I realized how comfortable they were with each other. It was clear they danced together often and that she trusted him. With the way my chest squeezed, it was also clear that this ridiculous jealousy wasn't going away.

After I dropped her off, I focused on my brother again. I hadn't called my father yet, but it was inevitable. First, I needed to find out whether or not Gabe had gone to the police with what Rosie told him. If he had gone to them, it could potentially pose a threat to all of us, and I wasn't sure how my father would react to that kind of news. If Gabe had gone that route, maybe he didn't deserve my loyalty, but the asshole would have it anyway. Deep down, he must've known that.

The only person we had on the inside that I actually trusted was a homicide detective who happened to be Rocco's brother. He didn't make it a habit of telling us much about his cases unless he thought we were somehow linked to them, in which case he'd call Rocco to ask. I imagined that to be both frustrating and nerve-racking for someone like Michael Marchetti. It wasn't like Rocco would ever confess to anything, but if he did, what exactly was Mike supposed to do?

We'd been sitting in the Newport Centre parking lot waiting for him for almost thirty minutes and as annoyed as I was about it, we all knew he could make me wait three hours and I wouldn't drive away. When he finally opened the door and slid into the backseat, Rocco and I turned as much as our seats allowed. The look Mike gave us made me feel like he was liable to murder us and pin the crime on someone else. Despite his chosen line of work, he had Marchetti blood flowing through his veins, so I wouldn't put it past him to be on some Dexter-type shit.

"What the fuck have you gotten yourselves into now?" he asked, eyes dropping to the cup holder. "One of those coffees better be mine."

Rocco sighed, making a show of it as if he hadn't been the one to pick up his brother's coffee of choice. "Gabe's missing and he's allegedly been working with the cops."

"What cops?" He took a sip of his coffee.

"We don't know. I don't even know if he's working with cops or not," I said. "If he is, it could be anyone, regular cops, the FBI. We don't know."

"Where did you hear this?"

"Roselyn Vega."

"Vega? Little Rosie from back home? The dancer?" Mike frowned deeply. "Santiago's kid?"

"That one. The one Dom had a crush on," Rocco supplied. I glared at him.

Mike let out an unamused laugh. "Funny how we tried to get away from each other and ended up in the same place."

I'd had the same thought when I saw Rosie at that nightclub. The aftermath of what happened was a blur. Rocco and Mike moved down here with their dad. It shouldn't have been a surprise that Rosie's dad did the same since they had family nearby. Yet it never occurred to me. When I convinced my father to let me move back here, he agreed as long as it was New York, and only because Lorenzo was here and would take me under his wing. At the time, Loren had been in law school and working closely with Silvio Costello. Silvio had him mostly looking for people, hunting them really. He'd look for them, pluck them from wherever they were, and deliver them to Silvio's men. I'd learned that skill from him, and soon Lorenzo was practicing law and I was the one doing the hunting for him.

I'd been all over New York, including Costello territory, which was why it was mind-blowing that I'd never run into Rosie. When Loren got out of his uncle Silvio's inner circle, he stopped sending me to Costello territory. I was a De Luca, not a Costello, and Silvio and my father butted heads too much, but for the sake of keeping the peace, they came up with an agreement. We wouldn't go into their territory, and they wouldn't come into ours. Since all of Santiago Vega's bodegas were in Costello territory, I was sure I never would have crossed paths with Rosie had it not been for this.

"Gabe left this voice message," I said after a moment and played the message on speaker.

Dom, I'm sorry. I need a favor. Go to Tempt, VIP area bar, look for her and take care of her. And don't fuck her.

It must have been the hundredth time I'd heard it, but this time, when it got to the *"don't fuck her"* part, I felt myself shake a little inside. After today, I wasn't sure that was possible. Shit, after last night when I'd all but felt her up, I knew it would be impossible. The memory came back to haunt me. *What was I thinking pinning her down in her bed like that?* And then I'd threatened to tie her up. Jesus. She probably thought I was a monster. *What was I thinking setting her up in the room next to mine?* I had another guest room downstairs that she could have easily stayed in, but I hadn't even considered it as an option. I told myself it was for her protection, but if this was how I felt on day one, I had the feeling that the only person she'd need protection from was me. I proceeded to show Mike the surveillance videos before he handed me back my phone.

"Where's the proof that he's talking to authorities?"

"I don't have any. Rosie seems to think he might be. Apparently, he told her if he ever felt like he was in danger, he'd go to them."

"Why wouldn't he come to us?" Rocco asked. I shrugged. I'd wondered the same thing, which was why him being on a business trip made sense.

"Was he in danger?" his brother asked.

"I don't know, Mikey. That's why we're sitting in a goddamn parking lot talking to a fucking cop."

"Detective," he corrected.

I rolled my eyes. Rocco let out a sound that sounded like a laugh. That pissed me off more. This wasn't the time to be funny.

"Why would he involve Rosie in any of it?" Mike shot me a disbelieving look. "Are they together again?"

I grit my teeth. One of the many decisions I'd made when it came to Rosie was that it wasn't good for me to think about anyone's hands on her, including my brother's.

"We don't know for sure, but they were definitely in touch," Rocco said.

"I'll see what I can find out, but I can't make any promises." He started moving to the door when he turned back to look at me and from the amused expression on his face, I knew whatever came out of his mouth next was going to make me want to punch him in the face. "Try not to fuck your brother's girlfriend." With a wink, he left.

Rocco laughed. I punched him in the arm, which made him laugh harder.

"Fuck you both." I set the car in drive and headed back.

"You going by the gas stations today?" Rocco asked as I drove back to his car.

"Nah, I have something to take care of at Oui."

I was glad he didn't question me, not that he had reason to. I owned the damn place, after all. It was originally Gio's, but he'd sold it to me last year when he decided to set his focus on other business ventures. I had Veronica and Patty running Oui, so I only really looked at finances and approved or denied things they brought to my attention. We usually took care of everything through email exchanges unless there was anything more pressing to address, in which case I went into the office. This felt urgent.

CHAPTER TEN

"**Y**OU'RE JOKING." MY MOUTH FELL OPEN WHEN I STEPPED INTO the office and found Dominic sitting behind the desk.

"Life has a funny way of sneaking up on you, huh?" his eyes twinkled.

"Yeah, I'd think that was funny, but you aren't Alanis Morissette and there's absolutely nothing cool about this."

He looked over my shoulder. "Marco, you can go. Evie, shut the door on your way out and don't let anyone come in here until I'm done."

I caught Evie's eyes widening when I glanced over, but she merely nodded quickly as she left and shut the door. I turned back to Dominic. All he'd done was throw a black blazer over his black t-shirt, and somehow that made him look put together. I wasn't sure there was a look this man couldn't pull off.

"You own this place?" I stepped forward until I reached his desk. He hadn't invited me to sit, but I did anyway.

"Yep."

"So that was how you knew about my interview?"

"Yep." His eyes were dancing, and I couldn't decide if I wanted to jump over the desk and pounce on him or slap him for a second time this week.

"I was told I was meeting with Veronica to go over my paperwork."

"She's busy, so you're stuck going over it with me."

"Okay." I took a breath.

"Unless you're not comfortable with going over these

questions with me. If that's the case, we can discuss payment and you can wait for her to go over the rest." He searched my eyes for a moment.

He was giving me an out. The questions were extremely personal, but if I was going to talk about it with a complete stranger, it might as well be him, right? Besides, it wasn't like I was embarrassed by any of it.

I shook my head once. "Let's get this over with."

He looked at the computer screen and clicked something. His eyes scanned the screen. I figured he was going over all of the things I'd written down, which made me nervous for some reason. I tried to think of all of the questions. *Are you on the pill? When was the last time you checked your sexual health? Are you comfortable with touching, and if so, to what extent? Are you comfortable with sex? If so, please provide a list of things you will not do. What days are you free? Are you comfortable with a man not wearing a condom? Are you comfortable going out with the same sex?* The questions went on and on, and now that I was remembering the extent of it and knew Dom was reading my answers, I couldn't help the blush I felt on my cheeks. When he glanced over at me, I expected him to make a smart remark or make fun of something on that page, because surely he had enough ammunition to do so, but instead, he was completely serious. This was Dominic in business mode.

"You didn't specify an age range."

"I don't really have one."

"In question five, you wrote down 'maybe' for sex."

"I also wrote that I wouldn't do it until the fourth time I met with the person."

He looked slightly amused. "What's the difference between the first or the fourth if you're going to do it anyway?"

"Because I don't know if I'm *going to do it anyway.* I have to meet them first and go from there." I shrugged. There was logic to it; I just didn't know how to explain it to him.

"You do realize this isn't a dating service."

"Fair point." I pursed my lips. "Maybe I should just say no to question five for now."

He gave a nod. Clicked something on the computer. Looked at me again. "We run continuous background checks on everyone, so you shouldn't have an issue there." His eyes dropped to my neck. Thankfully the temperature had dropped overnight, and I was wearing a scarf, but we both knew what was underneath. "It says here that you won't be available on weekends. At all?"

"Nope."

"Are you aware that you get paid more on weekends?"

"Yep, but I'm performing five shows each weekend, and higher pay or not, there's no way I'm giving that up."

"Oh." His brows shot up. "That many shows?"

"Yep. Until mid-December."

"This is starting to make sense."

"My scheduling?"

"You wanting this job at all."

I bit my lip and looked away briefly. "Have you found anything out about Gabe?"

"Not yet, though I did hear that Tommy's out of the country."

"Since when?" I asked, trying to think back to my last days at Tempt. "I'm pretty sure I saw him after I saw Gabe."

"Rumor has it he's trying to get rid of his club and Gabe would have access to all of the financial statements."

I sat back in my chair. "So it could be a work trip he's on, after all."

"That's what it seems like."

If that was the case, Gabe's warning to Dominic about me would definitely have to be because of Anthony, because of how he saw him treating me, and not because of what I'd told him about Tommy's company. That would be good news since it meant he was safe, but what if Anthony found out about his scheme? What if he found out that was the reason I'd left Tempt to begin with? What would that mean for my dad? For Gabe when he came back? My phone buzzed in my purse and I jumped in my seat. Dominic gave no reaction, but it seemed like he was curious to see what my next move would be. I breathed a little easier when my phone stopped buzzing, but it started again shortly after.

"You may want to look at that. It could be your boyfriend."

I rolled my eyes. Telling him that I didn't have a boyfriend was on the tip of my tongue, but I bit back the information and pulled my phone out of my purse. It was from the correctional facility. My heart pounded loudly in my ears, but I didn't automatically answer since we still weren't finished with our meeting.

"It's not him," I said, glancing up at him.

"You can answer it if you need to." He shrugged. "This isn't a test to see whether or not you'll take the call, if that's what you're thinking. You already have the job."

I answered it quickly, pressing the button to accept the call. I stood and walked to the other side of the office. It wasn't very big and didn't give me much room away from Dominic, but having my back turned to him felt a little more private.

"Are you okay?" I whispered.

"I'm fine. Why wouldn't I be?" he asked.

I wanted to scream. The only reason I was in this room right now finishing up paperwork to work for an escort service owned by Dominic De Luca, of all people, was the man on the other side of the line and he was acting like I shouldn't be worried about him. He was the reason I'd let Anthony Costello touch me, hurt me, and the reason I'd poured my heart out to Gabe. Basically, the reason for all of this crap, and even though he was the one behind bars, from where I stood, I felt like I was the one losing in this scenario.

"Just checking," I said, swallowing back my frustration.

"I'll be out by Christmas."

My heart stopped. "For sure?"

"Yes, for sure. My lawyer confirmed it yesterday," he said. His lawyer. Another debt owed to the Costellos. "You still haven't gone to la bodega, right?"

"No, you asked us not to."

"Good. And your brother?"

"He's in Mexico visiting Vicky's family and going to Cabo and all that. He'll be there for the next two weeks."

"Good, good. No need to worry about me," he said. "What's up with the debt?"

"I'm almost done paying it," I whispered, glancing over my shoulder at Dominic, who was watching me like a hawk. I looked away quickly.

"You know I don't agree with what you're doing, but I can't thank you enough." He breathed out into the phone. "I owe you my life, you know that?"

"Yeah. I do, actually." I wiped my face with the back of my hand. I hadn't even realized I'd started crying.

"When I get back, I don't want you to come over right away. Wait until I know it's safe, okay?"

"Yeah."

"I love you. If you speak to your brother, relay the message."

"I will. Love you too, Papi." I swallowed against the emotion that built in my throat each time we said goodbye. It always felt like the last time we would, and I hated it.

"I can't wait to see you. I can't wait to rejoin my softball league, to walk the park again, to take the subway. I even miss the smell of the streets and the impatient people on the sidewalk."

At that, I smiled. "Can't wait to hear you complain about that last one."

He laughed. "See you soon."

The call ended and I focused on composing myself before turning around. Even though I wasn't looking at him, I felt

Dominic still watching me. When I finally went back and sat down, I folded my hands on my lap and met his gaze, struck by the intensity in them.

"Thank you for letting me answer that." I cleared my throat. "What else do you need from me?"

"Your bank account information." He slid a sheet of paper over to me. I knew this all by heart, so I jotted it down and slid it back. "You always did have a great memory."

"Some things never change." I tried for a smile, but it felt sad so I stopped.

I wasn't going to fake anything with Dom. He'd known me when I went through my awkward tween phase, when my entire face broke out with pimples, and when I had braces. It wasn't like I wanted to impress him. I wasn't sure that I could even if I tried. The man had it in his mind that I was dating his brother, or maybe he knew I wasn't and just wanted me to outright admit it for some reason. With the way he blatantly flirted with me, that was the only plausible conclusion. That, or he simply didn't care whether or not I was dating his brother or anyone else. There was no telling with him. Unlike his brother, Dominic was not an easy person to figure out.

"Does the company pay you per performance or are you on some type of salary?"

"Per performance," I said sadly.

"That's a bad thing?" He searched my face and I knew there were a million more questions he wanted to ask me.

"It's not," I said. "Not really. I'm grateful that I still have the opportunity, even if it is a temp role."

"Did you have a steady role before?"

"I was on salary, yes."

He waited for me to expand on that, and when I didn't, he asked, "How much do they pay you for temporary roles?"

"It varies. For this, they're paying me eight hundred."

"So you'll make four grand the weekends you have five shows."

"Yep."

"And you still need to escort?" He squinted at me.

"Do we live in the same city?" I asked.

I didn't want to tell him about my father's debt, but needing more money wasn't far-fetched. He'd seen my tiny studio apartment. It was nowhere near as nice as his townhouse, not that I'd ever complain about it. I was proud of my apartment. Besides, he wasn't entirely wrong. On my dancer salary, I did afford my bills, but I couldn't afford to pay my bills and Tommy Costello back at lightning speed. I wasn't going to divulge that information to him, but I knew he'd find out if he wanted to. He stared at me for what felt like an eternity, his eyes never leaving my face, and yet somehow he made me feel like I was sitting here completely naked. I really didn't want to break the stare first, but I couldn't take it. I felt too vulnerable when he looked at me. I felt *everything* and that was something I could not handle coming from him. I dropped my eyes to the large wood desk between us.

"I'll match that price. How does that sound?"

I blinked up at him. "It sounds great."

"You start Wednesday."

"Perfect."

"Good." He gave a nod and tapped his knuckle against the desk. "You can go."

"Um, thanks." I stood up and grabbed my purse. I was halfway to the door when something occurred to me. I turned to him again. "How will I know what to wear or where to go?"

"You'll be sent an email with all of the information a few days before and a follow-up the day of."

With that, I left. When I stepped out into the hallway, I nearly ran into Veronica, who I'd met the other day. She was holding a folder in one hand and a cup of coffee in the other.

"I'm so sorry," I said, shutting the door behind me.

"No biggie. Nothing spilled." She smiled. "Are you ready? I know how awkward it is to answer all of those questions, but I promise I'll make it as painless as possible."

"I just did that."

"You went over the paperwork?"

"Yeah. I *just* finished."

She blinked. "With whom?"

"Dominic. He said you were indisposed."

"Did he now?" Her brows rose.

"Yep."

"Dominic went over paperwork," she said, as if completely dumbfounded by this.

"Yeah," I said quietly. "Was he not supposed to?"

"Technically, he can do whatever he wants," she quipped. "But I've never seen the man do any kind of paperwork. I'm a little impressed."

"Oh. Well, he said I'll start Wednesday."

She was looking at me weirdly, as if I was speaking a language she was familiar with but couldn't quite understand in its entirety. "Sure. I mean, hey, he knows what he's doing, right?"

"The way you're saying this makes me think he doesn't."

She laughed. "It'll be fine. We'll be in touch soon." She smiled one more time before turning and opening Dominic's office without even knocking.

I left and got in the car. Dominic was having Marco drive me around as a precaution, which I had to admit was kind of nice. The rides themselves were pretty quiet though. Marco was always focused on ESPN Radio and wasn't much of a talker, which was fine by me. The less I knew about their lives, the better. I pulled out my phone and found Yari's last text.

Me: I took the job

Yari: HOLY SHIT YES BITCH

Me: lol

Yari: when do you start?

Me: Wednesday

Yari: we'll celebrate after? Or maybe Thursday?

Me: 100%

Yari: AH! Love you. See you soon

I sent my brother a long text about my conversation with Dad before setting my phone aside. No matter what I did, my thoughts kept drifting back to Dominic. This was not good. I'd dated his twin brother, for God's sake. And yet, Gabe didn't make me feel any of these things. He'd been the safe bet. Dom made me feel like I was in over my head, and I wasn't even *in* anything at all with him. I groaned. This arrangement couldn't end fast enough.

CHAPTER ELEVEN

"**S**INCE WHEN DO YOU INTERVIEW PEOPLE?" IT WAS THE FIRST thing Rocco asked when he walked inside my house.

I shook my head. "Veronica has such a big mouth."

"Yeah she does, but seriously, I can't even picture you doing paperwork." He shot me a look, then brushed past me and headed straight to the fridge. "Oh shit, someone went grocery shopping."

"Via my phone. You should try it."

"Nah, I like seeing what I'm buying. Besides, you don't know what those delivery people do to your food. One minute you're eating an apple, the next you're passed out and they're robbing your house." He closed the fridge, picked up a Granny Smith apple and smelled it before walking over to the sink.

"You don't seem too worried about that."

"I figure if I go down, you'll rescue me." He grinned. "Besides, they can't tranquilize *me*. I'm worried about you."

"I'm two inches taller than you." I shot him a look.

"It's not about height. It's about endurance." He switched off the water, dried the apple with a paper towel, and bit into it. He raised it. "This shit is good."

I sighed heavily, taking a seat on the barstool at the corner of the counter.

"Nothing on Gabe?"

"No, but I don't feel sick to my stomach, so that's a good sign."

"You and your twin shit."

"It's real."

"If you say so." He bit the apple again. "It's a good thing Mikey and I don't share that. Can you imagine? He'd have the guiltiest conscience."

"Or you'd be a saint."

"Right." He laughed. "Does your dad know Gabe's missing?"

"Yep." I'd finally called him and told him every detail, minus the bit about Rosie.

"And?"

"He doesn't seem too worried."

"Huh."

"Exactly." I frowned. "Something about the way he said it made me think he knows where Gabe is, but he didn't want to tell me."

"Maybe Gabe's working for him."

"Why wouldn't they tell me?"

"Maybe they think you'd get pissed that Gabe's involved in any of this kind of shit." Another bite, another crunch. "You're a little overprotective of your siblings."

"I guess."

"Speaking of which, what's up with your sister?"

"In the process of transferring to Columbia."

"Why?"

"To be closer to us?" I shrugged. "I think she thinks it means she'll have a little more freedom or something."

He scoffed. "She should know by now that Giuseppe will set up an ivory tower to keep her locked up no matter where she goes."

I nodded gravely. Our father had everything planned out for Lenora. It was disgusting and something I hated for her, but there was very little I could do to help her. Her mother—our stepmother—had been in a similar situation. Much like me and Gabe, Lenora was practically bred for this life. We tried not to think about it in those terms, since it felt like we were cattle and not human beings, but that's how things were. It was worse for Lenora since she was a woman. Dad controlled everything from her haircut to keeping her a virgin until her wedding night. It wasn't like I didn't like the idea of my little sister being protected, but it was all so antiquated.

"Is your dad still hell-bent on picking her husband?" He finished the apple, tossed it in the garbage, and opened the fridge again. "What else do you have in here?"

"She talked him into letting her choose. He has a list for her, but he's hoping she picks the Italian nobleman."

"Nobleman?" Rocco looked over his shoulder. "It's like a fairy tale. The little principessa will be so pleased."

"You know she hates it when you call her that." I felt myself smile thinking about the way my sister shot daggers at Rocco each time he did. "Speaking of fairy tales, what's going on with Crystal?"

He let out a forced laugh. "She finally got a boyfriend, so I'm hoping that means she's found a new obsession."

"For your sake, I hope you're right."

"What's going on with—" His sentence was cut short by the beep of the front door. His gaze swung in that direction and the moment his jaw unhinged, I knew Rosie was home. He glanced at me and muttered a low, "What the fuck?"

"Nice to see you again too, Ol' Blue Eyes," Rosie said, walking into the space.

I felt my lips twitch. I hadn't heard anyone call him that in a decade and from the look on his face, I was sure Rocco hadn't either. It was what all of the parents called him back home. He looked nothing like Frank Sinatra, but his eyes were blue and that was all it took for the name to stick. I didn't turn to her immediately. It was difficult enough having her sitting across from me at Oui. It had been even more difficult to ask her those questions and pretend I didn't care at all, when in fact I wanted to drill her for more information. I wanted the names of every person she'd ever been intimate with so I could look them up. For their sakes, it was best that they remained faceless. For mine, it was best I didn't think about it much. She was becoming an obsession. A liability. Neither was something I could afford, but it was too late for that. I knew that even if I could take her home today, I wouldn't be able to walk away.

I finally made myself look at her and instantly wished I hadn't. Her long, dark hair was up in a sleek bun that I was itching to undo. She was wearing a black sports bra and the tiniest pair of black biker shorts I'd ever seen. I was sure if she turned around, I'd be able to almost see the tips of her ass. When she walked toward the fridge, I confirmed it and nearly threw myself over the counter to cover Rocco's wandering eyes. I couldn't blame him for looking, though. Her ass looked incredible in that poor excuse for shorts. *She* looked incredible. This wasn't helping my trying not to drag her into my bedroom.

"I was not expecting to see you," Rocco said after a long moment, still looking at her as she opened the fridge and pulled a bottle of water out along with a huge container of mixed fruit. She downed the entire bottle of water in what seemed like two huge gulps and opened the container, standing in front of it and eating.

"Are you going to share that?" Rocco raised an eyebrow.

Instead of answering, Rosie looked at me. "Do I have to?"

"No, you don't have to." I felt myself smile, the smile widening when her eyes fell to my lips.

She looked away with a blush as if she'd done something wrong. At the very least, I knew she was as affected by me as I was by her. It occurred to me that when she looked at me, she very well may be seeing my brother, and that soured my mood instantly. The way Rocco was blatantly checking her out soured it even more. I'd kill him for this.

"Don't you have places to be, Marchetti?" I said after a moment.

He looked at me, eyes dancing. "Nope. Can't say that I do."

"Well, you should leave anyway."

"I think I'll stay a bit longer." He turned and went back to the fridge.

I turned my attention to Rosie, who had already eaten half the bowl of fruit. I was impressed. I could eat that in one sitting, no problem. Rocco could inhale it from just looking at it, but Rosie was tiny.

"Do you want actual food?" I asked after a moment.

"You're going to make food?" Rocco turned around and looked at me. "Because if that's the case, I won't be leaving any time soon. I'm not going to miss that shit show."

"Fuck you." I shot him a look before looking at Rosie again. She smiled, and fuck, it was so disarming that I lost my train of thought for a second. "I have pizza and a few other things in the freezer. There's also two ready meals in the fridge."

"Oh, I love those ready meals." She kept eating her grapes. "Maybe after I shower."

She looked up at me and right back down at the grapes, a light blush creeping on her face, and I swear time froze. I knew she wasn't inviting me to shower with her. I knew she wasn't because I was a sane person who was capable of logical thought, but the way she said it and looked at me, it was the only thing I could picture. When she was finished, she grabbed the container and tossed it into the recycling bin.

"How's your little brother?" Rocco asked as she went over to pick up her bag.

"He's good." She smiled at the mention of her brother. "Really good."

"How's your dad?"

"He's . . . good." Her smile faltered for a moment. I thought she'd leave it at that, but she indulged him by answering honestly. "He's in jail on a bullshit charge. He was supposed to serve twenty-four months, but he's getting out soon because of good behavior."

"Damn. I'm sorry to hear that. I heard he has some bodegas."

"Yeah."

We'd just found all of this out and I wasn't sure where he was going with this interrogation, but it was obviously making her uncomfortable and I didn't like it.

"Have you been holding shit down at the bodegas while he's away?"

"No. I don't go there anymore." She looked away, but not before I saw the discomfort.

Rocco shot me a look, wordlessly asking me if I caught it.

"Well, it was good to see you, Roc. Maybe next time you can tell me how Mikey became a cop, and you became a convict."

"To be a convict you have to be convicted, sweetheart." He winked.

Even though her reaction was to roll her eyes and laugh as she walked away, I wanted to pound Rocco's face into the ground. He looked back at the open fridge. At the rate he was going, I was going to start charging him for my fucking light bill. The moment she grabbed her bag, walked upstairs and closed the door, Rocco shut the fridge and whipped around to face me.

"Are you fucking kidding me?"

"Are *you* fucking kidding me? *Sweetheart?* A wink? And could you make it any more fucking obvious that you were checking her out?"

"Oh, so you're mad that I'm checking out YOUR BROTHER'S GIRLFRIEND?"

"Keep your fucking voice down." I stood quickly, the barstool screeching with the force. "Next time you call her sweetheart and wink at her, I'll murder you and I won't be using a fucking apple."

At that, he grinned and shook his head. "You're so fucked.

I'm only going to state the obvious once. A woman should never come before a brother."

"She won't." I felt myself scowl.

She wouldn't.

It wouldn't come to that.

Besides, she wasn't his.

CHAPTER TWELVE

Dominic

FOR ROSIE'S FIRST ASSIGNMENT AT OUI, SHE WAS ACCOMPANYING AN old lady to the MET. It was exactly why people should withhold judgment about things, escort services included. Billie's husband died six years ago, and she'd been using Oui since. Her kids lived out of state, so she called us to send people to accompany her to museums, the zoo, wine and painting nights, you name it. I had to jump through hoops to make sure she ended up with Rosie, trading people's schedules and making sure no one got screwed over because of it. The look on Rosie's face when she saw her date was priceless. I signaled Marco to make sure he stayed with her as I got in the backseat of the SUV Nico was driving. If it weren't for the other things I needed to take care of right now, like the status of her father's bodegas, I would have probably stayed and watched her myself.

After speaking to my father again this morning, I knew Gabe wasn't in any real danger. It didn't make me feel any less uneasy that he'd been doing business with Dad, though. Giuseppe De Luca might think he had his children's best interests at heart, but anything he was involved in came with a price, and I was sure whatever job Gabe was doing was no different. I wasn't sure what any of it meant for Rosie. Every time I'd tried to find out who put those marks on her neck, she shot me down, and that bothered me more than I cared to admit. I thought about the conversation I overheard between her and her father and how she'd obviously told Gabe what was happening and something in my stomach twisted. I didn't like thinking about how deep their relationship went or that he'd once been her boyfriend. I wondered if this was how Lorenzo felt when he'd been chasing Catalina, or how Gio felt when Isabel did stupid shit behind his back. I reminded myself that this was different. It was. I wasn't in love with Rosie. I just didn't want anyone else to have her. There was a difference.

Now I was on my way to case out her father's businesses to see what I could get on the Costellos. It was yet another distraction I couldn't afford, but this one could affect all of us and we needed to get to the bottom of whatever Tommy and Anthony were into. By the time Nico pulled up two blocks from the bodega where I was meeting Dean Russo and Rocco—Dean for information; Rocco for backup in case shit went south—I was practically bouncing off the walls. We'd parked a couple of blocks away because this was still Costello territory. As their namesake, Lorenzo may have been welcome once upon a time, but these days none of us really knew what would happen if we were caught lurking here. As I got out of the SUV and walked down the street where Dean was leaning against his car smoking a cigarette, I figured this was as good time as any to find out. Rocco was standing in front of him, nodding his head at whatever Dean was saying to him. They looked over when I reached them.

"Tell me you have something for me to work with."

"Tommy's back in town," Dean said.

"Is he really trying to sell the club?" Rocco asked.

"I guess we'll find out soon enough."

"What's up with this area now that Silvio's gone?" I put up a finger and whirled it around.

"Everyone is still loyal to the Costellos. They revere Anthony like he's some kind of second coming of Jesus and shit." Dean flicked his cigarette.

Rocco looked around, jaw set as if he was trying to contain all of the thoughts running through his head. He'd made it clear that he was against starting a war, and this felt like the beginning of one. He thought that we should leave the past behind and hand Rosie over to his brother so he could put her in a safe house until further notice. I couldn't argue that it was a bad plan, but the only way Rosie was going to a safe house with the feds was if I was bleeding out in the street. I had my men with her, and I knew we could take care of her better than anyone else. Besides, a safe house meant she'd have to stop doing ballet and that was out of the question.

"Who's running the bodega while Santiago's in jail?"

"He has a few kids working it, but Tommy's the one pocketing the money."

Dread sank slowly into my stomach as I processed that. The way we ran things in our gambling rings was fair. The owners of the bodegas or laundromats kept a large percentage of their earnings. It was the easiest way to keep things fair and ensure that no one stepped out of line. If Tommy was pocketing all of the money in his rings, it was just a matter of time before someone either slipped up or started to borrow money, which meant they'd be completely indebted to Tommy.

"Who's running the bodegas?" Rocco asked again, trying to wrap his head around this as well. "Not the gambling ring."

"Tommy's in charge of both." Dean flicked the last of his cigarette away. "Vega took the fall for him as a way to pay back some of what he owes Tommy."

"Roselyn was working at Tommy's club," I said, trying to make sense of why.

"If I had to guess, she was probably there paying off some of her father's debt." Dean shrugged. "It makes sense, considering she never deposited one check in her bank account."

"You went through her bank statements?" Rocco asked, sounding a little too concerned for my comfort. I shot him a look. "Dude, I'd expect you to be mad if he did it to the girl I was trying to fuck."

Dean's brows rose. "The plot thickens."

"I'm not trying to fuck her."

"We don't believe you," Rocco said.

"I don't give a shit whether or not you believe me. I'm not."

"Right. Because she's fucking your brother," Dean said, and the gleam in his eyes told me he was fucking with me and winning, because that little statement made my blood run cold.

"How many men do the Costellos have now?" I snapped.

"Enough. He recruited some of Bonetti's men when he died."

"Fuck," I breathed.

Charles Bonetti was a stone-cold killer and he'd surrounded himself with a very particular group of men. They wouldn't be the easiest to get rid of or control. I looked around again. There wasn't much to see. In the evening, most businesses were already closed.

"He owns three bodegas total?" I kept my eyes on the one down the street.

"All within a few blocks from each other."

That gave me pause. "How much money could he have possibly borrowed?"

"No idea." Dean pushed off the truck and straightened.

I turned toward the bodega in question. We really didn't have a clear line of vision from two blocks away, but the lights were on and that was enough. Would Anthony go in there today to collect payment? Was that where he set his eyes on Rosie? She said she didn't go there anymore, but that didn't mean she hadn't before. As if reading my thoughts, Dean's voice broke through them.

"According to my guy, neither Rosie nor her brother has been around here since Santiago was locked up."

Did her father want her to avoid Tommy or Anthony? If that was the case, why work at Tempt?

"Crazy how she was here all along," Rocco mused. "Not even ten blocks away from us."

I'd been having the same thought way too often lately. We were standing right at the edge of their territory now in a safe zone, though safety was an illusion. I wondered if she'd been living around here, surrounded by concrete, while I'd been living in my father's sprawling Italian estate, on land that would someday belong to me. I thought about the sense of responsibility I felt for my father, for Gabe, and for Lenora, who was barely twenty-one. Rosie must have felt the same way about her brother. She probably felt that way about her father, even though it should've been the other way around. I thought about everything my tiny dancer had given up to make things right for them, and that same knife that had been twisting in my gut since I heard the voice message from my brother, twisted again. He'd told me to take care of her and I would.

I looked at Dean again. "Thanks."

"Don't mention it." He swung his key ring around his finger. "I know the way you two operate, and I think you should wait until we know exactly how many people we're up against before you put on your masks and capes and start doing the vigilante shit you love to do."

Rocco laughed. I felt myself smile.

There was no use in denying that it was exactly what we were itching to do.

CHAPTER THIRTEEN

I HADN'T SEEN DOMINIC IN TWO DAYS. EVIDENTLY, OUR SCHEDULES didn't coincide at all, which made me wonder if he'd moved everything out of the way that day he took me to rehearsal. I thought I'd at least hear him on the treadmill when I woke up in the early morning hours, but either I'd shockingly slept through it, or he hadn't been running in the mornings. My time was taken up by studio time since Josh and I were finally on the same schedule for rehearsals. Opening weekend was two days away and we were getting butterflies over it. The thing about playing the role of Sugar Plum Fairy was that you sat around ninety percent of the time and danced ten. It was also one of the most memorable and tough, albeit random, roles in the ballet. The moment we picked up our lives and moved here, I decided that the one thing no one would ever take away from me was dance. After years of hard work, I'd been thriving in the company, which was why it killed me to hit pause on all of it. Thankfully, Madam Albert understood that I couldn't fill the role of principal dancer right now.

Not until all of this was over.

Thankfully, she didn't push or question too much. Madam knew I would never say no to a promotion unless the situation was dire, which it was. Besides, I was only taking a short break, and not even much of one obviously, considering that the moment she called to offer me the role of Sugar Plum Fairy, I'd screamed and jumped and readily agreed. *"Only if you can,"* she'd said. *"Don't take it if it will overwhelm you."*

I'd been trying to move mountains to take that role and I'd be damned if I gave it up because of an asshole like Anthony Costello. Whenever I thought about him, my stomach flipped, and not in a good way either. Not in the way it flipped whenever I saw Dominic. I was trying really hard not to feel this way about him. Not because of Gabe, but because I'd spent the last ten years of my life trying to erase my past, and when I couldn't do that, I decided to focus on the things I could control. At the top of that list was not falling for a man like my father. Like Anthony. Like Dominic. Those were the kind of guys responsible for what happened that Tuesday.

At 4:13, when I shot up in bed, I heard him leave his room and soon after, the sound of the treadmill. I pushed the sheets off me and stopped by the bathroom to brush my teeth and fix myself a bit. I was wearing an off-the-shoulder Grey's Anatomy shirt with four last names written on the front and matching shorts that barely covered my ass. I had no qualms about nudity, though. I opened the door to his little gym and froze, wondering if seeing him shirtless would ever not affect me this much. It was his back, I told myself. He had a wide back and a body that people trained hard to achieve. He was perfection, truly. He was running at a speed of seven point five again and somehow kept his breath steady. I shook my head.

"You must be half man, half machine." I walked over to the front of the treadmill like I did the other day.

"Do you want to find out which half is what?" He threw a wink at me.

I felt myself blush and looked away. People did not make me blush. I was a dancer. I'd spent the last ten years of my life in a neighborhood where questionable-ass dudes were constantly whistling and hollering remarks when I walked by.

I cleared my throat. "Do you run a certain number of miles or by time?"

"Time."

"Hm."

He slowed his pace to walking speed, then shut it off completely, using the t-shirt hanging on the treadmill to wipe the sweat off his face and neck as he stepped down in front of me. I watched the way his throat worked as he downed his water, watched the way his arm flexed before forcing myself to look away. I needed to stop this.

"I always thought people who enjoyed running liked to show off how many miles they conquered," I said finally.

"Interesting." He set his water down and searched my face for a moment. "There are a couple of things I'd like to conquer. Running a ton of miles isn't on my list."

"What's on your list then?" I asked, and my voice sounded flirty to my own ears.

"You." He stepped forward, further invading my space. "Your pussy."

My jaw unhinged. He smirked, taking a step back. I had no words. Who said things like that and how the hell could I even respond to it? Instead of trying to come up with something, I focused on settling my heart into a normal pace and breathing. He picked up his water and tossed the shirt over his shoulder. I pushed away from the door, walked sideways to give him space, and bumped into the bench. People did not make me blush. People did not make me nervous. Somehow, Dominic managed to do both.

"You can't say things like that," I said once I found my voice.

He ignored me, his gaze falling to my shirt. "Who the fuck are those guys? A band?"

"They're not all guys." I laughed. "They're Grey's Anatomy characters."

"Huh."

"Santi gave it to me for my birthday even though I haven't watched since season five or something."

"I don't like it."

"The show?" My brows shot up. "I'm surprised you've seen it."

"I haven't. I heard it's dramatic and tragic."

"You don't like tragedy? Really? In your line of work?"

"What's my line of work?" His eyes danced.

"I don't know. Whatever it is mobsters do."

At that, he laughed.

"So, what don't you like?"

"Your shirt."

"What's wrong with my shirt?" I looked down at my perfectly cute shirt.

"My name's not on it."

"I can't believe I didn't see that one coming." I laughed, shaking my head. "You want me to get a sharpie and write your name under O'Malley?"

"Fuck no. I want it over Grey and while you're at it, you can cross all of theirs out and just keep mine."

"That's a little possessive, don't you think?" I asked, pretending that didn't make my heart skip three beats.

"Maybe I'm a little possessive with what's mine." His expression shifted from playful to all-consuming in a way that threatened to take me under. I waited, heart pounding. He took one step forward, leaning down. I held my breath. Was he going to kiss me? Was he trying to kill me? He pressed his cheek against mine. I shivered at the stubble on his face. "When you let me conquer that pussy, I'll make sure to draw my name on it with my tongue."

My jaw dropped as he walked out, shutting the door behind him.

I pressed a hand to my chest.

Holy fuck.

CHAPTER FOURTEEN

Dominic

I YAWNED BUT DIDN'T TAKE MY EYES AWAY FROM THE BAR THAT ROSELYN was currently at with her friend Yaritza. As far as I could tell, this was her only friend. I'd met her once when I'd been at Oui, dropping something off in the safe I kept there. I didn't know much about her, but Veronica said she was one of the best people we had. Watching how she made Rosie laugh, all carefree and light, made me smile. I couldn't seem to take my eyes off Rosie. She'd taken her hair out of the bun she had it in when she went to the MET earlier. It was down now, dark brown hair hitting her elbows in waves. I shut my eyes and inhaled for a moment, smelling the memory of the flowery shampoo from here. I'd kept my word and stocked up on it.

She hadn't verbally thanked me, but after my workout this morning, I walked into the Jack-and-Jill bathroom and found a "thank you" scribbled on the fogged-up mirror. The note made me think about her naked and wet in the hot shower and that visualization made me so hard that I couldn't go back to my workout. I was actually starting to think Rocco was right about this being a terrible idea. I wasn't sure what was making me crazier, the fact that I wanted her as much as I did and knew I shouldn't or that he was right about something. My phone buzzed on my lap, and I looked down to see a text from him.

Rocco: how's the stalking going?

Me: I'm not stalking

Rocco: you aren't sitting outside watching her without her knowledge?

I felt my brows furrow. Was that the definition of a stalker?

Me: mind your business

Rocco: k I'll leave you alone while you stalk your brother's girlfriend

I scowled at my phone and tossed it beside me in the seat. "Ready to go, boss?"

I met Nico's gaze in the rearview. I'd been his boss for a little over eight months now. That was how long it had been since the five of us created the new Famiglia. The only Famiglia, as far as we were concerned. It still felt weird when Nico called me "boss," though. He wasn't much older than me, but still. Even though I'd started as a soldier, I'd risen up the chain quickly because of who my father was. I also had Lorenzo's backing, which held a lot of weight because of who he was and who his father was. There were men who'd been around longer than I'd been alive and would remain in the same position forever, while guys like us rose quickly in rank. That was maybe one of the only good things about being a De Luca, a Marchetti, a Russo, and a Costello.

"Boss?" Nico repeated.

"Not yet." I tore my gaze from his and glanced back at Rosie, noticing that three guys had joined them now. I shifted in the seat, sitting up straighter.

Nico said nothing and went back to the book he was reading on his Kindle app. Two seconds ago, I'd been tired and yawning, but suddenly I felt wide awake. I watched one of the guys clink his glass against Rosie. She was smiling at him, and I decided I didn't like it. Who the fuck were these idiots? The guy next to Yari was holding her hand as he apparently read her lifelines. I rolled my eyes at the lame pick-up attempt, but then one of the guys next to Rosie decided to do the same to her. I stiffened. What was it about this woman that made me forget all reason? She seemed to have my heart in a chokehold. I'd never been an asshole as a kid, but to her, I was the worst. I'd never cared to make anyone jealous, but when I knew she'd be around, I made sure to have the hottest girl in the school on my arm. Well, second hottest. None of them ever compared to Rosie. Rocco used to think I was crazy, even back then, for feeling this way, but I couldn't help it.

A rush of anger spread through me as I watched the guy keep her hand in his. He was saying something to her, probably commenting on how soft her skin was or some shit. My fists clenched on my lap. Fuck. I already knew I was going to get out of the car and fuck this up. I also knew no amount of deep breaths or counting would help stop me from leaving this car and going over there. I thought about my brother and how I was going to have to explain that I fucked his girlfriend, because I would. I'd made up my mind about that right then and there as I watched another man flirting with her. Gabe shouldn't have left her in my care if he wanted another chance with her. What was he thinking?

I thought about his voice message again and all the things she'd said. I thought about the way her brows pinched every time I mentioned her boyfriend or my brother being her boyfriend, and made up my mind about them not being together. She had something going on with Anthony and my brother obviously knew about it. How could he be okay with that? I wasn't even okay with it. I breathed a little more. I'd almost calmed down when the guy, who I decided would not be keeping his fucking hands or face after tonight, leaned in and smelled her hair. Her hair which smelled of the shampoo that I'd bought her. The fact that I was thinking about the six-dollar bottle of shampoo confirmed that I was spiraling, but it was what it was. I opened the door.

Nico set his phone down and looked back.

"I'll be back," I said before I jogged to the other side of the street.

CHAPTER FIFTEEN

Rosie

For a moment, I thought my mind was playing tricks on me. Or maybe it was that third tequila shot that Yari made me take. I wasn't always a lightweight. A few years ago, I could outdrink the best of them. These days, I was an easy lay. I preferred it that way when I needed to be. Still, three tequila shots did not get me drunk, but I did have to blink out of a haze when I saw Dominic walking directly toward us looking like the opposite of a knight in shining armor. He was wearing a black t-shirt with a slight V-neck that gave a peek of his hard chest and tattoos. His dark eyes seared through me, locked on me so intently that it was as though he had blinders to block out everyone else around us. As if he didn't register them at all, though his corded muscles said otherwise. My pulse raced in my neck, in my ears, between my legs. I knew that the people that had surrounded me two seconds ago were still there, but I couldn't bring myself to pay attention to them. His gaze held me prisoner, and even if I could look away, I didn't want to. I felt a sudden slap on the back of the hand I had set on the table and jolted, looking over at Yari.

"You okay? Where'd you go?" she asked, turning her head to look in my line of vision. "Who'd you . . . oh, fuck." She looked away, saw Dominic, and looked at me again, mouth agape for a second. He was readily approaching when she practically yelled, "*That's* your guy?"

I swallowed thickly, eyes still on his. From the way his lips twitched slightly, I knew he heard what she said. I shook my head quickly to deny it, because he wasn't. He wasn't *my* guy. I hadn't even referred to him as such to her. I'd just mentioned that I was staying with Gabe's brother and that he was making me feel things I shouldn't. I'd never called him *mine*.

"No?" Dominic asked, a fire in his eyes as he stopped in front of me.

My mouth parted slightly. I shook my head again, slower this time. Where was my voice? Why couldn't I find it? The guys who'd been flirting with us two seconds ago suddenly seemed to have lost their voices. The entire area of the bar seemed to have quieted with his arrival. It wasn't my usual hangout. Whenever I found time to go out and have fun, it was with the dancers at the company, and we always went to bars near the performance center. Dominic merely looked at the guy to my left, Terrence, who had his arm up against mine and suddenly it was no longer there, and he was saying goodbye to us. His two friends followed suit. Everyone around us kept talking, in hushed whispers now, and I wondered who the fuck Dominic De Luca had become to warrant that kind of reaction in this neighborhood. His brother certainly didn't, but then again, his brother hung out with rich assholes who partied at high-end nightclubs and dabbled in recreational drugs. I had no idea who Dom hung out with besides Rocco, and those two together hadn't been a good idea back when we were teenagers. I couldn't imagine much had changed there.

"What are you doing here?" I asked once I finally found my voice.

"Not your guy?" He quirked an eyebrow, still stuck on that. "So it wouldn't bother you if I went and flirted with another woman here?" he asked, not taking his eyes off me. "Maybe took one of them home?"

My heart pounded even harder. I tore my gaze from his and looked around, finding a lot of the women looking at him like he was a snack, and that bothered me beyond reason. It shouldn't; I knew I shouldn't feel this way about him, but I couldn't help it. At the thought of him with another woman, I saw red. I looked at him again, and from the way his mouth tipped up on one side, I knew he read the answer in my expression.

When I didn't say anything, he took his eyes off me for the second time since he got here and looked over at Yari. "Hello, Yaritza. I'm sorry I scared away your company."

"Are you really?"

"I am sorry I scared away *your* company." His lips twisted. "Not hers."

At that, Yari laughed. My heart skipped again.

"I'm going to the bathroom," she said, looking between the two of us. "And then I'm going to find one of those guys you just scared away because I kind of liked him." I stared at her like I was going to kill her for abandoning me like this. Her response was to smile wide. "Should I tell Terrance to come back over here when Dominic leaves?"

I was about to ask her what the hell she was talking about when I realized what she was doing. I looked up at Dom who was watching me closely. Only because of what he'd just said to me, what he'd made me picture, I made my lips move and said, "He was kind of cute, right?"

"So cute," she said across from us, egging him on. She winked at me as she walked away, and I couldn't help but laugh. He took a step closer.

"Why are you playing with me?" he growled.

"I don't know what you're talking about."

"I think you do." His eyes darkened, jaw twitching.

"What are you doing here, Dominic?" I asked again.

"What, I can't check in on my brother's girl?"

My heart stopped for a solid beat. "I am *not* his girl."

"No?" His smile bloomed slowly, and when it reached its peak, my pulse raced.

"No."

"Is that why you want Terrance to come back over here?" He spit the name out like it was a bad word. The intensity in his eyes made my knees feel weak. I had to remind myself to breathe.

"I can't concentrate when you look at me like that," I said quietly.

"Like what?"

"Like you want to eat me for dinner."

He chuckled, a low sound that sank its claws deep in my belly. He moved so close that I had to crane my neck to continue to meet his eyes. He was so tall. Too tall for me, I decided. Too handsome. Too dangerous. I wished my body would hurry up and catch up to the logic my mind was trying to feed it.

"Oh, tiny dancer." He lowered his head, bringing his mouth to the shell of my ear, the light beard on his face grazing the side of mine, his cologne invading my senses. "If I had you, I'd eat you for breakfast, lunch, and dinner. And maybe even snack in between."

I inhaled sharply. When I was little, I had asthma, which thankfully I'd grown out of by the time I was a teenager, but this was how I remembered it feeling, like I couldn't get enough air in my lungs. It was the kind I'd treat with albuterol every four hours or else run the risk of it being too late and going into a full-on asthma attack. I hadn't felt this way about a guy in . . . maybe ever.

"Dominic," I whispered. He inhaled deeply as if he was trying to consume me through his nose, before pulling away slightly. "Why are you doing this?"

"Doing what?"

"This."

"Flirting?"

"Flirting?" My jaw dropped momentarily. "This isn't flirting. This is foreplay."

He chuckled, leaning in again. "Are you admitting that I'm making you wet?"

"No." I swallowed, tilting my chin up slightly. It was a total lie, but what the hell? *Who said stuff like that?*

"No?" He pulled back and raised an eyebrow. "You sure about that?"

"Dominic." It was supposed to be a warning, but my voice shook.

He reached a hand out and brushed the top of my chest with his knuckles, where the bruises had been. I shivered. He held my gaze. "Come home with me."

"No."

"We live together." His eyes danced because he knew exactly what he was doing to me.

"We don't live together." I took a shaky step back and it had nothing to do with tequila. "I'm only there because God knows what Gabriel has gotten into."

At the mention of his brother, he finally—*finally*—tore his gaze away from me and let his hand drop. I'd have to remember that. Gabe would be my albuterol. Dominic turned sideways and steepled both hands at the edge of the table, which was as tall as my chest but made him look like even more of a giant somehow. He let his head hang and breathed out as if he was trying to work out a battle in his head. I decided that I didn't like seeing him like this. I lifted my hand and placed it on his forearm, which twitched underneath my touch. He lifted his head and looked at me. I wasn't sure what I expected to find in his eyes, but the carnal need in them rushed through me and settled in the pit of my stomach.

"I love my brother." He straightened slowly and faced me, the motion making my hand drop back to my side. "But I want you." He took a step closer, closing the gap I'd created. He searched my face. "And I know you want me too. I see it every time you look at me. Tell me I'm not making this up. Tell me I'm not crazy."

Other men shot their shot and moved on or skirted around

as they tried. Dominic infiltrated until he was settled so deep inside your walls that you couldn't even think of the reason you'd tried to keep him away in the first place. I could've told him he was crazy for thinking I wanted him. I could've made myself laugh and walked away then. I could've told him a lot of things, but they'd all be lies, because the truth was that I did want him. God, I wanted to give in so badly. I wanted to know what it felt like to be in this man's arms, in his bed. A part of me wanted him to consume me, but the logical side of me screamed that it was a terrible idea. In the end, I threw caution to the wind, because why the hell not? I'd had a hard life and the last few years had been awful. I'd given up too many things that made me happy and right now, I just wanted this one thing. Him.

"You're not crazy." I shut my eyes for a second and took a breath. "I want you so bad."

"Fuck." He ran a hand over his face and let out a laugh before pinning me with his stare. "Let's go home."

I tried to ignore the way I felt when he said home, as if it was ours. I tried to ignore how much I loved that idea. I felt myself nod. I wasn't sure if he was aware of it, but no matter what he asked of me in this moment, the answer would be yes.

CHAPTER SIXTEEN

Dominic

I T TOOK US TEN MINUTES TO FIND YARITZA AND SAY OUR GOODBYES. I'd met her once before, and that time, she looked at me like she wanted to climb me and fuck me in the middle of the office. Tonight, the lust in her eyes had been replaced with a clear warning not to hurt her friend. When we turned to walk away, she grabbed my arm to stop me.

"Do not mess with her emotions. She's been through a lot."

I gave a nod and kept walking, wondering if she knew how long Rosie and I went back. I wondered if she knew about my brother and what she thought of him. Rosie had obviously talked to her about me. When I got to the bar, Yari had asked her if I was her guy and I saw the answer clear as day in Rosie's eyes. I was the one she'd been talking about. She'd called me her guy. If everything else hadn't already put me over the edge, that would have, because fuck, I really wanted to be her guy. Outside, I found Rosie pacing up and down the small area of the sidewalk in front of the bar. Behind her, Marco and Nico stood by the SUVs, waiting. She stopped pacing when she saw me, and I knew what was coming before she even said it.

"We're taking separate cars," she announced.

I shrugged, trying to look unbothered by this decision, and walked over to the one I'd arrived in. I didn't like the idea of separate cars at all. We were three blocks from my house. Three blocks by car at this time would take maybe four minutes. Four minutes apart was more than enough time for her to regret accepting my proposal and take it all back. It was enough time for me to think things over and back away from it, but I wouldn't. My mind was made up. Was it an asshole move? Maybe. Did I give a shit? That would be a resounding no. If Gabriel was serious about me not fucking his girlfriend, he shouldn't have set his eyes on the one woman he knew would make me break that promise. The idiot practically served her to me on a silver platter.

By the time we pulled up and parked, my anticipation had reached an all-time high. After Nico cut the engine and got out, I stayed in the car a moment longer, clearing my head. When my brother came back, I'd come clean but I wouldn't apologize. If Rosie wanted to apologize, so be it. I thought about my mother. My favorite person in the entire universe, who'd been ripped from our lives prematurely, unfairly. What would she say about this? She'd probably slap me in the back of the head and berate me for it. She used to go on and on about how it was me and Gabe against the world and if a woman ever came between us, we needed to cut her loose because even if she had a golden vagina, it wouldn't be worth losing a brother. Her exact words. People said time healed all wounds, but it seemed like I missed her more with each passing day, month, year. I pushed thoughts of my mother aside and went back to the basics. Rosie was mine first. With that thought, I got out of the car and went inside the house.

She wasn't in the kitchen or living room like I expected her to be. I found her upstairs in the Jack-and-Jill bathroom, looking at her reflection in the mirror. Her brown eyes cut to me when I entered the room. I leaned against the door frame, crossing my arms and keeping space between us.

"This can't happen," she whispered.

I didn't say anything, didn't let my thoughts on the matter show on my face. I just stood there. I'd been expecting her to say that. If it weren't for the way she was looking at me, like she wanted me to convince her otherwise, chest rising and falling with quick breaths, mouth parting as she looked at my lips, I wouldn't have pushed off the door frame and walked over to her. The fact was that whether she wanted to or not, Roselyn Vega wanted me as much as I wanted her. I walked up and stood behind her, setting my hands on the counter on either side of where hers were planted, and leaned to breathe her in. I watched her reflection, heard when she gasped, felt the way her back arched and her perfect round ass hit my cock.

"This can't happen," she whispered again, shutting her eyes.

"Babe." At the sound of my voice near her ear, her eyes popped open and met mine in the mirror. "It's already happening."

"Oh, God." She closed her eyes when I nipped her shoulder, pushed herself onto me again, inviting me.

I took my hands off the counter and swiped her hair to one side of her shoulder with one while the other traced the curve of her body. She was wearing a dress with shoulder straps that fell off her shoulders. I brought my mouth to the back of her neck as I hooked a finger under one of the straps. I didn't dare take my eyes off her face in the mirror. She was watching me back, eyes blazing.

"You want this, Rosie."

She nodded her head slowly, lips parting.

"Tell me." I bit down on her shoulder blade lightly and ground my cock against her ass.

"Fuck." She groaned, throwing her head back, giving me more access. "I want this. I want you, Dominic. Please."

"Hm." I smiled against her skin and continued my exploration of her neck, her jaw, her back, relishing the way she inhaled sharply when I reached certain spots.

I couldn't wait to see what she did when I buried my face between her legs. Would she even breathe then? I continued dragging the dress down, my mouth following each patch of skin bared to me as I went. Once I was on my knees and reached her ass, bare on either side of the stringy thong she had on, I pulled back and closed my eyes on a groan. How many times had I pictured this ass in my hands, in my face, with my dick inside it? I'd lost count. I'd watched too much porn as a teenager, but while my friends were picturing Jenna Jameson when they jacked off, I pictured Rosie. I didn't want to. I tried not to. Sometimes I hated myself for it, but I couldn't help myself. I bit each of her ass cheeks now, licked where I bit, and did it again. She kept moving, groaning, moaning, hissing, each time I did it and I decided I'd teased enough. I slapped her ass hard as I stood, finding her eyes wide on me in the mirror.

"I can't believe you did that," she whispered.

"What?" I slapped her ass again. "This?"

She nodded, eyes hooded.

"You like it."

"No." She shook her head, nodded, and shook it again as if she couldn't decide. I slapped her other ass cheek, then gripped both in my hands, squeezing. She gasped.

"You fucking love it, Rosie. Look at yourself."

"I don't." Her voice shook.

I brought a hand to her front and dipped it into the front of her thong, my cock growing impossibly hard when I felt how wet she was. I tried not to show it on my face, but there was no use in playing that game; there was no use in hiding how much she affected me. I didn't expect her to know that I never went after women with this persistence. I didn't expect her to know just how much I needed her. I slid two fingers between her folds.

"You don't like this?" I asked, fingers sliding against her. I wouldn't sink one in yet, I wouldn't rub her clit yet, either. Maybe I wasn't done teasing after all. Maybe I'd drag it out until she screamed out my name and begged me for it. "I can't wait to see how wet you get when you actually like something."

"Dominic," she gasped, pushing her ass back onto my cock. "I need . . ."

I waited, paused my teasing.

"I need you." She ground against me.

"Need what, baby? Tell me."

She shuddered. I wasn't sure if it was the term of endearment that earned the reaction, or the way I'd bit the shell of her ear, but I vowed to do both again.

"Tell me," I said again.

"I need you to make me come." She shivered at her own words, cheeks flushing as if she couldn't believe she'd spoken them. I hid my smile against the side of her neck as I sucked.

This was going to be so much fucking fun.

CHAPTER SEVENTEEN

I KNEW IT WAS A BAD IDEA BEFORE WE STARTED, BUT THE ORGASM HE gave me in the bathroom confirmed it. He lifted me and carried me to his room, opening and shutting the door with his foot. He walked to the king-size bed and dropped me in the middle of it. My body bounced up once and I set my elbows up to both steady myself and look at him. I wanted to look around, I really did, but I couldn't take my eyes off Dominic. I'd never admit it, but I couldn't think of a time he didn't make me feel a certain type of way when he looked at me. Before I started dating his brother, he'd looked at me like I was the most beautiful thing he'd ever seen. After I started dating his brother, he looked at me with contempt, like he hated my existence. Ten years later, he looked at me with a mix of curiosity, affection, and the kind of lust that threatened to set me on fire from the inside.

Tonight, he looked at me like he wanted to fuck me every type of way he knew how and discover ways he didn't yet know of. He hadn't bothered to turn the lights on, but the streetlight that sat a few feet from his bedroom gave us just enough light. He was still fully dressed, standing in front of me, dragging those dark eyes down my completely naked form in a way that made me want to cover up. I started moving my knees closer together, but he shook his head slowly, took a step forward, and used both hands to spread them further apart than they had been. He licked his lips as he looked between my legs but still hadn't said a word. I wasn't much of a talker during sex, but this man made me want to demand things, say things, scream things, and because I trusted him, because he *knew* me, I did.

"Dom."

"Give me a moment, baby."

My heart sped up when he called me that. Who would've known? I would've laughed at myself if I wasn't so wrapped up in the fact that despite how much I wanted him, I knew it was a terrible idea.

"I don't think I can handle another moment," I said. He grinned. "You're still fully dressed."

He kept his eyes on mine as he lifted his shirt over his head. I knew great bodies. I was surrounded by them, but none were like Dom's. I'd seen him shirtless, of course. I'd seen the lines on his hard stomach and the V on his pelvis. I'd seen the tattoos that covered his torso and arms, but I hadn't really *looked*. Or rather, I'd tried hard not to look. His jeans were gone next, exposing the kind of muscular thighs I'd only seen on soccer players. Back then, Dom had been an all-around athlete, getting medals and trophies for every sport he'd played, but people lose that drive as they get older. I wasn't sure if he'd lost the drive, but he definitely had kept the body. I zeroed in on his boxer briefs, also black, at the tent there, which was massive, and held my breath. My eyes snapped back up to his as he dragged those down and stepped out of them, tossing them aside. I licked my lips but didn't look back down. I wasn't ready.

I wasn't even sure why I was still looking him in the eye. It wasn't the norm for me. I avoided eye contact, avoided kissing if I could, avoided any kind of connection that wasn't purely physical. I hadn't always done that, of course. I'd had a boyfriend from when I was eighteen to twenty-two, who I'd loved and given myself to completely. I thought Ray would be it for me, but then we broke up and I found out the hard way that loving someone wasn't the same thing as being in love with someone. Since then, I'd had one more serious relationship that ended in a less-than-ideal manner, when he'd decided to date another dancer in the company, and after that, I hadn't really been with anyone until Anthony. I shut my eyes briefly at the thought of Anthony right now and pushed it away quickly. Even though I meant to keep tonight casual, I didn't want to tarnish it with bad thoughts. At the feel of his hands on my knees, my eyes popped open.

"Where'd you go?" He spread my legs wider, setting a knee between them, right against my pussy, and leaned forward on the bed, hands on either side of me as he brought his mouth down to my jaw, my cheek, my neck. He hadn't kissed my lips yet and I wondered if he had the same conflict as me. The feel of his thick, hard cock against my belly made me shiver.

"Nowhere," I whispered, bringing my arms around his neck and encouraging him to keep exploring my body.

"So impatient." He chuckled against my neck, dragging his mouth to my chest, swirling his tongue around and over my left nipple before sucking it into his mouth.

"Oh, God." I hissed, arching my back, pushing myself further onto him. His dick pulsed on my stomach, and I groaned again. "I need you to fuck me."

"*So* impatient," he said again, another dark chuckle leaving his mouth as he moved on to my right breast.

"Please." I bowed my body onto him as much as I could. He brought one hand to my waist and set me flat against the bed, pulling away from my chest to meet my eyes.

"Stop moving." He squeezed my hip. "I've waited too long for this just to have it be over in one minute."

"Okay," I breathed. "Okay."

It wasn't okay, since I didn't think I could take any more of this teasing, this torture, without release. I wasn't used to this, but I'd try. He didn't let go of my hip as his mouth traveled back to my chest and down my abdomen. Only once he'd settled between my legs, did he let go of my hip and bring his hands to my inner thighs, stretching me. I got back up on my elbows and looked at him, heart pounding, pulse racing when he met my eyes and I saw all of the dark promises in them. Without taking his eyes off mine, he dipped down and licked the length of my slit. My hips buckled. He did it again and again until my legs shook.

"You like that?" He took his tongue off me and pulled back slightly.

I nodded feverishly; my fists clenched painfully on the bed on either side of me because I didn't know what to do with them in this instance. He searched my face for a moment. I wasn't sure what he was looking for or waiting for, but whatever it was, he must have found it, because he dipped his head again and this time, took my clit into his mouth. My legs shook harder. No way. There was no fucking way he was going to make me come and this quickly. I shut my eyes as his mouth worked on me, sucking my clit, licking me everywhere, his hands moving from my inner thighs to my ass and holding me slightly off the bed as he did so.

The term "eat me out" was tossed around frequently, but that wasn't what Dominic did. Dominic feasted. My orgasm started at the tip of my toes and rushed through the entirety of my body until I felt it burst. I screamed something. I didn't even know what I was saying at that point, as I shook uncontrollably. He slowed down, licking me lightly, nipping and licking the insides of my thighs as he set me back down on the mattress. I kept my eyes screwed shut for another moment before opening them. He was rolling a condom onto himself. I felt his eyes on my face as I watched his hands move. I bit my lip, felt my breathing grow heavy in anticipation. He leaned down and I braced myself, but instead of thrusting inside me, he set a kiss on my mound, grabbed both my legs, and flipped me around. He slapped my ass, a little more gently than he had in the bathroom, and I growled my disapproval. He chuckled, then slapped the other cheek.

"Ass up, baby." He grabbed my hips when I didn't comply right away and kept his hands on them, even as I did as I was told, pushing my ass up and planting my hands on the comforter. His hands left my hips and moved over the backs of my thighs. He spread my legs a little more and went back to rubbing my ass cheeks with his rough hands. I glanced over my shoulder and watched as he leaned down and bit my right cheek. I gasped, moving forward, but he gripped my hips again and stopped me.

His eyes met mine. "Don't fucking move."

"Do something." I tried to push myself toward him, but he gripped harder. I groaned. "Please, Dominic."

His mouth spread into a grin, an evil smile, and I felt it all over my body. I looked back down at the white comforter beneath me because I didn't want to look him in the eye any longer. I couldn't. He moved slowly. I felt the head of his cock first, then inch by inch he stretched me. He groaned deeply once he was at the hilt, and I felt like all of the oxygen had been sucked out of my body. He stayed that way for a moment, an eternity, without moving. His grip loosened on my hips. I pushed back then, wanting more, needing more.

"I told you not to fucking move." Dominic hissed, his grip tightening again.

"I can't. I can't. I need more. I need—"

Before I finished the sentence, he started to fuck me. His movements were no longer slow or gentle. He fucked me like he was trying to exorcise something out of me, like he wanted to touch each one of my organs, like he'd been waiting to do it his whole life. He slowed his thrusts and brought his mouth to my back, kissing the length of my spine. I rolled my neck forward, my hair spilling onto the bed between my arms. His arm came around to my front, his fingers teasing my clit and he thrust in and out of me. I threw my head back with a moan when he bit my shoulder, and his mouth came up to my ear, licking.

"I've been dreaming about this pussy more times than I can

count," he said, voice strained. I shuddered, legs starting to shake. "I've dreamed about my cock inside it just like this." He thrust hard as if to show me. "About licking and sucking and playing with this clit." He pinched me there. I groaned, my legs shaking even harder. "Have you dreamed of this, baby? Have you thought about my cock inside you?"

I nodded. There was no use in denying it.

"Tell me." Another thrust.

"Yes." I gasped. "Fuck, Dominic."

"That's right, baby. Dominic is fucking you." He bit the shell of my ear. "How do I measure up to my brother? I bet he's all sweet and quiet when he takes you." Another lick.

I didn't know why that was such a turn-on, but the orgasm hit me like a wave. Not one of those tiny little waves that hit the beach every so often. A huge wave. One that took me under and took the strength from my arms. Somehow, Dom kept fucking me.

"Fuck." His movements slowed. He took his hand away from my clit. I felt his dick pulse inside of me. "Fuck. Fuck. Goddamn, Roselyn."

The sound of my name coming from his lips when he was groaning like that, made me come again.

CHAPTER EIGHTEEN

Dominic

S HE WAS AVOIDING ME. I BET SHE THOUGHT I WAS SLEEPING WHEN she left my bed in the middle of the night and went back to the guest room. I let her think I was, not because I didn't want to drag her back into my arms and pin her down and fuck her senseless until she couldn't tell what was right from wrong, but because I knew not to push her. Some women you could smother into submission. Rosie wasn't one of them. Instead of working out at home, I grabbed my things and headed to the gym. Rocco and Gio would be there at this time. Sometimes Lorenzo joined. Dean rarely did. He had a state-of-the-art gym at his huge mansion anyway; it wasn't like he needed to leave the damn place for this. I checked in at the front and headed back to the weight section. Gio was spotting Rocco as he benched. I looked at the weights on either side of the bar.

"You added another plate to your set," I commented. "Impressive."

Gio snorted. "Be impressed when he doesn't need me to spot him, because he can barely lift his arms five times."

"Fuck you." Rocco let the bar hit the rack and sat up on the bench as G laughed. From the look of his shirt, I could tell they'd been here a while.

"How was your ridiculously short trip?" I looked at Gio, who shrugged.

"It was nice until the hurricane decided it was heading straight toward us and we had to run home."

I laughed. "I bet you're upset it's going to miss the island entirely."

"I am. Isabel isn't." He rolled his eyes but smiled. "I guess one of us has to be nice, right?"

"Right."

"You haven't been here in a while," Rocco said.

"I needed a change of scenery." I walked over to the power rack and set up the bar for my squats.

"I told you not to face the treadmill at the wall. If you face it out, at least you'll have a window to look out of." Rocco picked up his jug of water and started guzzling.

"You look at the wall when you run?" Gio frowned. "Why?"

"Because not all of us have a treadmill that faces the entire city," I said. "Besides, the treadmill has a built-in television. Rocco's just being an asshole."

Gio shook his head and moved on to the free weights. "Still nothing on Gabe?"

"Nothing." I set the bar a little higher than it was and locked it, turning around as I stood beneath it. "Nothing is good, though. My dad doesn't sound worried."

"Huh." Gio didn't sound convinced by this.

I started my squat exercise. Radio silence meant that he wasn't kidnapped for ransom. If he'd been kidnapped at all, someone would have already found out and told us about it. That was the thing about all of these wannabe gangsters. They liked to show off and boast about the things they did. It was how they ended up locked up. Or dead. Sometimes in that order. So no, I wasn't worried about Gabe. I was a little pissed off at him, but I wasn't worried.

"Have you been to *The Nutcracker* yet?" I looked at Gio, who was doing curls.

He was a donor at the ballet. At a few of them, actually. He'd say it was because of his sister Catalina. We all knew it was because he wanted to fuck all of the ballerinas. Well, used to, past tense. He'd been married almost a year now and I swore that even if the finest Playboy model walked in here naked, he probably wouldn't care to look. He was ridiculous, but that was G. Once he committed to something, he was all in.

"Not yet." He lowered the weights to the ground and picked up lighter ones. "Isabel wants to go with Cat, so I'll probably sit this one out."

"Look at you being all loyal and shit," Rocco said with a laugh. "It used to be that you were there before, during, and after to check out the new dancers."

"In another life." Gio lowered the weights to take a break. I went back to my next set of squats. "I don't give a shit who's on stage or off."

Rocco shook his head. "So whipped."

"Guilty," Gio said, curling his right arm again.

"What's up with your house guest?" Rocco asked.

"Are you here to work out or chit chat?" I glared at him, standing up straight and locking the bar again.

"I already worked out. Now I'm here to chit chat."

"Well, I'm not." I unlocked the bar and started again.

"By the way, Anthony collects payments tomorrow," Rocco said casually, taking out his phone.

"What?" I stood up straight again and locked the bar. "Do you know at what time he usually goes?"

"Nah. I just know it's on Thursdays."

"Huh."

"Is this about Gabe? Or the Rosie chick?" Gio asked. I glared at him. He smiled. "The Rosie chick then."

"Her name is Roselyn. Stop calling her the Rosie chick like you're Russo or something," I said. "And this is about my brother."

"Right." Gio switched weights.

"Did you tell him she's staying at your place?" Rocco asked, looking at Gio who was on the verge of laughter. "To 'take care of her.'"

"Right." Gio chuckled. "Like it isn't *you* she needs to worry about."

I scowled, finished my set, and moved on to the bench, ignoring them.

"Tommy's people have been quiet about the club thing," Gio said. "He either got a relative to buy it and kept it in the family or changed his mind. I guess we'll find out soon enough." He glanced over at me. "I hope that doesn't mean Rosie will go back there. I heard the escort thing is going well for her."

Rocco laughed and I knew these fuckers knew. I was going to kill Veronica for this.

"She won't go back there," I said, setting the bar on the rack and breathing out.

"Of course, she won't. Not when she's on geriatric duty," Gio said.

At that, we all laughed hard. I wasn't going to deny it. All of the clients I'd set her up with were over eighty. She had two shows today, one in the afternoon for a field trip, and another in the evening. She'd gotten a ticket for Billie to go watch her show tonight. The topic of conversation moved back to business, and amongst the topics, we discussed the theoretical possibility of taking over everything from Amsterdam to Riverside, if Tommy just so happened to forfeit it or disappear for good.

CHAPTER NINETEEN

WHEN I ASKED YARI IF ALL OF HER CLIENTS AT OUI WERE OLD, she'd laughed loudly and agreed that Dominic was definitely the reason for my schedule being a little on the older side. I wasn't sure if he was doing it for his benefit or mine, but I appreciated it. I hadn't seen him since we slept together and if it were up to me, I wouldn't see him again. Ever. Even with my back turned to him, even without kissing him, even without looking him in the eye, he'd made me feel things I had no business feeling. Not with him, anyway. I was opening the back door to the theatre when my phone buzzed in my hand. I glanced at it. Normally, I didn't pick up the phone for unknown numbers, but it could've been my dad. My heart sped up as I answered.

"Rosie." It was Gabe.

I let out the longest breath. "Oh my God. Where are you? Are you okay? What happened?"

"I'm fine. Everything is fine." His words were rushed. He sounded like he was someplace windy.

"Where are you?"

"I can't tell you. I had to drive across a border to even make this call from a burner." He let out a laugh. "I'm okay, though. I'm here willingly, for a job."

"What kind of job?"

"Accounting."

"But you left without a trace. Everyone's been worried sick," I said unnecessarily, as if he didn't know what the fuck he did. "I didn't know if you were on some kind of drug binge or working or what. Your co-workers don't even know where you went."

"I know. I'm sorry. I swear I'm completely sober," he said. "Are you okay?"

"Yes. I'm fine."

"Is Anthony still hurting you?"

"Wh . . ." Before I denied it, I sighed into the line. "No. I haven't seen him. I quit Tempt."

"I thought you couldn't?"

"I found a better paying job and I'll be able to pay Tommy back quicker."

"He just let you go, just like that?"

"I'm not sure." I felt myself frown.

"Has my brother been in contact?"

"Yes. He's making me stay with him."

A stretch of silence greeted me.

"Gabe?" I said, after it felt like he was quiet too long.

"Anthony won't bother you again then," he said.

"Because of Dominic?"

"Dominic and his crew, yes."

Now, it was my turn to stay quiet a while. "You mean Rocco?"

"Rocco is one of many, but yes." Gabe let out a laugh. "You know what they call Dom and Rocco?"

"What who calls them?"

"Everyone. Behind their backs, they call them Ghost Assassins, because you never see them coming, and once you do, it's too late." He said it casually, but I could tell it bothered him more than he'd ever admit. My heart squeezed. I understood that feeling. The moment my dad started getting involved with Tommy Costello, I felt the same way.

"Should I be scared?" I whispered.

"You? Of my brother?" he asked. "Never."

"I meant whatever is happening with you." I licked my lips

and looked around to make sure no one was in the hall. I lowered my voice and pressed the phone closer to my face. "I told you everything. I thought maybe someone found out or—"

"No. I didn't tell anyone what you told me," he said. "The only thing you need to know is that I am okay. I'm safe. Well, safe for now." He let out a forced laugh. The wind picked up wherever he was.

"What does that mean, safe for now? You think they'd kill you?" My heart stopped as I waited for the answer.

"I'm not really worried about that," he said nonchalantly. "They know if they do, my brother will retaliate twice as hard."

"You have a lot of faith in him."

"I trust him with my life. It was why I told him to take care of you."

I frowned. "If you haven't told anyone what I told you, why did you have Dominic come to me?"

"Because, Rosie, I've seen your face whenever Anthony steps into the room, and I've seen his. The last time I saw eyes like that, the man killed my mother."

"And mine," I whispered, though I'd never seen the attacker's faces. I stood up straighter. "But Dominic is also *that guy*, Gabe. I'm sorry to have to say it, but it's the truth."

"I know it is," he said. "But sometimes to fight evil, you have to become it, and I couldn't help you."

I swallowed. "Your brother isn't evil."

"I think he does a good job at turning it on and off." He let out a forced laugh. "I can't even try."

"You sure you're okay wherever you are?" I asked.

"I'm positive. I have to go, Ros. I just wanted to make sure you were okay and away from Anthony. I'm glad my brother's taking care of you. I knew he would. I have to go, so I can call my dad to discuss a few things with him. When I get back home, I'll call you so we can grab that dinner I promised you."

I smiled at the smile in his voice. And the promise. It meant he really was fine. "I'd love that."

He ended the call. I lowered my phone and stared at the screen. I was about to scroll through my contacts when I realized I didn't even have Dom's number. I took a step toward the door to ask Marco for it but looked at the time and gasped. I was going to be late.

CHAPTER TWENTY

Dominic

I COULD SEE WHY GIO LIKED THE BALLET. WATCHING THEM MOVE ON stage was intoxicating and I hadn't even seen her yet. I looked at my pamphlet again and leafed through it trying to pinpoint when she'd make her appearance. I'd never seen *The Nutcracker* before, so I had no idea what to expect. I definitely didn't expect to see a giant mouse on stage.

"She'll be out later in the show," Catalina whispered next to me. "Like much later."

I shut my pamphlet and glanced over at Isabel, whose phone was on silent but wouldn't quit lighting up. I rolled my eyes. Gio might as well have come along if he was going to be such a fucking stalker. She'd ignored most of his messages; you would think he'd get a clue. I looked back at the stage.

"She said she only comes out in one part," I replied, voice lowered but not whispering. We were in a fucking box. Who was going to hear us?

"Yeah. It's a tough role," Cat said. "Kind of annoying since you mostly sit around and watch everyone else dancing, but if the performance is stellar, it's the one most people remember."

"If it's stellar," I repeated.

"Unfortunately, it isn't always."

"I don't remember that part," Isabel said. "But I've only seen this twice and both times it was on field trips, and I was either shushing kids or waking them up since they'd fallen asleep."

"In that case, whoever performed as Sugar Plum wasn't stellar." Cat shrugged. "Trust me, you'd remember."

"Were you ever the Sugar Plum Fairy?" Isabel asked.

Cat smiled wide. "Once."

"And let me guess, it was memorable," I said.

"They wrote about me in *Broadway World*." Her smile grew. "But I never did it again. It's a tough role, and since I did it so well the first time, I decided to bow out while I was hot."

"You're almost done with the remodel of the ridiculous theatre your brother bought you, so I hope you don't bow out now." I took a sip of my whiskey. That was another thing about the ballet, they had a full bar and snacks.

"Nah, I'll definitely perform." Her eyes were on the stage the entire time she spoke. She seemed to be analyzing every move they made and how they landed. I shook my head, grateful I wasn't under her scrutiny.

"How's the school year going, Iz?"

"It's going. I'm counting down the days until we go on break," she said.

"I can imagine."

"You're coming to the house for Thanksgiving, right?" Cat asked, looking at me.

"Yeah, I guess I will." My heart squeezed at the thought of Gabe not having a Thanksgiving meal. Fuck. Where the hell was my brother? Maybe he'd be back by then. He wasn't one to miss our football games, the meal, or the NFL games.

"Don't bring anything," Cat said.

"You say this every year. I know."

The reason she didn't want anyone to bring anything was that she cooked the entire meal. Well, Loren was in charge of the turkeys—one fried, one baked—and she did everything else. Once, I'd taken pumpkin pie, and someone—probably Gio—said the one I took was better than the one she made, and she flipped out over it. Now, she didn't allow outside food.

"Is Emma going to be in town?" I asked.

"Did I tell you she got a job with the *Miami Herald*?" Cat asked, looking at me for the first time since this thing started.

"Nope."

"Well, she can work remotely, but she's living down there for now."

"So she's not coming?" Isabel frowned. "I thought she was."

"Oh, she'll be there. I just wanted to show off a little." Cat smiled. "I can't believe she actually got a real job."

I laughed. "You say it as if she wasn't making money from her crime blog."

"She still does that, but it wasn't what my parents . . . what my dad would have wanted," she said, clearing her throat.

Isabel and I shared a quick look. Catalina's mom was someone we never brought up these days. Joe Masseria, on the other hand, had become somewhat of a legend. We looked back at the stage. My phone buzzed on my lap and I turned it over quickly.

Rocco: Anthony picked up the $ at all three bodegas

Rocco: Tommy met him at one of them

Huh. So Thursday nights, then. We had to watch him one more week or get someone working the bodegas to give us more information to confirm that. I flipped my phone back over and looked up at the stage again, but it buzzed again.

Dean: Tommy didn't replace the kids who work the bodegas with his own people, they were all hired by Santiago

I flipped it over once more. On stage, a male dancer that wasn't the guy I'd seen with Rosie was doing his thing.

"This is the part. This is the part." Cat sat up straighter, if that was even possible. She did a little clap as she looked at me. "This is the part."

My heart beat a little faster in anticipation. Rosie had already come out once in a pink tutu and crown, but it was brief and she was back off stage too quickly for my liking. This time, it seemed like the stage was for her, and her alone. I recognized the song immediately from Home Alone, and wondered if this was why it was memorable, but then Rosie started moving and I forgot how to breathe.

I'd never watched her dance before. I wondered how often Gio had seen her perform without even knowing her name. For some reason, the thought of him seeing her dance before I got a chance made my blood boil. I wondered if my brother had seen her, not now, since she said this was her first role this season, but back then. Back then, when she was his. Thinking about it now made me feel sick, not because I felt guilty for wanting her, for needing her, for fucking her, but because I didn't like the idea of her being anyone else's. She was meant to be mine and mine alone.

I wanted to see Cat's reaction to Rosie's solo dance, but I couldn't look away from her. Why the hell was she side-hustling? As far as I was concerned, there were two places Rosie belonged: the center of that stage, and my arms. Anything outside of that wasn't acceptable. Not the escorting or the bartending or whatever else came along. When the number finished, I stood up to clap and noticed that Cat and Isabel had done the same. I looked down and saw that most of the audience was also standing. A wave of pride shot through me, and I felt myself smile so wide it hurt. We sat down and let the show continue. This time, Rosie was dancing with the male dancer who had danced alone before.

"What do you know about that guy?" I asked Cat without looking away.

"He doesn't have a name."

"I mean in real life." I shot her a look. She was still looking at the stage.

"Oh. His name is Josh." She shrugged. "He was never in Madam Costello's company, so I don't really know him; I only know of him, but I've seen him dance."

"It looks like he's pretty close to Rosie."

"I bet they are."

The way she said that didn't sit well with me. "Didn't you used to date one of your dance partners?"

"Oh, God." Cat laughed, shaking her head. "Don't say that in front of Loren. He just came around to the fact that Justing and I weren't going to stop being friends just because he was jealous."

I couldn't imagine how Loren stood there and watched Cat dance with that guy knowing they'd fucked. As I looked at Rosie and Josh, I felt jealousy bubble up inside me. They seemed to know every single movement the other would make, and I knew they'd rehearsed endless hours for it, but they made it look like it was more than that. They made every step, every leap, every embrace look effortless.

"You think she's hooking up with Josh?" Cat asked after a moment, her eyes still on them.

My chest squeezed. "No."

"Yeah, I wouldn't think so." Cat spared me a glance. In my peripheral vision, I caught the smile on her face. "He was engaged to one of the guys in Madam Costello's company. I think they ended up getting married, actually."

"Hm."

I kept my eyes on him, the way he moved, the way he touched her. I wanted to hate it, because despite knowing he was married, he still had access to her like this, and I didn't. Yet, I couldn't deny that they danced damn well together. The whole show came to an end shortly afterward and we all stood up and clapped for each dancer who bowed. When Rosie and her partner bowed, I clapped even harder. Cat and Isabel cheered beside me.

"So?" I turned to Cat. "How'd she do?"

"Brilliant." She was smiling wide, shaking her head. "She was fucking brilliant."

I grinned but stopped when my phone buzzed.

Gio: when are you giving me my wife back?

Me: you have issues. The show just finished. We're still in the box.

I opened my camera app and set it on selfie mode, telling the girls to pose for a picture, then I sent it to Gio.

Gio: that would've been a cute pic, why'd you ruin it with your face?

I laughed but didn't respond. Not even one second later, as if he'd timed the show, Lorenzo texted.

Loren: are you still with Cat?

I sighed, shaking my head, and they wanted to make fun of me and call me a stalker?

"I'll walk you to your cars. I don't want Loren or Gio on my ass about letting you take the ten steps it takes to go from the front door to the drivers waiting for you."

They laughed but didn't argue, because they knew it was true. On our way out, I kept looking around, hoping Rosie would jump out at any second, even though I knew it wasn't likely.

"Where do they leave through?" I asked Cat, as I opened the door for them and held it.

"Side door." She nodded her chin toward the right.

"How long after the end of the show?"

"It depends on whether or not she showers here. Most people just go home, but some people like to shower and change here so they can go about their day or night."

Knowing Rosie, she'd probably shower. As I approached the SUVs where Tony and Carmine were waiting, I spotted Billie getting into her own car. Once Isabel and Cat drove off, I texted both of their psycho husbands to let them know they were on their way home. Neither of them thanked me for the intel. Assholes. I walked over to Nico, who was on his phone while he waited for Rosie to come out. He'd parked on the other side of the street and didn't have a clear view of the door, but enough that she'd definitely see him when she exited the alley. We were making small talk about Thanksgiving when I spotted someone walking toward the alley. I took my hands out of my pockets. Was that Anthony Costello?

"Nick, am I seeing things, or is that Costello?"

He looked up from his phone. "It looks like him, but to be fair, it could be anyone."

I nodded slowly. It could be, but my gut said otherwise. Still, I waited, watching. Finally, Rosie walked out. I straightened and opened the door to the backseat to pull out the bouquet of sunflowers I'd gotten her on the way here. Gio suggested I get her roses, but these were Rosie's favorite. At least they used to be.

"Uh, boss," Nico said.

The uncertainty in his voice made me turn around quickly. I looked across the street and saw the man, who now I knew for a fact was Anthony Costello, push Rosie onto the wall. I threw the flowers back in the car and made my way across the street. Anthony had his hand on her throat and just before I reached the sidewalk, his mouth covered hers. I thought I'd felt rage, thought I'd felt anger, but none of what I'd felt in the past compared to this. Rosie's eyes widened when she spotted me and before Anthony even got a chance to look, I pulled him off of her and threw him on the floor.

"What the fuck, De Luca?" He spat as he stood up.

I charged, grabbing him by the throat and pushing him onto the brick wall behind him. I'd seen the way he'd done it to her, but I knew I'd done it twice as hard. I knew that if I wanted to, I could bash his head open right now. He must have known it too, with the look he was giving me.

"Dominic. Stop." Rosie grabbed the arm I was using to pin him down. I spared her a look and saw the fear in her eyes, the unshed tears. "Please stop. Please."

"Step back, Roselyn." It was my only warning to her, and I hated the way her expression changed as she let go of my arm.

Hated the unfiltered fear I saw in her eyes as she took a few steps away from us. I didn't have time to apologize or tell her it would be okay, though, because I still had this asshole in front of me.

"You're a dead man," I said, voice low. His eyes flashed, but the fear in them was undeniable. "I don't like witnesses, but next time you even look in her direction, it's on."

I pushed him one last time before letting him go. I saw the surprise in Rosie's eyes when Anthony didn't even lift his eyes to her and scattered away. Fucking coward. He knew better than to defy me, though. Anthony may have a reputation for being a bully, for hitting women and strong-arming everyone who dared give him trouble, but he wasn't me.

CHAPTER TWENTY-ONE

I WAS CATCHING MY BREATH, MY EYES LOCKED ON DOMINIC'S SHOULDERS as they rose and fell. I'd seen him run on the treadmill at high speeds and never take breaths like this. I'd never seen him like this at all. I shouldn't have been surprised. I knew who he was and could only imagine the kinds of things he probably did, the tactics he most likely used, and it wasn't like Anthony didn't deserve his wrath, but still. This was Dominic, the charming jock, the one who would get his hand slapped by his mother every time we all had dinner together because he started before we finished saying grace. I knew he was no longer that guy. I wasn't an idiot, but this version of him was a lot to take in at once. To make matters worse, I feared that what he'd just done could get my father killed.

Dominic whipped around suddenly and grabbed my arm to walk me out of the alley. It was so sudden that I nearly tripped on a crack on the sidewalk. It took me another second to process the pain the grip was causing me. I yanked my arm, yelling his name, but he didn't seem to notice. If he did, he was ignoring me. Finally, I planted both feet on the ground and fought against his current.

"Stop." I yanked away from his grasp and backed away a few steps, needing space.

The look in his eyes was dark, wild, barely contained. It took me another moment to reconcile that. I'd hated Anthony for what he did to me, hated the Costellos for what they did to my father and countless other people in the neighborhood. I knew

Dominic would never hurt me, not physically and not emotionally if he could help it, but it didn't take away from the fact that he was hauling me to the car like I was an object. Hauling me the way Anthony had done countless times when he wanted to be alone with me in dark hallways of the nightclub. The thought sparked the anger that had been buried underneath my fear and suddenly, I snapped.

"You do not get to manhandle me!"

"No?" His voice was quiet as he took a step forward, his eyes dark as coal. "I don't get to manhandle you?"

"No." My entire body shook with anger.

"But that asshole can?"

"That asshole is the only reason my father is alive right now!" I screamed it and choked on the last word, feeling the sob that I'd been holding back finally escape. His jaw twitched. For a moment, he just stared at me like he was barely holding on and was about to snap back. I thought he would, but when he spoke again, his voice was quiet.

"How so, Roselyn?"

"Because. They're waiting for me to fuck up. They have people in jail just waiting . . ." I held my stomach. I was so close to being done paying the damn loan. Dad was so, so close to getting out. "Oh, God." I took a steadying breath and met his gaze again. "Anthony has guys on the inside just waiting to kill my dad if I get out of line."

"Is that what he told you?" He let out a laugh that held sharp edges and made my blood go cold. He took another step toward me, and I took one back. His eyebrows furrowed. "You let him touch you, yet you cower from me?"

"Please, Dom." My lip trembled. "I've had a really, really long day."

He stared at me for a long moment, and I swear I saw sadness flicker in those dark eyes. He glanced away and looked at the SUVs, which were now parked on this side of the street, a few steps away.

He was still looking at the SUVs when he cleared his throat and said, "Go on, then."

I didn't wait another second. I rushed over to Marco as he opened the door for me. I got in so quickly that I nearly sat on top of a bunch of sunflowers. I picked them up with both hands, the cellophane crinkling in my fists as I stared at the large brown anthers and long, beautiful yellow petals.

"He got those for you," Marco said as he started the car and drove away from the theatre.

Tears instantly filled my eyes. I felt my heart crack a little more. The look on his face when he thought I was scared of him would haunt me forever. The worst part was that I could never be scared of him, but seeing him like that made me feel like I was looking at a stranger. I thought about my conversation with Gabe, which I hadn't even had a chance to tell him about yet. He'd warned me. He'd told me what people said about him and Rocco. I knew, deep in my bones, what Dominic was capable of. He stood for everything I stood against, for everything *he* should stand against, and probably would if his mother was still alive and his father hadn't gotten to him.

"You can drop me off at my place," I said.

Even though the last place I wanted to be was the apartment where Anthony would surely know to find me, I couldn't just go back to Dominic's place. Not after this. What would I even say to him? What was there to say?

Marco met my eyes in the rearview. "Do I look like I have a death wish?"

I shivered, sinking back into my seat. Was everyone scared of this man? If so, I'd just seen a preview as to why.

He wasn't home when we arrived. He didn't have a vase, so I put the flowers in the largest glass jar I could find, my heart sinking deeper with each stem I cut. I got some water and a bowl of fruit he'd just had delivered today and went over to the couch. For a while, I flipped through previews before settling on *Peaky Blinders*. Fucking ironic. I must have fallen asleep because the next time I opened my eyes, it was 4:13 and I was lying in the guest bedroom.

CHAPTER TWENTY-TWO

I HADN'T SEEN HIM IN TWO DAYS. I WISHED I COULD SAY IT DIDN'T hurt, but every waking second I felt the knife dig deeper into my gut. Every time I was in or out of the house, he was on my mind. When I danced, he was on my mind. When I worked out, he was on my mind. When I ate, he was on my mind. When I stepped into the guest bathroom, all I did was relive the things we'd done in there. I'd left him a detailed note of my conversation with his brother, leaving out the part about him and Rocco. I wanted to go home. I *needed* to go home. At least if I was home, I could pretend none of this had happened. I could pretend that I'd never even seen Dominic or Gabe or Rocco and never got sucked back into that life. It was a lie I told myself, of course. I'd been sucked back into that life the moment my father chose to do business with Tommy Costello. He was really to blame for a lot of this, but I didn't choose my father. I chose to let Gabe back into my life and Dominic was a direct result of that.

I was stretching my feet before my performance when my phone buzzed on the chair next to me. It was Yari.

"I have a show tonight, so I can't talk," I said upon answering.

"Oh shit. I forgot. I'll talk to you later. I just called to see how you were doing."

"Fine." Not fine.

"You want to go out for drinks tonight?"

I bit my lip. "I don't know."

"K. I'll tell you where I end up and you can decide if you're up for it when you finish."

"Thanks." I smiled.

"Break a leg," she said. "I still think that's a stupid thing to say to someone, but whatever."

I laughed. "Thanks. I'll talk to you later."

"K love you."

"Love you." I hung up and shoved my phone in the pocket of my bag so I could focus.

After tonight's show, I had five days off before I performed again during a Saturday matinee. The three previous shows these last two days had sucked. Well, I'd sucked. I knew the dance and could perform it in my sleep, but my movements felt stiff. Even if I hadn't felt that way, Joshua sure as hell did. He pointed it out to me twice already. He told me the next time, he'd pinch my ass to wake me the fuck up. I hadn't even laughed. How could I, when the only thing I wanted to do was cry? This was exactly the problem with the Dominic thing. If this was the way I felt now, I couldn't even imagine how I'd feel if we started dating and broke up. I could barely stomach the thought. And we hadn't even kissed. Or held hands. Or cuddled. We'd only had sex. Yet every time I looked at him, I felt my stomach flip.

"You ready for round four?" Josh asked, appearing in the doorway. "Maybe this time you'll actually let yourself feel the fucking music."

"I will." I took a deep breath. "I'm good. I'm ready."

"Do you want to go see the little girls?" He leaned against the door. "Maybe they'll remind you what hope feels like."

I felt something heavy settle in my chest, but I nodded as I stood up and followed him, because he was right. The kids in this show were fantastic and they all looked at me like they couldn't wait to one day be the Sugar Plum. The last show was our best of the last two days. Once I finished, I walked to the shower with some of the other girls, talking about plans for Thanksgiving. I had none. I didn't even have anyone to celebrate it with. I was sure Dom would do something, if not with his dad or little sister, then definitely with his band of brothers. I thought I'd be sad at the prospect, but last year, Dad wasn't here to celebrate, and Santi had been gaming the entire day, so I was practically on my own anyway.

I was meeting Yari at the bar. I figured I could do that or go home and cry into my pillow. I'd probably still go home and cry into my pillow, but at least I'd be drunk when I did it. When I got to the bar, Marco was hot on my heels. Apparently, he wasn't allowed to stay by the car anymore. Now, he had orders to follow me like white on rice. Even with him nearby at all times, I was looking for Anthony. I don't know where I expected him to be hiding, but I couldn't let the feeling go. When I finally spotted Yari, I was happy to see her sitting down, rather than standing by one of those tall tables. I wasn't sure my feet could take any more tonight. I'd already iced them and still felt like I needed to do it again. When she saw me, her face lit up as she stood and wrapped her arms around me.

"How'd it go?" She sat down. I took the seat across from her. "I ordered you a martini."

"Thanks, and it went okay."

She sighed. "You weren't into it again?"

"Not really." I took a sip of my drink and looked around. "This place is cute."

"Are things not going well with Dominic?"

My eyes snapped to hers. "There's nothing going on with Dominic."

"Please." She rolled her eyes.

"I'm serious."

"Last time we were out, he showed up and all but carried you over his shoulder like a caveman, and let me tell you, it was hot as fuck," she said, "But, I don't want you getting hurt."

"I won't." I already was.

"You already fell for him." She let out a laugh. "At least it's not one-sided."

"What do you mean?" I asked, even though I knew what she meant. I felt what she meant, and yet, I needed to hear the words aloud from someone outside of my head.

"Do I need to repeat my previous statement?" She raised an eyebrow. "Or the fact that he picks your schedule at Oui and only lets you see the oldies."

"I like going out with Billie." I smiled when I thought about her. "She went to my show the other night."

"My point is that he's obsessed with you, and it's not low-key, either."

"And you're scared that he'll take over my life and I'll lose myself to him?" I took a sip of my drink. It sat heavy in my stomach.

"No." She scoffed. "You're not going to lose yourself to no one. I'm here for all of it, if this is what you want, but you already have to deal with Anthony and—"

"Had to deal with Anthony. Past tense." Another sip, this one bigger.

Her jaw dropped. "What happened?"

"Long story short, Dominic threatened to kill him if he ever looked at me again."

She continued to gape at me. "Is he insane?"

"I think he might be." I felt tears prick my eyes, but I breathed them away.

I was not going to cry. We spent the following two hours drinking and talking about lighter things, like a new client she had who kept requesting her back, and Thanksgiving. She was going to the Dominican Republic to visit family. I was so jealous. I hadn't been since I was a teenager, since before Mom was killed. I felt that thing in my chest get even heavier.

"Ros." She set her hand over mine. I looked up at her

through glassy eyes. "Hey, I'm here for you, girl. If you want me to cancel my trip, I will."

"No." I wiped my tears with my free hand. So much for not crying. "Don't be stupid. I just . . . this is why I don't drink tequila. You know how I get."

"All emotional and sappy? Yeah." She smiled sadly.

I squeezed her hand back. "I love you."

"I love you too. Now, are your feet in too much pain to dance? Because this is my jam."

I laughed and stood up. Hell yes, my feet were in pain, but never too much to dance.

CHAPTER TWENTY-THREE

"**C**AN WE GO?" ROCCO ASKED BESIDE ME, ANNOYED. "WE EITHER go inside and get a drink or go take care of business, but I refuse to sit here like a fucking stalker."

I sighed heavily and looked away from the bar that Rosie and Yari were in. They'd been dancing for half an hour and drinking for much longer. She looked so free, so happy, with her hair pulled up into a high ponytail as she threw her head back in laughter. Seeing her like this did something to me. It made me wish I'd put that smile on her face. It was a gift, seeing her this unfiltered, and a curse, knowing I couldn't provide that kind of peace. We'd all worked hard to go completely legit, or at least as legit as we could get. Russo liked to call it the eighty-twenty method, like it was a fucking diet. Eighty percent legit, twenty percent dabbling in shit that could put us in jail if we weren't smart about it.

We had the gas stations, the import and export businesses, the escort service, the nightclubs, gambling rings in the laundromats and bodegas, two casinos, a private sanitation company, a trucking fleet company and as of now, Loren was also working with his friend Enrique to invest in a private jet company. These were all things we'd either inherited or started with the money we made from the things we'd inherited. Instead of keeping everything close to our chests, the way our fathers did, and only coming together once in a while to meet with the other bosses, we decided to bring it together. We agreed there was less of a chance that any of us, or our kids who would inherit this from us, would stab each other in the back and try to take it all.

Lorenzo's father was on board, probably since he was at the tip-top of the command chain and knew it wouldn't affect him. My father, on the other hand, didn't agree with it, which was understandable. Some people are afraid of going into business with their lifelong friends, and since my father had both screwed over and been screwed over by his, he thought this was a stupid idea. We liked to think we were better than our fathers, though. We also had a shit-ton of lawyers on retainer and every single business decision was reviewed by them. The sanitation company was something we'd been having issues with lately. It had been handed down by the old Marchettis, who lost a lot of employees to the city. We were trying to win over the next generation and bring them back to our side. That was the reason Rocco was sitting in the backseat of my SUV right now.

These companies were legitimate, tax-paying companies. I knew I could explain this to Rosie until I was blue in the face, though, and she'd still argue that it wasn't safe. The worst part is, deep down, I knew that I couldn't provide the kind of peace she deserved. She'd always have security with her, always have a driver, always have me looming over her. I wasn't sure how she felt about any of those extra things. A big part of me wanted to take over her life despite all of that, but this was Rosie. I fucking cared what she thought.

"Let's go," I told Nico after indulging in the sight of Roselyn dancing a moment longer. I turned to Rocco. "Run this by me again."

"We go there, talk to these guys, shoot the shit a little, and tell them to jump ship and come work for our private sanitation company."

"Why would they do that?" I asked.

Back in the day, when Marchetti's uncles were heavily involved, the sanitation and construction industries were controlled by organized crime. These days they had unions. They knew how valuable they were and even though I liked the idea of private sanitation, I couldn't knock these people for going out there and protecting themselves.

"They're on strike again. We're going to pay them more, give them better benefits, better vacation time. If they want to stay working for the city that'll be their choice, but I know I wouldn't turn this down," Rocco said, "Besides, some of these guys are part of Costello's crew. If we get them on our side, it'll be one more thing we have over Tommy."

"Huh." I felt myself smile for the first time in days. It was a win-win all around. "We're going to steal them away and gain control of the industry again."

"Exactly." Rocco grinned. "And then we can tell Mayor Hamilton to kiss our fucking asses."

"Pretty sure G beat us to it."

"It never hurts to remind these assholes who's really in charge."

I couldn't argue there. We were silent for a while before he spoke again.

"I went by the location we talked about the other night."

"And?" I glanced over at him.

"I think we should do it."

I smiled. "Good."

We'd been talking about opening up a secret bar for a while now. The kind that you needed to pay a membership fee and use a password to get in. I'd been on board from the beginning. The other guys agreed to pitch in as well, but Rocco was still thinking about it, mostly because he'd be the primary owner. I'd help, of course, but the space was owned by his father, and following his death, by him and Mikey. Mikey agreed from the get-go to sign over the property. He said he'd go have drinks when we opened up, but he wanted no part in the actual business. Their father used it as a meet-up for him and the old bosses. It was meant to be handed down to us for the same purpose, but because everyone knew about the location, we'd moved our meetings elsewhere. Because of the reputation built around the original location, we knew that we'd get enough memberships within the first five minutes of launching the website to pay for the renovations it needed. It helped that we had tour buses pointing out the location and adding to its mystique.

I looked outside and thought about Rosie again, wishing like hell that I could turn this car around. I'd get out, walk into that place, and pull her to dance with me. I wasn't much of a dancer, but for her, I'd dance to anything. Everything. After the other night, I'd been trying not to think too much about the future. Whenever I did, I felt like I was slowly losing her, and I wasn't sure what I was going to do with myself if she really walked away from me.

CHAPTER TWENTY-FOUR

I REMEMBERED THE MOMENT I FELT MYSELF DRIFTING INTO SLEEP BUT made no move to go to the room. Part of me wanted to catch a glimpse of Dominic, but the main reason I stayed on the couch is that I was really, really exhausted. I wasn't sure how long I'd been sleeping before I felt myself being scooped up off the couch. My eyes popped open and suddenly Dominic's face was right beside mine. I shut my eyes again as I held onto his neck and set my cheek against his beating heart. I could've sworn he kissed my head as he walked upstairs, but I doubted it. I was sure he was still mad at me for the other night. He probably hated me and wanted me out of this place but was tolerating me for the sake of the promise he'd made his brother. I hated that thought more than anything. When he stopped in front of the guest bedroom, I tightened my grip around his neck. He pulled back and looked at me, questioning.

"Can I sleep with you tonight?"

He stared at me for so long, I was sure he'd say no. So many thoughts had muddled my mind since the other night, and at the forefront, the fact that we'd never even kissed. We'd had amazing sex. He'd kissed my entire body, but never my mouth, and even though I hadn't kissed anyone in well over a year, it was just as well since the only man who'd been all up in my business for the last year was Anthony, and the thought of his mouth anywhere on me made me want to vomit. No kissing never bothered me, but for some wild reason, I wanted to be kissed by Dominic. He didn't say a word, but after a long, silent moment, he continued to his room, shut the door behind him with his foot, walked over to the bed, pulled the comforter back, and set me down on the right side of it. I pulled the comforter over myself as he walked away and settled into the pillow.

He disappeared into the bathroom, shutting the door behind him. I heard the water switch on in the shower and felt myself drift into sleep again. When the bed dipped beside me, I opened my eyes again. He'd switched the television on but had it muted. When I turned on my side, I found him already turned to his, watching me. My pulse raced at the sight of him. I didn't understand why I felt nervous suddenly. Maybe deep down, I knew whatever happened next would make or break whatever this thing was between us, and even though I knew it was a terrible idea and definitely not something I could do long-term, I didn't want it to end just yet.

"I never got to thank you for the flowers," I said quietly, after a moment.

"I wasn't sure if they were still your favorite."

I nodded against the pillow and smiled at him, but then I remembered the message I was supposed to relay to him. "Did you get my message?"

"About my brother?"

"Yeah."

"I did. He spoke to my father as well."

"And you think he's really safe?"

"Yes."

"Well, that's good."

"Do you miss him?" he asked. Even though his expression hadn't changed from blank and nonchalant, he seemed like he was waiting for my answer on bated breath.

"Your brother?"

He nodded.

"Why would you ask me that?" I whispered.

He sighed heavily, as if that was the confirmation he needed, and I hated that he'd jumped to the wrong conclusion once again. Before I could say anything, he said, "You don't have to worry about your dad. He'll be safe and taken care of."

My heart dropped. "Dom."

"Just trust me."

"Did you kill Anthony?"

"Would it bother you if I had?"

I moved to my back. I wasn't going to sit here and pretend that I didn't have horrible thoughts about Anthony's demise, but I wasn't sure how I felt about being the reason he met it. I turned over again and licked my lips. "I wouldn't miss him."

He didn't smile, but the coldness in his eyes seemed to thaw a little.

"I'm not scared of you, you know?" I whispered.

"You looked terrified the other night."

"Is that why you've stayed away?"

He shut his eyes for a solid moment. When he opened them, his gaze seared into me. "I can't stay away from you, Roselyn."

I shifted in the bed, scooting closer to him until we were sharing a pillow. I lifted my hand to the side of his face and ran my fingertips over the prickly hair on his cheeks. He made a rumbled sound in his throat as he closed his eyes.

"I don't want you to stay away from me," I said after a few seconds of just touching his face.

There was a fire in his eyes that made my heart skip when he opened them again. "You never answered my question."

"About Gabe?"

"Yes." He brought a hand to my left hip and started drawing light circles with his thumb.

"Do I miss him? Not really, no." I bit back a smile, but he didn't. His lips spread into that slow, wolfish grin of his. Before he could say anything or ask anything else, I added, "You know I was never with your brother, right?"

His hand stilled on my hip. "What do you mean?"

"I've never had sex with your brother."

"Roselyn." His grip tightened. "If this is a joke, I'm going to slap your ass ten times."

"I'm pretty sure you slapped it more than ten times, last time." I laughed but stopped when the expression on his face morphed into one that made me lose my train of thought. When he pulled me flush against him, chest to chest, I lost the ability to speak.

"Tell me again."

"I never slept with your brother."

"Not now or not ever?"

"Not ever." I pulled back and searched his eyes, wondering what he was thinking. His jaw was set, but he was giving away nothing. "I'm not saying we wouldn't have, but we were only together for like five months. We never even made it to third base."

"I skipped all the bases. Remind me what happens in third."

"Touching under clothes, sex, oral, you know, the big stuff." I hissed when I felt his calloused fingers move underneath my loose t-shirt. He said nothing as he ran his fingers lightly against my back, my side, and finally, squeezed my breast lightly. My back arched when he started rolling my nipple between his fingers.

"Not this?"

I shook my head, unable to speak through my gasp.

His hand traveled down my stomach slowly, dipped into my shorts, under my underwear. He slid his long fingers through my folds. "Not this?"

"God. No." I gasped loudly when he sank a finger inside me and hooked it.

"Not this?" He used his thumb on my clit, his other finger working inside me.

"No. Fuck." I squeezed my eyes shut and arched my back as fireworks went off inside me.

He slowed his fingers but kept touching me as he leaned in and kissed the hollow of my throat, my neck, my jaw. He took his hands out of my underwear slowly, dragging the evidence of my arousal up my abdomen. I opened my eyes to find him watching me, his face just inches from mine. The way he looked at me was enough to send my pulse racing, and then he inched closer, his thumb caressing my jaw. When he pressed his lips to mine, it felt like the entire world stopped spinning. I gripped his arm and pulled him closer, and that was when he began to kiss me. The kiss was the opposite of everything he appeared to be. It was soft and inviting, his tongue sneaking its way into my mouth hesitantly, as if asking for permission, dancing against mine in an all-consuming way. The kiss felt like an erotic poem, beautifully written, with the power to set your insides aflame. I never wanted it to end. I never wanted him to stop touching me. I never wanted to stop feeling his tongue against mine or stop hearing the way he groaned into my mouth as if I was the best thing he'd ever had.

After what felt like an eternity of kissing and touching and somewhere along the way, undressing and discarding our clothes, we pulled apart and lay naked as we faced each other, in the same position we'd started. He watched me as he climbed over me, pushing my legs apart with his and settling between them. He held his dick in his hand, his hand moving slowly on it, as he looked into my eyes. I couldn't keep eye contact for too long, but only because I wanted to see the movement. I bit my lip and pushed myself up. He rocked back in his heels and watched me as I leaned forward and took his hand away. He hissed on an inhale when I sat up a little higher and licked the tip.

I glanced up and smiled at the hunger in his eyes, before going back to my task. I swirled my tongue around him a few times, teasing him the way he'd teased me last time, before taking what I could of him into my mouth. There was no way for me to take all of him, but I did what I could, encouraged by the way he was breathing, by the way he gripped my hair and groaned my name each time I moved up and down. He pulled my head back, pulling himself out of my mouth completely, and tilted my face to his.

He looked at me for a beat, two, seeming to search my eyes for something, and brought his mouth to mine again. It wasn't a sweet kiss. It was possessive, carnal, like he was trying to invade and conquer every ounce of me, as if he already hadn't. I pushed myself up to my knees to try to gain some leverage, but that was impossible with a man like him. He slowed the kiss, nipped my lips, my jaw, and pulled back to look at me again.

"Do you want me to use a condom?" His hands were still framing my face as he searched my eyes. "I've been tested, but I will, no questions asked, if you want to use one."

"I don't . . . are you . . . I've never done it without one," I whispered. He let go of my face and reached over to the night-stand, but I grabbed his arm quickly to stop him. "I don't want you to use one."

His eyes seemed to darken at my words, and my pulse quick-ened. "I've never gone without one either."

"Are you just saying that?"

"Do I ever just say things?" He shot me a look.

I shook my head, my heart thrashing inside the confines of my chest. I wanted to ask him, why not with me? But I couldn't form the words. Instead, I leaned into him, wrapped my arms around his neck, and pulled him into a kiss. I used our height dif-ference to my advantage and stood on the bed, positioning my-self right above his cock as he sat back on his heels. We didn't break the kiss until I pushed myself down slowly onto him. I broke the kiss and threw my head back to take a gulp of air be-cause I felt so full, and he felt so fucking good. I moved slowly, giving myself time to acclimate to his length, his girth.

"Fuck, baby." He gripped my hips and took control over my body, thrusting and pulling me onto him until I screamed and my legs started to shake. "I love how you ride my cock." Thrust. "I could do this all day with you." A deeper thrust. He groaned deeply, gripping my hips tighter. I couldn't breathe, legs shaking uncontrollably now.

"Look at me," he growled, pulling back slightly. I shivered when I lowered my eyes to his. He nipped my bottom lip, sucked it into his mouth, his thrusts slowing as he looked at me. "You're fucking mine, Rosie. Your pussy, your smiles, your tears, your gasps. Everything. Mine." He thrust harder, deeper, hitting a spot that made me feel like I was burning up, a fire licking every inch of my insides. "Tell me."

"Dom." I gasped, spasming on his cock. "I'm yours. God. Yes."

"Fuck, Rosie." He grabbed my face with both hands, unwilling to let me take my eyes off his as we moved against each other.

Tears pricked my eyes but I held them back, not wanting to complicate or ruin the moment. This was unlike anything I'd ever experienced before and for a split second, I felt out of my element, completely terrified, but then he threw his head back slightly and started growling out my name with each thrust, and I got lost in him again, feeling another zap of electricity jolt through me. His entire body stilled underneath me, and I felt him empty himself inside me, the sensation making me grip his shoulders even harder, the tips of my short fingernails digging into his skin. He brought his eyes back to mine for a second before he kissed me thoroughly again, wrapping his arms around me, his cock still pulsating inside me.

I felt full of him even moments later, as he pulled out and lay me on the bed before going to the bathroom. I was still catching my breath, reeling from what happened, when he walked back and cleaned me thoroughly, gently, before disappearing again. As I closed my eyes, I heard the sound of water, but could barely keep my eyes open. When I felt him again, he was covering me with the comforter as he nestled into his side of the bed and turned my body toward him.

"Hey." He touched the side of my face with the back of his

hand. I opened my eyes and did the same to his before dragging my fingers down, feeling each wave of muscle in his arm and each indent on his chest. He raised an eyebrow. "I don't think you're ready for round two yet."

I smiled. "And you are?"

"With you?" He let out a laugh. "I've been waiting ten fucking years, so I'm ready whenever you want me to be ready."

I felt myself frown. He'd said something like that before and I'd ignored him, but now it felt important, and I was too curious not to ask. "What do you mean ten years?"

"It doesn't matter. I have you now." He leaned in and pressed a kiss to my forehead. I decided to drop the topic for now. "Have you had a lot of boyfriends since?"

"Not a lot." I smiled against his chest. "What about you?"

"Not really. No one I saw myself settling down with anyway."

"Hm." I didn't like the idea of him being like this with anyone else, but it would be hypocritical of me to say that, so I didn't. "I haven't been with anyone in a couple of years. Hadn't. Until this year," I whispered. I hated that the person had been Anthony and hated it even more that I was bringing him up now, but I wanted to be honest. "He always used a condom. We never kissed. It wasn't . . . it wasn't . . ."

I was going to say consensual, but I couldn't bring myself to. I'd never said the word "no" to Anthony. He hadn't really given me a choice, though, with his threats. Every time he touched me, he'd started with "your father" or "you wouldn't want your little brother to—" I didn't want to say that to Dom, though, not here. I didn't want to discuss Anthony at all.

"Like this," he said, leaning back to cup my face and tilt it up to look at me. "It wasn't like this."

I shook my head. Definitely not like this.

"Nothing has ever been like this for me." He kissed me again and I felt butterflies explode inside me. When he pulled back, he searched my eyes. "Before tonight, I hadn't been with anyone in nine months."

"That seems impossible."

"Trust me, I've been counting." He chuckled with a sigh as he pulled me into his chest. "I got tired of feeling empty after sex."

I thought about the gravity of those statements, what they meant individually and how they came off when said back-to-back. Even as a kid, Dominic had never been one of those people who wasted words or lied about things. He'd been sneaky, sure, but never a liar. Having him say those things to me made my chest inflate in a way it never had before. I'd had one serious boyfriend, the only one who'd come over for dinner at my dad's and took Santi to baseball games, but even he didn't make me feel these things. I'd always thought what happened to my mother broke me in that way. That maybe my ability to get attached had been stripped from me that night, but it was clear I'd been wrong. I'd pushed that away, tried to bury it underneath the rubble of my broken emotions. I closed my eyes, inhaling him. I loved the way he smelled, loved the way I felt in his arms.

"What are you doing for Thanksgiving?" he asked after a moment.

"Nothing." I yawned, not opening my eyes. "I have to work that weekend."

"You don't have dinner plans?" he asked. "What do you normally do? What'd you do last year?"

"I took Santi to Niagara Falls." I smiled at the memory.

"You went to Canada to celebrate an American holiday?"

"Yeah." I opened my eyes and laughed at the bemused expression on his face. "It's just another Thursday, right? I don't really care for holidays anyway."

"It's not about the holiday." His brows furrowed. "It's supposed to be a day spent with people you love."

"Santi's in Cabo with his girlfriend. Dad's in jail." I let out a laugh as I continued. "My family in Union City is going to DR. Yari's the only other person I'd hang out with, but she's also going to DR." I shrugged. "Like I said, it's just another Thursday."

He searched my eyes for a moment but didn't say anything until I shut my eyes again. "Do you ever go back to Providence?"

"No." I felt my body tense, my senses rearing up for a flight response. If he brought up our Thanksgivings together over there, the lid on the emotions I'd been trying to contain may just pop. I'd tried to keep only the good memories from back home, but after the tragedy, even those looked like lies. "Do you ever go back?"

"No."

"So you've never seen the memorial or visited the graves."

"It doesn't interest me. Mom's not there. *They* are not there," he said, pulling back slightly. I opened my eyes and met the sadness in his.

"I know," I whispered. "I kind of want to go, though. Just to see the memorial at least once."

"If you go, I'll go." He leaned in and planted a soft kiss on my lips.

"Even if it doesn't interest you?"

"You interest me." He smiled. It was a charming smile that made my heart flip. It reminded me of the boy who used to visit the ice cream shop all those years ago. "And you're spending Thanksgiving with me."

"What?" I blinked. "Where?"

"With my family."

I froze momentarily. He'd said it was a day that was supposed to be spent with people you love, but surely, he didn't mean . . . no. Definitely not. He was definitely just being kind.

"With your family where?" I asked warily, remembering that he'd left for Italy after the tragedy to live with his father and remaining family. "I don't have a valid passport, and I really do work Saturday. I can't go to Italy just like that." I snapped my fingers for show.

"Relax." He chuckled. "Unless Palermo has relocated to Greenwich, you should be back in time for your performance."

I breathed against him and felt myself relax, finally going to sleep.

Rosie

DOM HAD BEEN GONE ALL DAY, SO I ASKED MARCO TO DRIVE ME TO the grocery store. I needed to get something to take to his friend's—family's—house. He'd said the couple lived in an apartment on the Upper East Side but had a second home in Connecticut, which was where we'd be spending Thanksgiving. He'd also told me to pack a bag since we'd been staying overnight. For some reason, that made me even more nervous about all of it. I couldn't help thinking how awkward it would be if they hated me or vice versa.

In the car, I checked my email to make sure Veronica hadn't sent me any clients. I wasn't surprised to find an email from her that just wished me a happy holiday weekend. Billie's kids were picking her up for the week and the man, Jack, that I'd accompanied to dinner, had a son in town. The fact that I'd only had two clients while I'd been working at Oui was something Yari endlessly made fun of. She knew it was Dominic's doing and she found it *"both hot and annoyingly machista."* I was starting to think it was messed up since it meant I was making less money, but Yari reminded me that the company capped at two clients a week and that went for everyone. Besides, I couldn't quite complain about the money, since I was making one thousand on behalf of the company and close to one thousand on account of tips and gifts provided by both Billie and Jack. I was so close to setting aside ten thousand, I could taste it. Once I had it all, I'd meet with Tommy himself and be done with all of this.

I was in the wine aisle and had no clue what I could buy,

since I had no idea what was good and what wasn't, when a man appeared in the same aisle. I glanced up and saw him. He was wearing a jean jacket and a baseball cap, his back facing me as he looked at the after-dinner bottles. I went back to my task, walking up and down this section. France, Italy, Spain, California, what was good? I glanced over at the other side of the aisle, where Marco stood. I would've asked him for help, had he not been closer to my brother's age than mine. I knew for a fact he didn't know about this stuff either. I sighed and started reading each description. Thankfully, the employees had rated and given their thoughts on some of them. Based on the logic that I would probably be having dinner with a bunch of Italians, and they might appreciate the gesture, I narrowed my search down to Italy. I heard a shopping cart coming down the aisle, but thought nothing of it, until it sounded louder, faster, as if a kid was riding it and letting it glide. I looked up too late, my entire body pushed back as the cart hit me on the side. I inhaled sharply, looking at the cart which was filled with boxes of sodas, probably the reason it felt like I'd just been hit by a ton of bricks and would definitely bruise. My eyes traveled up to the man in the baseball cap and I was met with Anthony's cold blue eyes. I opened my mouth to scream, to say something, but he turned and walked away quickly, leaving the cart where it was.

He didn't have to say anything. The warning was clear. My mind raced and landed on my father. I needed to speak to him again. I needed to make sure he was okay, but he hadn't called and that didn't sit well. At the sound of footsteps behind me, I turned, on edge, to find Marco rushing toward me. He looked at me, looked at Anthony, who was turning the corner, and finally decided to keep his focus on me.

"Are you okay?" He moved the shopping cart and touched my arm. I was shocked to find genuine concern in his eyes and wondered if it was concern for me or for himself, if he had to deal with Dominic's wrath on behalf of this. It was why I nodded despite the pain.

"I'm fine. Just an accident," I said, reaching for a random bottle of Italian wine. All that concentration, and it came down to desperation.

"You're sure?" He hadn't let go of my arm, hadn't looked away from my face, though I couldn't quite meet his eyes. I did then.

"I'm positive." I smiled. "I just need to grab a bottle of tequila as backup and then we can go."

❦

My knee hadn't quit bouncing. Instead of going in an SUV like I expected us to, Dominic had them follow us as he drove his regular car. Well, his expensive as fuck "regular car." Even the leather smelled expensive. I closed my eyes and inhaled it for the third time. Dominic chuckled, reaching for my hand and linking his fingers through mine. It was a simple gesture, but it made my heart gallop uncontrollably nonetheless.

"I take it you like the car." His eyes twinkled as he glanced at me.

"I love the car." I smiled. "The leather smells so nice, like an expensive purse. Definitely not like the inside of those stores on Mott Street."

He laughed harder. "I can assure you I didn't buy it in Chinatown, baby." I didn't know why, but every time he called me this I felt myself blush. He took notice but hadn't said anything. From the way his lips twisted in amusement now, I knew he would. "You like it when I call you that, don't you?"

"Maybe." I bit my lip and looked away as he stopped at a red light.

"Tell me." He leaned in, invading my space, and suddenly I was filled with the scent of him and the leather, and it smelled like what I imagined heaven would, if there was such a place. He kissed my neck, the side of my face, and bit my earlobe. "Baby," he whispered huskily. My stomach flipped. "Tiny dancer," he said, licking the shell of my ear. "Mine." My heart beat faster and faster. I turned my face toward him, and he captured my lips in a dizzying kiss.

The car behind us honked the horn three consecutive times. Dominic pulled away, searching my eyes as if he had all the time in the world. The car drove around us, a man flashing us his middle finger. I laughed against Dominic's mouth.

"I think you need to move, *baby*," I said, emphasizing the word.

His eyes flared as he sat back in his seat. "Next time I fuck you, I want you to call me that when you come."

"Okay," I whispered, my heart skipping another beat.

Someone else honked. This time, it was Marco. Dominic started driving and lowered his window to stick his middle finger out. In the rearview, I caught both Marco and Nico laughing.

"Are they having dinner with us?" I asked. "Marco and Nico, I mean."

"Of course." He shot me a look as he got on the highway. "They're family."

"So it's safe to assume this family is an organized crime family."

"I don't assume anything, but if you want to assume that, go ahead." He grabbed my hand again, kissing the back of it. It would probably be the closest thing I got to a confirmation. "They're the only family I know. The only family I have."

I let his words hang for a moment. I knew he would have said more if I'd pushed, but I didn't want to. After a moment, I went back to the topic I wanted to discuss and had yet to bring up again.

"So you've wanted me for ten years."

"I knew you wouldn't drop that."

"Of course not. One minute we were friends, then we were flirting, and the next you were a total asshole to me and now you're saying you liked me?" I tried taking my hand from his, but he gripped it a little tighter, not letting go.

"I was only an asshole because I was pissed," he said. "And because I thought if I was an asshole, my brother would stop seeing you."

"Really?" I shot him a look. "That sounds incredibly dumb."

He shrugged. "I was seventeen."

"You know I had a massive crush on you, right?"

He glanced at me quickly. "When you were dating Gabe?"

"Before that. Like, the biggest crush ever. I never even wore makeup unless I thought I might see you, and I only did because all the girls you hung out with wore makeup."

"And because you couldn't have me, you decided to date my brother?"

"No. I mean, he was really persistent." I felt my face heat up. "And he wasn't bringing all of his dates into the ice cream shop only to ignore them and flirt with me in front of them."

"Gabriel is a fucking asshole." His lip twitched as he shook his head. "I told him I liked you and he talked me out of asking you out. I swear two weeks hadn't even passed before you started dating."

"You're kidding."

"I wish I was."

"That's so messed up." I felt my brows pull in as I thought back on it. "Did you hate him for it?"

"A little," he said. "I tried to tell myself you were just a girl."

I scowled. "You definitely had a lot of them back then."

"And yet, I wanted you."

My heart dipped. "Dom."

"Like I said, I have you now, and that's what matters." He kissed the back of my hand and chuckled as he lowered it. "I still can't believe you never made it to third base with him."

"Your brother is a perfect gentleman."

"Well, then. It's a good thing I'm not." He winked.

My heart dipped again.

Ugh. I was so screwed.

CHAPTER TWENTY-SIX

WE PULLED UP TO LOREN AND CATALINA'S GREENWICH HOUSE at nine in the morning. I watched as Rosie took it all in, eyes wide, mouth dropped. She was amazed at the house, and I decided I was going to buy one on this block just for her. For *us*. The homes we grew up in were pretty damn big, but not like this. This was a waterfront home with an iron gate, a fountain, a sprawling front and side yard, and a backyard complete with a beautiful pool. It was a dream, for sure. It had never been my dream, but if it was Rosie's, I'd make it a priority. Fuck. I sounded like Lorenzo. Like Gio. And I couldn't even deny or say I hated it. As far as I was concerned, Rosie was it for me. I tried to think about what my brother would say about all of this but pushed it aside. I'd deal with it when he called, or when he finally came home. It wouldn't make a difference anyway. I looked up at the sky and silently asked my mom to forgive me for the thought. God, I wish she was here for all of this. She'd know exactly what to say to me, to Gabe, even to Rosie. I met her on her side of the car. She was still looking around.

"This is insane," she said, "I mean, we've been to big houses, but this . . . people our age own this place?"

"They're a little older than us, but not by much." I bit back a smile. If Loren had been out here, I'd say he was much older just to fuck with him.

"I would ask what they do for a living, but honestly, I'd rather not know."

At that, I grinned. I threw an arm around her and headed

toward the front door. "He's a lawyer and she's a ballerina, so not much to tell."

She glanced up at me and the look on her face told me she didn't believe me.

"I'm serious." I squeezed her to my side and kissed the top of her head. Damn, her shampoo was intoxicating. Or maybe it was just her.

"And that's where their money comes from?" she asked wearily.

"Not *all* their money, but you said you don't want to hear about that part." I pulled away and winked at her as I opened the door.

"Oh." She shook her head as she walked in. "Do you just open the door to people's houses? Shouldn't we ring the doorbell?"

"Nah." I glanced back at Marco and Nico, noticing two gift bags in Marco's hands. "What are those?"

"Oh, I brought that," Rosie said. "We can't just show up at someone's house empty-handed, especially if they're going to feed us."

I looked up at Marco, who shared the same look as me. He'd been here the last time I tried to bring something to Thanksgiving. I just hoped Cat wouldn't automatically hate Rosie because of the gesture. I couldn't imagine anyone hating Rosie though. I reached for her hand. I'd never been a hand-holder; I'd always thought it was stupid, especially inside a house. Like, what is the person going to do, run away from you, go hide in the bathroom? What was the point of holding their hand? But here I was, doing yet another thing I didn't normally do because, with her, I wanted to do it, and yeah, I didn't want her to run away from me. We walked into the kitchen, which smelled so good already, and found Lorenzo doing something to the turkey, Cat and Emma preparing a recipe as Isabel washed dishes and Gio dried them. They all looked so fucking domestic. Rocco and Enrique walked in through the back door, having a quiet conversation. The fact that Enrique was here wasn't totally shocking. He and Lorenzo went way back, but he'd never spent Thanksgiving with us. The only one missing was Dean, but he lived down the block and always got here late.

Gio glanced up first. "Great. Dominic is here. Hide the bread."

"Fuck you."

Everyone stopped what they were doing and looked over at us. I didn't miss the way some jaws seemed to unhinge at the sight of Rosie's hand in mine. Suddenly, my chest felt a little heavy. It hadn't occurred to me that while I thought everyone should like Rosie, it didn't mean that it would definitely be the case, and it mattered. What they thought mattered more than whatever Gabe would inevitably have to say about it. I spent all of my time with these people. They were my people, the ones I could completely let my guard down in front of, and I really wanted Rosie to fit in, because as far as I was concerned, she'd be mine forever.

"This is Roselyn." I cleared my throat and started pointing around the room. "Rosie, this is Catalina, her husband Lorenzo—I think you've met him before—Giovanni, his wife Isabel, Emma—who's Gio and Cat's sister—that's Enrique, and you already know Rocco."

Rocco raised the beer in his hand. Rosie let go of my hand and took a few steps forward. I didn't take my eyes off her as she approached Catalina with that effortless grace she had about her.

"It's so nice to meet you." She smiled as she set a hand on Cat's shoulder and kissed her cheek. "Thanks for letting me crash. You have a beautiful home."

"You're welcome." Cat smiled wide. "By the way, your pas de deux was fucking phenomenal."

"Oh my God." Rosie laughed lightly and glanced down, a

slight blush on her face before she looked at Cat again. "That means so much coming from you."

Cat set a hand on her arm. "We'll talk dance later."

"I'd love that." Rosie smiled and moved on to each and every person, kissing their cheek and saying hello.

Something in my heart unlocked as I stood there, watching the way they all smiled and laughed—some at my expense, but who the fuck cared? They'd welcomed her so easily. I realized that I'd been smiling and laughing more in the short time I'd been with Rosie than I had in years. I was a jokester, sure, but my laughs were forced sometimes, and my jokes hid pain all of the time. I hadn't faked it in Rosie's presence, though. That free feeling, the one she seemed to experience when she let her hair down and danced? I had it with her. I loved her.

The realization shouldn't have hit me as hard as it did. It should've been obvious, considering the same crush I had on her ten years ago came right back the moment I saw her at the nightclub, but it was different. That was a crush, though. This was so much more than that and those were three words I'd only ever said to my mother, father, little sister, and brother. They were three simple words that I wasn't sure I'd ever say to a woman. I'd hoped for it, sure, but I hadn't found her until now.

CHAPTER TWENTY-SEVEN

Rosie

THE GUYS SPENT THE AFTERNOON PLAYING FOOTBALL, WHILE THE girls and I waited for everything to finish baking and made margaritas with the tequila I brought. They were so easy to talk to, so much fun. Yari would love them.

"Sorry we're late." A woman said behind me. Emma, Isabel, and Cat smiled wide, and I turned to see a Black girl with short platinum hair and John behind her. She zeroed in on me, sizing me up. She was tiny, but there was a sharpness in her eyes that made my stomach flip.

"Petra," Isabel said, walking over to her. "This is Dominic's girlfriend, Rosie."

I hadn't expected to be introduced like that. His girlfriend. The little flip my stomach had done when Petra sized me up happened again for a completely different reason. Under any other circumstance, I would've killed to have been Dominic's girlfriend, but given the one we were in, where he did the things he did and I tried to avoid people like him as a life rule, I wasn't sure. Still, I couldn't deny that I liked being called that by his friends.

"No shit." Petra's brows rose. She looked at me again. This time, she smiled wide.

Isabel laughed, turning to me. "Dom never brings anyone to Thanksgiving."

"I'm Petra." She walked over and shook my hand, nodding behind her. "My brother, John."

I smiled. "I know John."

He smiled back, walking around his sister and giving me a quick side hug. "I hear you're practically doing geriatric work."

I laughed. "Oh, God."

"This is her?" Petra said, laughing. "Oh, girl, you have Dom wrapped around your finger."

I glanced away. My cheeks hurt from smiling so hard. "He's a good guy."

"First time I've ever heard that." Petra went over to Emma and Cat. "Where's my drink, bitch?"

John set a bag on the table and looked at Cat. "It's home-made mac and cheese, my grandma's recipe, so don't you dare scream at us."

"I would never." Cat smiled, but the blush on her face told me she was guilty. Once John went outside, she looked at me. "Last year, Dom brought apple pie from Trader Joe's and not to knock them, because it is delicious, but I'd been working in the kitchen all day and someone said his was better than my home-made, so I flipped and banned people from bringing things."

"Ah." I nodded. "It makes sense now. He was being weird about the bottles."

"Oh. Drinks are welcome. I just don't want to be upstaged by something that comes in a box."

I laughed. "I see your point.

Dom and I sat in the middle of the massive dining room table. The dining room itself was the size of my apartment. The bed was like two of Dom's king-sized beds put together. I could see why, though. This was a big family. I thought people were fin-ished arriving, but right after Petra and John got here, some guy named Dean showed up. Now I kept looking at the door, fully expecting someone new to walk in at any moment. The dining room was full of chatter as we ate, commenting on how good the food was every so often. It really was incredible. Sitting here felt like being transported back to Providence. It felt like the next generation of what our parents started, the bond that our mothers had been trying to ensure we had before they were ripped from us. Was it possible for a heart to swell with happiness and break at the same time? That was what I felt like sitting here. They were all so gracious, welcoming with open arms like I belonged here. It felt like I did. It felt like I'd known them my entire life. It felt like the thing I'd been trying to avoid my entire life, because I couldn't do this. I couldn't go through what happened last time I felt this comfortable with this kind of company. Because despite how nice and funny they were it didn't take away from the fact that they were involved in it somehow.

Once the food was cleared from the table, Emma and Cat brought dessert out. Cat leaned over between Dom and me, as she set one down in front of us.

"Dominic's special request," she said. "I hope my pumpkin pie is better than the ones you buy at the store."

"I'm sure it will be."

"I guess we're about to find out." She straightened. "You never even eat the pumpkin pie."

She walked away and Dom reached for a plate and a knife, cutting a piece. He set it down and reached for the vanilla bean ice cream on the table.

"Another special request," Catalina announced from the other side of the table, using the knife in her hand to point to the ice cream. "I got the one that looked the best."

"Thanks, Cat." Dom smiled at her and went about serving a scoop on top of the pie. My mouth was already watering when he set the plate in front of me.

My eyes snapped to his. "For me?"

"I really don't eat pumpkin pie." He winked.

"You remember that I like pumpkin pie?" I whispered. An

emotion I'd desperately been trying to avoid rushed through me and took hold of my throat.

"With vanilla bean ice cream."

I glanced down at the plate. I couldn't remember the last time I'd cried in public, but in this moment, right now, I just might have. I pushed it down and hoped it would wait until later. I took a couple of deep breaths and once I knew I could speak again without shedding any tears, I looked up at him.

"How could you possibly remember that?"

"I remember everything about you." He kissed the tip of my nose and went about serving himself apple pie, which had always been his favorite.

His mother used to make it from scratch every year. It was one of her contributions to the table on Friendsgiving. I felt eyes on me, and when I looked up, I found Rocco openly staring at us. I wondered what he had to say about this relationship. *Relationship*. Damn. I wasn't entirely sure how I felt about that. At first, I'd settled for the idea that he was just being nice bringing me, but even if the women hadn't called me his girlfriend, I knew this meant something to him. He brought me because he was serious about me. In front of them, he bragged about me like he was proud of the woman I'd become, and it made me feel all sorts of things. A slice of pumpkin pie with vanilla bean ice cream made me feel like I was at a crossroads and only had two choices. I could walk away, or stay in it for the long haul, because now I knew that's what it would be. I knew he was it for me and vice versa. I could feel it in my bones, and yet I wasn't sure it was the right thing for us.

CHAPTER TWENTY-EIGHT

DIDN'T GET PAST THE POINT OF BEING TIPSY OFTEN BECAUSE I DIDN'T trust anyone, but last night after dinner, Emma came up with a tequila-shot-taking contest, and I went way beyond my limit. So beyond my limit that I didn't remember half of the night. Or going upstairs. Or changing into my pajamas and going to sleep. I woke up with a groan, opening my eyes and turning to find Dom lying beside me.

"You know it's very creepy to watch someone without their knowledge, right?" I cleared my throat.

"So I've heard." He reached over and moved my hair out of my face. "I just woke up though, so I haven't been watching you very long."

"What time is it?"

"No idea." He sat up in bed and stretched.

I was itching to reach out and touch every single muscle on his body, but instead, I got out of bed and went to the bathroom. I loved bathrooms like these, with two sinks and a separate area to use the toilet. I found Dom brushing his teeth as I was leaving the little toilet room and walked over to wash my hands and do the same in the sink next to him. It wasn't the first time we'd done this, but again, the familiarity of it struck me, the way I didn't want to ever not have this peaceful moment in the mornings with him. That was the thought that finally sent me over the edge. I finished rinsing and left the bathroom in a hurry, unable to look Dom in the eye. All of the emotion that threatened to spill out at the dinner table came back to me.

It started with one tear, then two, and soon I was sitting on the little bench against the window that had a view of the front yard, silently crying. I wiped my face as fast as I could, not letting any tears reach past the tip of my nose. I didn't want him to see me like this and ask, because then I'd have to tell him what I was feeling, and saying it aloud would make it more real than it already was. I felt him come up behind me, closed my eyes tight when he wrapped his arms around me, and set his chin on my head.

"What's going on, baby?"

"It's stupid." My throat hurt when I tried to keep the sob in, so I let it out, my shoulders shaking, but his arms didn't shake, didn't move. He shifted so that he could sit down behind me. I was grateful for that. He wasn't making me look at him while I cried.

"Tell me."

"I don't think I can do this." I wiped my cheeks. "I can't be with you."

His arms tightened. "Don't say that."

"I can't, Dom." I moved out of his arms, sat on my knees, and turned to face him. I searched his eyes, hating the pain I saw in them. "I can't go through it again."

"We're not going to go through it again." He brought a hand up and wiped my cheeks with his thumbs. "Hey." He waited until I breathed deeply and calmed down. "We won't."

"How do you know?" I blinked. He caught more tears with his thumbs. "Doesn't it feel the same? All of us at that table laughing and sharing a meal? It feels exactly the same, Dom. Same shit, different generation. The only difference is that in this case, we're our parents."

"It's not the same, Roselyn."

I blinked at his tone and brought my hands up to grab his and take them away from my face. I meant to let them go, but instead, he held my hands between us.

He pinned me with his gaze. "Can't you just trust me?"

"I do trust you. This isn't about trust."

He sighed heavily, turning to look out the window. When his eyes returned to mine, he looked determined. He brought his hands back up to my face and pulled me into a kiss. It was hard, his tongue lashing against mine as if punishing me for the things I'd just said. It lit something up inside me and I started undressing him fast, my nails clawing against his skin. He hissed and pulled back when I ran them down his shoulder blades. He looked at me. The gleam in his eyes held a promise that made me shiver. He stood, taking me with him back to the bed. He tossed me onto it, pulling down my shorts, opening my button-down pajamas with such force that the buttons flew across the hard-wood floors. He pulled my legs apart roughly and pulled me to him, my pussy hitting his dick, the black boxer briefs he wore barely containing it. He bit down on his lip as he looked down at me, an unreadable expression in his eyes.

"You think I'm going to let you leave?" He pulled me again.

I gasped at the feel of him hitting me right *there*. He flipped me over so quickly on my chest that I struggled to get up on my hands. When I looked over my shoulder, I saw him pulling down his briefs, eyes on mine. He slapped my ass then. Hard. The whip of his palm stinging me instantly, making me wet in-stantly. Fuck. Why did I even like that? He slapped me again on the same spot, but before I could even register the sting, he was inside of me with one hard, deep, unforgiving thrust that took all of the air out of my lungs. I cried out, fists clenching the sheets beneath me, my eyes rolling back with each of his deep, hard thrusts. He wrapped my hair around his hand and brought my hands off the mattress as he leaned over, bringing his other hand to my clit as he continued to move inside me.

"Do you really think you're going to give this pussy to an-other man after me?" he murmured in my ear, biting it as he cir-cled my clit with his fingers and his cock hit me at the perfect angle, the perfect spot, making me spasm. "That's right. Come all over my cock, baby. It's yours, isn't it? This cock." He bit my ear again. "Answer me." The feeling started to rush through me again and I knew he was going to make me come. He slapped my ass, fingers still playing with my clit, cock still fucking me at a slower pace now. He knew exactly what he was doing. My eyes started rolling back on their own. He slapped my ass again. "Tell me. Do you want another woman to have this cock?"

"No. God, no." I groaned, pushing into him, the mixture of pleasure and the spark of anger pushing me over the edge again. "Fuck. Fuck. Dominic."

"That's right, baby." His fingers left my clit, and he pulled all the way out of me, the movement alone causing my legs to shake.

He flipped me over on my back and arranged my legs before settling back between them. This time, he slowed his thrusts and held my gaze, as if he wanted me to feel every inch of him, as if he hadn't already infiltrated me enough with his presence. His pace was languid. I tried to look away, tried to regain some kind of footing, but it was no use. The way he was looking at me, as if in complete awe that he had me at all, made my heart pound harder. I was on the edge again, the walls of my pussy closing tightly around his cock. He groaned, leaning in and capturing my lips and kissing me as deeply and as slowly as he was fucking me. When he pulled away, he set his forehead against mine, his rhythm not stopping for a moment, his pelvis hitting my clit every time he thrust in deep. I couldn't breathe. It was too much.

"You're not leaving me, Rosie," he breathed, pulling back only to look at me and drive the point home. "You can't leave me."

All of the emotion I'd tried to put away started rushing back when he looked at me like that. My legs started to shake again. I didn't know whether it was the fact that his dick was made for me or that he knew exactly how to fuck me, but I came with a gasp, holding his eyes. "Don't say you're leaving me." He pressed a soft kiss against my mouth as I spasmed. His words sounded softer now, unsure, maybe even a little sad, as he emptied himself inside of me. He kissed me again and pulled out slowly, walking over to get tissues and bringing them between my legs. He wiped me softly, his eyes back on me, on my body.

"What's this?" His brows furrowed as he brought his hand to my side, touching me gently, and I knew I'd bruised.

"It's nothing." I pushed off the bed and brushed past him, heading to the bathroom.

"It's not nothing." He was hot on my heels. "Was I too rough? Did I do that?"

"No. It's really nothing." I went into the little toilet room and started closing the door, needing space. I hated that he thought he was responsible for those marks. I hated that I felt the need to keep it from him. He stopped the door before it shut. "Dominic, I need to pee."

"So, pee."

"I can't with you standing here."

"Are you serious?"

"Yes."

He scowled but turned around and walked away. When I finished, he was in the shower. It was one of those double showers, with two separate rain shower heads and he had both of them switched on, expecting me to join. I sighed heavily and got inside, staying to the side he wasn't using. He didn't speak as he finished showering, didn't say a word as he walked over with the bottle of shampoo. He walked around to my back, and I closed my eyes when I felt his fingers in my hair, working the shampoo into my scalp. We didn't speak as he washed the rest of my body. He was extra gentle on the bruises and between my legs. When he was done, he switched off the water and led me to the plush white rug outside the shower. He brought a towel to my hair and dried it sloppily before patting it down my body and handing it to me. He wrapped another one around himself, right over the spot where the V-shape started on his abdomen. I was still staring at his chest when he set both hands on my waist, his touch gentle. I wanted nothing more than to grab the towel he'd set next to me and cover up, but I knew this was inescapable. When I dared meet his eyes, I expected him to be mad, but the only thing I found in them was concern.

"Tell me about those bruises." He brushed his thumbs slowly over both sides of my waist, his touch making me shiver, my nipples pucker, my breath quicken.

"It's really nothing," I whispered.

"Tell me."

I swallowed. "I went to the grocery store and a cart hit me." It wasn't a lie.

"What do you mean a cart hit you?" He dropped his hands from my waist and examined my hip with a frown on his face. "Unless the cart was moving concrete, I can't imagine how it did this." His eyes snapped up. "Tell me how this happened."

"If I tell you what happened, you have to promise not to take it out on Marco."

"Roselyn." The rumbled warning made me shiver underneath his scrutiny.

"I'm serious, Dominic. I begged him not to say anything."

His jaw twitched, but the concern in his eyes won over. "Nothing will happen to Marco."

"There was this man wearing a baseball cap, so we couldn't really see his face. He was nowhere near us. Marco was standing at the end of the aisle, waiting for me. The guy walked down the aisle and I didn't really think anything of it until I heard the cart moving a little faster and I saw it from my peripheral vision." I took a deep breath and let it out, dropping my gaze to my feet. "It was Anthony."

"Anthony Costello did this to you?" His voice was so quiet,

I barely heard him. When I looked up, his expression was dark, menacing.

I swallowed, nodding. "Marco ran straight to us, but he was faster and by the time either of us realized what happened, he was gone. It happened so quickly."

"What was in the cart?"

"What?"

"The cart he hit you with, what was in it?"

I frowned. "Boxes of soda, I think."

He looked at a spot over my head, seemingly lost in thought for a moment. I could see the darkness brewing. I could see that he was containing his anger so I wouldn't see him the way I had that night, so he wouldn't scare me. When his eyes met mine, they were clear of that darkness, but I could still see the anger, the concern. I threw my arms around his neck, pulling him down, pulling myself onto him, unable to stand seeing him this way. My towel dropped as I wrapped my legs around his waist. He groaned into my mouth as I kissed him, his hands gripping my hips as I deepened it. He pulled me away slightly, to rid himself of his towel, his cock hitting me hard on the slit of my ass. I moved, trying to position myself on him, but had to pull away from his lips to do so. We were panting against each other.

"You do things to me, Roselyn." He groaned deeply. "You have no fucking idea what you do to me."

"I think I have an idea," I replied breathily, rubbing myself against him.

He walked me back to the bedroom and laid me down on the bed. Instead of thrusting inside me, he lowered himself to his knees and spread my legs. I got on my elbows and looked down, my breath catching at the sight of him as he gave a long, hard lick up my slit before pressing his lips to my clit and sucking. The sensation made me arch off the bed. I reached out and grabbed his head, wishing his hair was long enough to pull on.

He continued to move his mouth on me, licking and sucking as if he couldn't get enough of me.

"That's it, baby. Grind that pussy against my mouth." He drew circles around my clit, up and down my folds, encouraged by each of my gasps, my moans. "Fuck. I want to devour you."

He pressed his lips back on me and did just that.

By the time we left the room, everyone was downstairs, looking at us with amused expressions that made me want to dig up a hole and die in it. I grabbed Dominic's arm a little tighter, which made him chuckle and drop a kiss on my head. He lowered his lips to my ear so only I could hear. "One minute you're begging me to fuck you, and the next you're blushing because you screamed my name so fucking loud that everyone heard you?"

A shiver raked through me. I slapped his chest, which made him laugh harder. He pulled me flush against him, holding me to his chest as if he was afraid to let go. I wasn't sure what scared me the most, opening up to this life, these people, or the idea of him ever letting me go.

CHAPTER TWENTY-NINE

I FELT ABOUT MONDAY THE WAY PEOPLE FELT ABOUT THE WEEKEND. Since we got back from Lorenzo and Catalina's house, I'd only spent maybe a full thirty minutes with Dominic, between performances, rehearsals, and his job. I had two days off, Monday and Tuesday. I was performing twice from Wednesday to Sunday, so this was a much-needed break. When I opened my eyes on Monday morning, I found him looking at me. He smiled softly when our eyes met. I wondered how often he watched me and why, instead of feeling freaked out about it, I was turned on by the idea that he was this enamored with me.

"You slept past four," he said.

I sat up slowly, noticing that he was fully dressed in jeans and a t-shirt. "What time is it?"

"12:30."

"In the afternoon?" I shouted, scrambling out of bed, even though I had nowhere to be.

"Where are you going?" He chuckled, following me to the bathroom. "Rosie."

"I . . . nowhere." I frowned and felt my lips twist when I saw the amusement on his face. "Holy shit. I can't remember the last time I had nowhere to go."

I could, actually. It was January 27th, but I didn't want to bring it up since there was no bringing it up without discussing Anthony, and I was done paying attention to that man. He gave me space to do what I needed to do, and once I finished and he knew I was ready, he walked over and hauled me off the ground, kissing me deeply. He tasted like strawberries. I picked my legs up and wrapped them around him, deepening the kiss, moaning into his mouth.

"Fuck." He pulled away, a wild look in his eyes when he met mine. "I was going to ask if you were up for a little trip, but I may cancel the whole thing if you keep moving your pussy against me like that."

I stopped moving. "Little trip where?"

"Providence."

That instantly iced my veins. I unwrapped my legs from him and set them down slowly. I'd thought about going back so many times and always came up with an excuse as to why I shouldn't. It wasn't like I had anyone to visit there anymore. I'd mentioned the memorial, though. It was one of those places I wanted to go in theory, kind of the way I thought about skydiving. I closed my eyes and pictured myself in the air, but I wasn't actually considering jumping out of an airplane. With Dominic, I might though. But then, another wave of fear gripped me. Could we just show up there? What if something happened? The big rumor was that Patriarcha had been responsible for what happened. I wasn't sure if people came to that conclusion since he'd been the big boss there, or because one of his guards had been killed, and not his wife. He swore he wasn't behind it. He'd gone to all of the funerals and paid his respects and continuously maintained his innocence. I was probably the only one who believed him, but that didn't mean I wasn't scared to show my face there. He must have seen my panic, because he set his hands on my shoulders and brought his face down to eye level.

"We don't have to go."

"What if something happens while we're there?"

"Nothing will happen."

"Dom." I bit my lip. "You can't know that."

"I do know that, Rosie."

"We're taking Nico and Marco?" I asked.

"Yes. Just taking me would suffice, you know?" He smiled softly. "But if you want me to put together a whole army to go with us, I will. We can even take Rocco if it'll make you feel better."

I snorted a laugh. "Hard pass."

Dominic chuckled, pulling me to his chest. "You know he's a badass, right?"

"I know. He's a Marine and all that, but he's still just Rocco Marchetti."

He laughed harder at that. "*Just* Rocco Marchetti. I'm going to say that to him whenever he annoys me."

"I want to go with you." I pulled away to look up at him. "I do."

The car trip felt way too quick, probably because I was dreading getting here. We went straight to the memorial. In the middle of the park stood a bronze sculpture of five women holding hands. My heart felt so heavy in my chest that I was afraid it would bottom out of me entirely. I was having trouble swallowing with the lump in my throat, and seeing through unshed tears, but I walked forward anyway. Dominic stayed a few steps behind me. I wasn't sure he'd get this close. The faces didn't look exactly like our mothers but definitely resembled them enough to make me gasp into my hand. I felt my knees give out and let myself fall to the ground. I stopped trying to hold back the tears and just let them flow. By the time Dominic's arms wrapped around me, my face was buried in my hands, and I was openly sobbing. His grip tightened, but he didn't say a word. He didn't shush me, didn't rock me, didn't tell me it would be okay. I think I appreciated that the most. He just held me as I let out the pent-up grief I held inside. When my shoulders stopped shaking and my breath started evening out, he pulled away and gave me a moment to drop my hands from my face. When our eyes met, he looked devastated. He brought both hands up to my face and wiped my tears with his thumbs before setting his forehead against mine.

"I've got you."

It was all he said, and apparently, the only thing I needed to hear, because I gained enough strength to stand and look at our mothers one last time before I let him take my hand and walk me back to the car.

"I want to drive by the house," I said, voice hoarse as I looked up at him.

Dominic's eyes flashed. "Roselyn."

"If you want to go in the other car I understand, but I need to see the neighborhood. I need to."

He looked worried, as if my seeing the neighborhood would cause a complete breakdown, and maybe it would, but I needed to go there anyway. I needed to. It didn't matter how many people I spoke to about this, or how many times I replayed it in my head as a reminder, I still hadn't let myself fully grieve. I'd always had Santi to look after. He'd lost a mother too, and he'd been too young to fully understand any of it. I still didn't fully understand any of it and I was now an adult. Then again, how do you wrap your head around something like this? I didn't think doing all of this would help the pain completely go away. How could it? For a moment, I wanted to stop running from it and just let myself feel it. After what felt like an eternity, he opened the door beside us and we got in the car. From the way his jaw was twitching, I could tell he was only doing this for me. The closer Nico got to the neighborhood, the more I felt like maybe this was a bad idea.

"I feel like throwing up," I said.

Dom's eyes snapped to me. "Do you want to stop the car?"

"No." I breathed. "I just . . . maybe this isn't a good idea after all."

"We'll just drive by, okay? We won't go into the cul-de-sac.

We'll stop at the corner, look, and leave." He searched my eyes and I realized that he needed this as much as I did.

I gave a nod. "Okay."

We'd been sitting with a space between us, but he took off my seatbelt, reached over, and dragged me onto his lap, cradling me as we both looked outside. We drove by our elementary school, our middle school, then our high school. Finally, we got to the cul-de-sac and Nico slowed down. He stopped just down the street. There were kids on bikes and parents putting up Christmas decorations. It was a lot. Maybe too much. But I watched them anyway. Dominic's arms tightened around me. After a few more seconds, he looked at Nico and told him to drive.

CHAPTER THIRTY

IT WAS DARK OUT WHEN WE GOT HOME, AND WE BOTH HEADED straight to the shower and bed. We hadn't said much on the way back. I'd like to think it was comfortable silence, but it just felt heavy. I wouldn't have done that for anyone but Rosie. I didn't even think I could do it if Gabe or Rocco asked me to. Seeing that sculpture was too much. Seeing the neighborhood was worse. I didn't know what she got from it, but I just felt angrier at the whole thing. It didn't matter. The only thing that mattered right now was that I was lying in bed with Roselyn.

"Do you ever think about that night, like, really think about it?" Rosie asked quietly. I squeezed her a little tighter to myself and breathed her in for a moment.

"Dom."

"What?"

"I asked you a question."

"Every fucking day, Rosie. Same as you do. Same as Gabe. Same as Rocco. Same as Mikey." I turned so that we were facing each other and swiped a lock of hair out of her face. "I can't imagine any of us don't."

"But I mean really think about it. I think about it every day, but after today, I don't know. It just made me realize details I hadn't paid attention to," she said, brows pulling in. "Like, it wasn't a robbery. They tied us up, but they didn't go through our things. They were masked but never spoke. Only women were killed. They didn't . . ." she took a breath. "They didn't rape them, but they killed them, one shot in the head, point blank."

"Yeah." I swallowed. "I think about that."

How could I not? There was no denying that what happened that Tuesday fucked us up, because it did, and no amount of therapy or hypnosis or even drugs helped because none of those things could bring our mothers back. That really tripped me up when I thought about it. They'd aimed for our mothers.

"Your stepdad died, though, and Patriarcha's guy also died, so I guess it wasn't only women," she said quietly.

"My stepdad only died because he stepped forward to protect Mom." I shut my eyes briefly, the image instantly coming back.

Sometimes I wondered if I remembered it correctly or if I'd made some of it up. What I knew for certain was that they'd come into our beds and tied us up there, while we were asleep and least expecting the attack. They didn't bother gagging us or doing any of the things I'd only seen in movies back then. Now, as an adult, after I'd done the things that I'd done, I looked back on that day and saw things I hadn't before, like what Rosie just said. The women were killed, they hadn't been raped, they hadn't been tortured. They were shot in a way that wouldn't make them suffer. The ones who suffered most were the ones who survived. Sometimes the aftermath of a tragedy is worse than the tragedy itself.

"Why do you think that is?" she whispered.

I wished I could erase the concern in her brown eyes, erase the pain and terror she lived with. I'd live with it doubly, triply, if it meant that she wouldn't feel it. I sighed. I could've said nothing. I could've told her I didn't want to talk about this, and that we'd already had a long day dealing with this. As it was, I'd only spoken to three people about this, including her. None of the women in my past knew, not by my account anyway. It was probably the reason I'd never been completely serious about any of them, not because they hadn't been fun or beautiful or great in bed, but because I couldn't open up to them. I didn't want to. But Rosie? Fuck. I'd do anything for Rosie. Maybe it was because she'd been there and could relate. Maybe it was just her. I couldn't say. I reached for her and pulled her a little closer so that her cheek lay on my heartbeat.

"It was personal," I said against her hair. "What's a home without a matriarch?"

"Who would do that, though?" She pulled back slightly to look at me. "I really don't think it was who they said."

"I don't think so either. If I thought it had been, or if I knew, they'd be . . ." I bit my tongue.

"Dead," she said, finishing the sentence for me.

I gave a nod and brushed her cheek with the back of my hand. This was one thing I didn't want to speak to her about. It was the reason she was reluctant to be with me, because of the things she thought I did. It was also one of the reasons I'd been reluctant to take her back there. I was nervous that it would drive a wedge between us and make her pull away more. She took a breath and leaned forward again, cheek resting on my heart.

"Hey, Dom," she said quietly against me.

"Hm."

"I feel safe with you."

My heart stopped. My grip tightened around her. She couldn't have known how much I wanted to hear those words, how much I needed to hear them. "You'll always be safe with me."

"I still worry," she said. "About you. I don't like the idea of you going out there and doing things that may get you killed."

"Would you miss me, tiny dancer?" I smiled against her hair. "Would you grieve me?"

"You know I would. You know it would kill me." Her voice broke. "That's why I'm afraid that this isn't—"

"Nothing will happen to me, baby," I said quickly, not letting her finish that sentence.

"How could you possibly know that?" She pulled away again, searching my eyes. I cupped her face, drawing circles on it with my thumb. I didn't want to stop touching her. I couldn't, especially tonight.

"I don't go around starting wars, Rosie. I don't go waving my gun around and killing people."

"No?" She shot me a look.

"No. I run legitimate businesses," I said, but when she raised an eyebrow, I corrected myself. "Legitimate enough that they won't lock me up for them. Is that better?"

"Not really. I'm almost afraid to ask what that means."

"Oui is legitimate," I said. "I legitimately own a few gas stations."

"So you don't, like, sell drugs?"

"Nope."

She searched my eyes. "You don't kill people for a living?"

"No." I let out a laugh. "Jesus, Rosie."

"Did you used to?"

That one gave me pause. I nodded my response. I wasn't going to lie to her.

"Like a made man?" she asked.

"Yes."

She gave a nod, letting that sink in. She knew what that meant. She'd grown up around all of us. She lived between Patriarcha and Marchetti. She'd shared dinners with them, with all of us, and even though they didn't bring up business at the dinner table, she would've heard the rumors like everyone else had. Some kids walk around idolizing doctors or astronauts. Some want to be superheroes and save the world. Where we come from, the mobsters were the heroes wearing capes. In the neighborhood where Rosie, Gabe, Rocco, Mikey, and I grew up, those guys were the ones we looked up to. Even Mike. The difference is, once he saw it for what it was, he wanted no part of it. I couldn't blame him. It was nowhere near as exciting as they pretend it is in movies.

"But you don't do that anymore," she said warily.

"Not anymore."

"You threatened Anthony. And the look you got when I told you about the grocery store? It didn't look very PG-13."

"PG-13?" I chuckled, though it sounded forced, because at the thought of Anthony, I felt my entire body stiffen. The asshole had been laying low lately and I didn't know what to make of it, but I didn't like it.

"You know what I mean, Dominic." She pursed her lips, unamused. "I don't want you doing anything that'll put you in danger and those people, Tommy, Anthony, and that whole crew, are dangerous."

"Oh, Rosie." I felt myself smile as I climbed on top of her, slipping off her panties and ridding myself of my boxer briefs. I put a hand between us, played with her pussy for a moment, until her breathing became ragged, and her eyes clouded the way they did right before she came. I took my hand away and she made a noise. I was sure she was about to complain, but I just wanted her wet enough that I wouldn't hurt her when I sank into her, because that was exactly what I was going to do to rid myself of the tension building up inside me. This wasn't going to be a sweet fuck. I positioned myself between her legs and thrust into her hard, deep. She yelped, bowing off the bed, her eyes rolling.

"Damn it, Dominic," she breathed, her fiery gaze meeting mine.

I pulled out slowly and thrust in hard again.

"Fuck." She threw her head back, fingers clutching my biceps. "Do it again."

I did. Again, and again, and again, until she was screaming my name at the top of her lungs.

"This isn't," she gasped, "going to make me," another gasp, "forget what we were talking about."

I stopped moving. Her fingernails dug deeper. She wanted me to move. She wanted me to fuck her hard and fast. "What were we talking about? I forgot." I thrust hard.

"Oh God," she moaned. "That they're dangerous."

"Hm." I ignored her and kept fucking her, bringing her legs up and stretching them across my chest. Fuck. My cock hit her deeper at this angle. I brought my hand down to her nipple, then spread her legs a little and slowed my thrusts so I could toy with her clit again. She started shaking the moment my thumb hit it, coming all over my cock. She felt so fucking good. So fucking wet. I started fucking her fast again until she was screaming so loud, I was sure she wouldn't have a voice tomorrow. My orgasm hit me hard, my come spilling inside her in spurts, saying her name as I came.

"Dominic." She was still breathing heavily as I brought her legs back down. There was a small frown on her face that I hated so fucking much. "They're really dangerous. I'm serious."

"I know you are." I chuckled at her concern and leaned in to kiss her. When I pulled back, I looked at her. "Don't you know who you're sharing a bed with, baby?"

She looked at me, and even though she didn't look scared or surprised, I regretted saying it. She'd already told me she had reservations about this, and it seemed like every time we took three steps forward and she seemed convinced that she could do this, something happened that made her hesitate again. I knew that until she committed to us one hundred percent, I'd always be on the cusp of losing her and that realization hit me right in the gut. I couldn't lose her. I wanted to shake her and tell her that she was brave and strong and belonged with me. Whether she wanted to see it or not, she was one of us. Her father may not be going around taking lives, but he was just as involved as the rest of us. She studied me for so long that I started to get nervous under her scrutiny.

"I know exactly who I'm in bed with, Dominic De Luca." She reached up and set a hand over my heart.

I didn't want to push my luck and ask her how she meant that, but when she threw her arms around my neck and pulled me in for a kiss, my nerves disappeared.

CHAPTER THIRTY-ONE

DOMINIC MASSAGED MY LEGS AND FEET FOR HALF AN HOUR BEFORE he told Marco to go get me bags of ice from the gas station. He'd kissed me and headed downstairs to make a phone call while I sat with my feet submerged in the icy water of the guest bathroom. I shut my eyes, forcing myself to keep my feet in the water, when my phone vibrated on the floor beside me. I reached for it, turning it over to look at the screen and nearly dropping it in the tub of ice when I saw my father's name and assigned picture on my screen. I pulled my legs out of the water and set them on the towel, standing shakily.

"Hello?" I held my breath.

"Mi hija," he said, voice booming. "You can come home now."

I felt my entire body go limp as I fell to the floor, tears pricking my eyes. "Are you serious?"

"I'll be making dinner tonight. Pescado con coco," he said. My mouth watered instantly. "You may want to get here before your brother eats all of it though."

"I'll be there." I felt myself smile wide. "Oh my God. I'll be there."

"See you soon." He hung up.

I looked at the tub of ice and debated not soaking my feet after all, but the throbbing convinced me otherwise. I'd just put them in there for a moment. I was lost in thought, texting back and forth with my brother, when I heard the commotion coming from downstairs. There was shouting and the sound of something crashing. I inhaled sharply, hands shaking for a completely different reason. I looked at the doors on either side of me, at the cabinet in front of me. Would I fit there? Did I have time to hide? Another crash. This time, I did drop my phone. I got my feet out of the tub quickly and set them on the towels I'd set down, walking over to the door of the gym. I rushed in there, grabbed a ten-pound dumbbell, and ran to the door next, trying to listen, to see. My heart pounded loudly. This was supposed to be the safest place in the city, but it couldn't be, right? Because in theory, Dominic may be able to protect me, but it was only a matter of time before things caught up to him. It was only a matter of time before this happened. I swallowed back my fear and tried like hell to think of something positive. Maybe he was fighting with Marco over the bruises, and if that was the case, I had to go down there. I opened the door slowly and tip-toed to the top of the stairs, heart in my throat. I listened to the voices, trying to make out who was speaking, or rather, screaming. Definitely Dominic. I braved a peek over the stairs and saw another version of Dominic. Somehow, I managed not to drop the dumbbell as I rushed downstairs.

"Gabe?" I set down the dumbbell as both brothers turned to face me.

I had to take a step back for a moment. I hadn't seen them side-by-side in ten years. Back then, they looked so much more similar, but now, the only resemblance they shared seemed to be a few features. I did a quick sweep of Gabe and breathed easier when I realized he was intact. When I looked at Dominic, his expression was intense. It was one that practically screamed *"mine."* I looked down at my feet for a second, hating that the room was filled with animosity, instead of joy and relief. Before I knew what was happening, Gabe was charging me and I was in his arms.

"I am so sorry, Rosie. Holy shit. I can't imagine what must

have gone through your mind. Are you okay?" He set me on the ground, but kept me facing him, his arms loosely around me.

I glanced over at Dominic and noticed that his face had gone from pissed off to murderous. I took a step back to set some distance between me and his brother.

"Yes, I'm okay. I thought you got killed or something. I thought maybe it was my fault for the shit I'd told you and then . . ." I shook my head and looked at him, really looked at him. "Did you get a fucking suntan?"

"Yeah." He had the sense to look embarrassed as he looked away. "I called Dom because I had to skip town on short notice, and I was worried about you. I kept thinking about Tommy and Anthony and—"

I pushed his chest with both hands, moving him back with the force. "We were freaking out about you, and you were sunbathing?" I pushed him again. He took another step back.

"I wasn't just chilling the entire time. It wasn't like that." He took a breath. "I'm sorry. That's why I called you. I didn't want you to worry."

I turned my attention to Dominic, who was still standing in the same spot. "Are you just going to stand there, staring?"

"Trust me, you don't want me to walk over there right now."

Gabe waved a finger between me and Dominic. "So this is a thing then."

"Yeah," I said quietly, looking at the ground. "He's good to me."

"Yeah." He let out a short laugh. "I bet he is."

"Gabriel." Dominic warned.

"No, you stole my fucking girlfriend." Gabe looked over.

"What?" I shouted. "I was not your girlfriend, you liar!"

"She was never yours to begin with," Dominic growled, and I could tell he was fighting to stay at a distance.

"We didn't even go on a date." I looked at Gabe. That was

when I saw the amusement in his eyes and realized he was joking. JOKING AT A TIME LIKE THIS. I pushed his chest hard again.

He chuckled but turned serious quickly. "I specifically asked him not to get involved with you."

"You can't ask that of him."

"I love him. I trust him with my life." Gabe nodded toward his brother. "But as your friend, and knowing everything you've told me about your life, I feel like I need to tell you that I don't think this is a good idea. You've been through enough. This isn't what you need."

"And you think you know what she needs?" Dominic asked, his voice short. I heard it a little closer now. "Let me guess, you want to offer her your services too."

"I mean," Gabe said, and I could hear the smile in his voice. "If that's what she—"

Dominic was just one step away from us in a flash. "If you finish that sentence, I swear to God, brother or not, I will fucking kill you, so choose your words very carefully," he said quietly, the warning clear.

"I should go," I whispered, crossing my arms so my hands would stop shaking.

I took a step back, distancing myself from both of them. Gabriel wasn't wrong, but I didn't expect him to warn me away from his own brother.

"I think that's a good idea." Gabe smiled. I turned and started walking to the door.

"You'll stay." The command came from Dominic.

I froze in my tracks and turned around. I looked up at him, meeting that dangerous gaze that everyone seemed to shy away from. Everyone except his brother, who obviously had a death wish, and me, since I knew he'd never hurt me.

"I'm going," I said, as quietly, as cutting, as clearly as he had. "You obviously need to work this out with your brother and my dad just called me, so I have my own family to visit."

I turned around again and walked toward the door, slipping my feet into the boots I had there. I grabbed my jacket and threw it on quickly, my bag next, and opened the door, pausing at the force of the chilly wind that hit me.

"Rosie," Dom said, his voice softer, closer now. "Don't go."

"I'll be back tonight," I said to the sidewalk.

"It *is* tonight."

It wasn't. It wasn't even six o'clock.

I didn't turn around, but I suddenly felt him at my back. He brought an arm around me, flat against my stomach, and pulled me flush against his hard chest. I felt his warmth behind me, slipping inside me and spreading, threatening to take over. I shut my eyes against the feel of it, fighting the tears that pricked my eyes, knowing that if I focused on how good he made me feel, I'd stay, and I couldn't. He must have known it, must have sensed it somehow, the way he seemed to sense everything else about me.

"Baby," he whispered against my ear.

"Dominic. Please don't." I shivered, screwing my eyes shut tighter. He wasn't playing fair.

"Baby," he whispered again, rougher this time, pressing his face into my hair. "Please stay."

"I'll be back." My voice shook.

I took a steadying breath and opened my eyes, grabbing his hands and lowering them as I turned around to face him. God, he was so fucking beautiful. I brought a hand up and ran the tips of my fingers over the perpetual five o'clock shadow on his face. He shut his eyes for a moment, as if savoring it. When his gaze found mine again, he looked raw, open, letting me see all of him in that split second.

"I don't want you to leave like this." He searched my eyes. "Will you come back?"

"I'm going to have dinner at my dad's." I smiled at him and wondered if my expression looked as torn as I felt. "But yes. I'll be back."

"Marco's going with you."

I didn't argue. There was no point. I took a step away from him when he caught me by the waist and pulled me to him, pressing his lips against mine. What started as a chaste goodbye kiss turned into a slow heat that ran down my spine, through my entire body, and settled between my legs. I broke the kiss first and watched as he opened his eyes ever so slowly. I loved this man. I really did. And yet my own fear, which Gabe had now confirmed, kept me from speaking those words. He pressed one last kiss against my forehead, his eyes torn, looking like he was struggling to let me go, but he did. I took a deep breath and turned around quickly, shutting my jacket tighter as I walked down the steps and headed to the car. It was colder than it had been in weeks, but the thought of seeing my dad and brother warmed me right up.

CHAPTER THIRTY-TWO

Dominic

"WELL, FUCK." THAT WAS GABRIEL.

I could kill him right now. I turned around and walked to my kitchen, ignoring him and his stupid comment. For someone who always had honors and AP classes, got into an Ivy League University, earned the degrees he had, and landed a high-paying job, my brother was one stupid motherfucker. Normally, when he pushed my buttons, I laughed it off, but tonight he'd gone too far. Way too fucking far.

"You're in love with her."

I looked him straight in the eyes. "What gave it away? Was it my threat to you, which, by the way, I meant every word of, or the way I kissed her?"

"Neither." His brows rose. "It was the begging. I didn't see that coming."

I shook my head and opened the fridge, grabbing one of those disgusting sour beers I stocked up on just because he liked them, and handed it to him. He held it up as a thank you and started drinking.

"Tell me about the job you were doing." I leaned against the counter.

"I will." He paused to take another sip of his beer. "But you're not going to believe me."

"Try me."

"I signed an NDA." He raised an eyebrow.

"Fuck your NDAs. I'm your brother."

"I asked you to take care of my girlfriend and you stole her from me." He raised an eyebrow and took a seat. "If that's what you do to your brothers . . ."

"She wasn't your girlfriend, asshole." I felt myself scowl, and scowl deeper when he grinned. "And she was mine first before you went behind my back and asked her out."

"I'll admit that it was a shitty move." He nodded, conceding. "Not that it matters, all things considered. I guess I'll let you have her for now."

"Gabriel." I stood up straight, pulse racing.

"Kidding." He chuckled. "Jesus."

"It's not funny." I took a breath. "None of what you said is fucking funny. She already had doubts about us, and you just gave her more reasons to rethink this whole thing."

"She needed to hear it." He sighed, shaking his head. "I wish someone had told Mom that before she got involved with Dad."

"Then neither of us would be here, moron."

"And Mom would be alive."

"And it wouldn't matter because you wouldn't be here, so she wouldn't be your mom."

"My point is, someone needed to tell Rosie. Not that it matters."

"Trust me, it fucking matters." I slammed my fists on the counter. The look on her face, the way she kissed me, it was all fucking me up right now.

"Did you see how she looked at you? She's fucking crazy about you. I don't think anyone's ever looked at me like that. She's one hundred percent yours."

"I know she's mine. I just want to make sure that *you* know she is." I glared at him. "What you just said will stick with her all night. She might not come back."

"She'll come back." His shoulders sagged slightly. "She's been through so much, D. Maybe you're the one who needs to reconsider."

"And give her up?" I shook my head. "I don't want to talk about this anymore."

I couldn't. I felt like an elephant was sitting on my heart.

"Fine." He set the beer on the counter. "If I tell you where I was, you're not going to like it, and if they find out, I may be the one floating in the river."

My eyes narrowed. "You really think I'd let anyone hurt you?"

"You've threatened me like three times since I got here." He raised an eyebrow. "You threw a fucking chair at me." He nodded over his shoulder as if I needed a reminder of the broken television and fucked up furniture.

"Because you stormed in here talking about Rosie, and she's not a topic of discussion unless you're going to allocate some of my money into a wedding fund." I scowled at the grin on his face. "You owe me a TV and a new chair."

He shook his head, still grinning, and because it was genuine, I felt myself loosen a bit, but my chest still felt heavy. I was going to try really hard not to fixate on the way she left, but the kiss tasted like a goodbye, and not just goodbye for now. That didn't bode well with me. She was with Marco though. He'd tell me if she made any strange moves. If she really wanted space, really wanted to sleep in her apartment tonight, or her dad's house in Washington Heights, I'd have no choice but to let her. I'd probably be sore as fuck from sleeping in the backseat of an SUV across from her building, but I'd do it for her. Fuck. If this was what love felt like, I didn't understand why anyone would want to willingly chase it. We're a masochistic society. There was no other explanation for it.

"I heard you're into drugs now. What the fuck, Gabe?"

"Jesus." He sighed. "Does she tell you everything?"

"You left without a trace. We were fucking worried. Dad had a team of professionals looking for you everywhere."

"Dad." He let out a laugh. "Have you spoken to him?"

"Yeah. That's another thing I want to talk about. He kept telling me not to worry about you, like he knew exactly where you were. Are you working for him now? Is that what this is?"

"I wasn't with him," he said. "I'm flying over there tomorrow. You should come with."

"For what?"

"Uh . . ." A short laugh left his lips. He scratched the back of his neck, the way he did when he was nervous. My stomach flipped.

"Spit it out, Gabriel."

"The job I was doing? Dad was pretty well informed about it."

"What do you mean?" My eyes narrowed on him.

"He set up the goddamn meeting."

My heart pounded harder. "Who's the client?"

He shook his empty bottle as if more beer was going to magically appear. I got him another one, set it down in front of him, leaned against the counter, and waited. My brother was one of those people who took thirty minutes to tell a two-minute story. I'd learned patience with him. That didn't mean I wasn't dying for him to get to the fucking point, though.

"A lot of these guys have very intricate operations. Not that I have to explain that to you," he started. "Rosie somehow knows about Tommy and some other guys, which is another reason I was worried." He paused. "This client, I work with his attorney. His name is redacted from most of the papers sent to me. I know all his financials, but I don't know his damn name. When he said he wanted to meet with me, I was obviously weary. I mentioned it to Dad a couple of nights before I left, and he told me to go. Even if he hadn't, I didn't feel like I had much of a choice. The client knew where I lived, where I hung out, he knew who you were, he even knew Rosie by name."

My heart stopped for a moment, but I let him continue.

"I thought, well, I guess I'll go. I mean, Dad knows about it, what's the worst thing that could happen?"

"You could've died," I said, my voice coming out much harsher than I expected it to. "How could you put yourself in that situation after everything we've lost? How could you let any-one like that find out about Rosie? Jesus, Gabriel."

He scoffed. "You're going to lecture me on safety?"

"It's different."

"It's not different. You know that feeling we used to get whenever one of us was in trouble? I have it every fucking day, Dominic." His voice cracked. I looked up and saw the fear in his eyes, the concern, and it made me feel like shit. "I worry about you twenty-four-seven. So, what if I go out and dabble with drugs and get drunk? I'm twenty-seven. I've been through hell. If you're going to judge me for it, you can go fuck yourself."

"Gabe." I sighed heavily. What the fuck could I even say to that?

"I stopped, by the way. I didn't do any drugs on my trip, and trust me, there was cocaine on every fucking surface."

"Did you meet with the big client?"

"Never did. I met with his associates, a lawyer, but never him."

"And you were in Colombia?" I asked. He looked taken aback by my question, and I had my answer.

"How the fuck—" He stopped talking, face pulling. "Everyone has coke at their disposal."

"On every surface? You come back with a suntan, Dad knew where you were and didn't start a war? Am I right?"

"Cartagena," he said after a moment. "Dad is very friendly with this person."

"The drug dealer?"

"They deal much worse things than drugs, Dom."

Oh fuck. I stayed quiet.

"While I was there, Tommy showed up, which was a total mindfuck, by the way, seeing him in another country," he said.

My jaw set. I didn't say anything because whatever I'd say would come out as a scream. My brother could have easily been killed over there. He would've been one of those people gone without a trace. I bit back my words and let him continue.

"This client of mine was looking into buying Tempt and the strip club Tommy and Anthony own. He wants in on this operation that he has going with other families. Russians, Turks, et cetera."

"The one Rosie told you about."

"Exactly."

"Did you at least get a name?"

"I got a last name, which is the main reason I'm telling you this."

"Well, don't keep me in suspense."

"Masseria," he said. "I figured you should know since you're close with Gio."

"It's not Gio." The room spun. I leaned a little harder on the counter and caught my breath, looking back up at my brother, who looked concerned now. "It's his father."

I knew of three people who handled both the drug and sex trade business out of Cartagena and all of them were dead. Masseria, though? It seemed impossible, considering, but if that was the case, it meant my father knew about it, it meant the Costellos knew about it. It meant that it was only a matter of time before shit hit the fan. I looked up at Gabe, catching the concern in his eyes. Not very often, but sometimes it really did feel like looking in a mirror.

"At what time does your flight leave for Italy?"

"Nine in the morning. You coming?"

"I might." I took my cell phone out of my pocket and dialed Lorenzo's number first. He was the one I was closest to. He and Rocco, but Loren had been my mentor, and he was Gio's brother-in-law. It was only right that he gave Gio the news that his father was still alive.

CHAPTER THIRTY-THREE

"**M**Y ROSIE!" DAD PULLED ME INTO A TIGHT HUG THAT I returned. I smiled against his shoulder. God. He smelled like fried food, like home. I squeezed him a little tighter.

"You're thin, Papi." I pulled back. "Too thin."

"Can you believe they didn't serve platanos in jail?" he asked. "Don't worry, I'll get my weight up soon."

I laughed and turned to Santi, hugging him next. I pulled back and looked at him. "You know you were dark without the dangerous sun rays, right?"

"Vicky isn't and I wasn't going to let her tan her ass in front of every guy on spring break."

"Of course," I rolled my eyes and walked over to help Dad set food on the table. "How was meeting her family?"

"Great, actually." He grinned. "Her dad's fucking loaded. He has a crazy estate in Mexico City."

"What does he do?"

"What doesn't he do?" Santi chuckled.

"That sounds . . . ominous," I said.

I set down the bowl of red beans and we paused the conversation to settle into our seats and for Dad to say grace. The minute he was done, I picked up a toston.

"He's not into anything illegal, if that's where you're getting at," Santi said. "At least, not that I know of."

"Speaking of illegal activity," Dad said. "I heard you're dating Dominic."

If he'd thrown something at me, I would have been less shocked than I felt at his words. "Where'd you hear that?"

"It doesn't matter where I heard it," he said. The tone in his voice made my stomach clench. I didn't dare meet his eyes. "I don't like him for you."

That made me look at him. "Papi."

"He does dangerous things, Rosie. Unforgivable things."

"Really? When did you start believing gossip now?"

"I stopped considering it gossip when Anthony Costello threatened me because of your relationship with him."

"What?" I breathed. "He went to the bodega again?"

"Sure did." Dad pursed his lips and went back to his food.

A part of me wished he'd been so spooked by Dominic that he'd just stopped going there, but Dad's bodegas were in Costello territory, after all. All it would take was for Anthony to start spreading rumors about me and Dominic, and he'd turn everyone in the neighborhood against us. That was how these people did things. They divided the city into squares and infiltrated them until everyone in them was bleeding out, money and actual blood.

"As far as I'm concerned, Anthony can rot in hell," I said after a moment.

"Let's hope he doesn't take us with him when he does," my dad said. If he wanted me to lose my appetite, he'd succeeded.

"Who's Dominic?" Santi asked.

"The boy your sister is never going to see again," Dad stated.

I laughed; it was unamused, though. Dom wasn't a boy, and I wasn't a little girl, and there was absolutely nothing funny about this situation.

"Dominic De Luca?" Santi asked, frowning.

"Yes." Dad's voice was short.

"He's your boyfriend?"

"He's a *friend*," I said, shooting my dad a look.

"Friend." Dad scoffed anyway. "He's a thug."

"You didn't think he was a thug before." I raised an eyebrow. "You loved him and Gabe."

"He wasn't a thug back then." He scowled. "You need to stay away from him."

"That's bullshit." I bit into another toston. I wasn't even hungry. I was angry-eating now.

"Roselyn." Dad slapped the table.

Santi and I flinched and went silent. Dad had never lifted a hand at us, but he didn't have to. Our defenses went up the moment his voice did.

"Sorry," I whispered.

"He has a reputation," Santi said quietly. "Dominic De Luca, I mean."

My gaze flashed to his. "How have you heard of him, if I didn't even know he lived in this city?"

"You probably haven't heard about him since you always stay in your lane." Santi's smile faltered. "Maybe Dad's right about this one."

A knot formed in my throat. I swallowed hard, but it remained. I looked down at my plate. I'd stopped eating and went back to playing with my food, my fork pushing the rice and beans from one side to the other. Having two of the most important men in my life not accept the third like this hurt, even though I knew they weren't wrong to worry. Who knew what Dad had heard about Dom from the people around the neighborhood. It couldn't have been anything good, which was the only thing holding me back from standing up and shouting how in love with Dominic I was. The only way they'd change their mind was if Dominic showed them who he really was. Well, who he was with me.

"I'm curious." Dad turned to my brother. "How do you know about him? Are you not staying in *your* lane?"

"What? Of course, I am." Santi scoffed. "Jochy told me about him. You know he's un chismoso."

Santi was a terrible liar, so I knew he was telling the truth.

"Let's move on. I've stated my piece about the thug," Dad said. I bit my tongue. "I want to apologize for what I did. For everything that happened and everything I dragged you into. I don't know what I was thinking."

"You already apologized."

"I want to apologize again. What I did was selfish and unfair to both of you."

"Rosie got the short end of the stick," Santi mumbled. "I was fine at school."

"Let's just put it past us and agree to never borrow money from anyone but the banks," I said.

"Right." Santi scoffed. "Let's not borrow money from regular thugs, just thugs in suits."

"Santiago," my father warned. Santi shrugged.

I shook my head. "By the way, the rest of the money is in that little black bag. Once he gets this, it's really over."

"Thank God," Dad said. "Thank you."

He set a hand on top of mine, I set mine over Santi's, and the three of us held hands for a few seconds, just grateful for this moment.

And then our front door flew open. We didn't have time to prepare for it. When the first shot rang out, we threw ourselves to the ground. Then came the second shot, then a third. My own screams were the last thing I heard before everything went black.

CHAPTER THIRTY-FOUR

Dominic

OUR PHONES WERE SUPPOSED TO BE IN AIRPLANE MODE WHILE WE sat at the table, but I kept mine on and continued sneaking glances at it in case Rosie texted to tell me she was home already. Isabel, Catalina, and Petra were taking turns playing the Pac-Man machine in the room behind us. They'd been with Lorenzo and Gio when I called, and the guys didn't want to leave them wherever they'd been. Isabel cheered and the other two groaned. Across from me, Gio and Loren smiled wide, looking over at them. Jealousy shot through me. I finally had what they had and I would've given anything to have Rosie join them in the other room, where I could see her, hear her, smell her.

It used to be that women weren't allowed in here, but a lot had changed since Charles's and Joe's deaths. When it came to Lorenzo and me, our fathers didn't know about the lax rules we held these days, but we knew they wouldn't be on board with any of it. They were all about holding up tradition and we would probably be ostracized for having women we respected in here and not just whores we fucked and discarded. It was one of the things that made me and Gabe nervous for our little sister, Lenora, or Nora, as we called her. She was technically our half-sister, but still our flesh and blood and we were very protective of her. Gabe said he'd heard Dad talking about arranging her marriage as if this was the fucking 1920s or some shit. There weren't many men in the old country that I trusted to treat my sister well. Then again, Giovanni and Isabel were set up that way and it had obviously worked out for them, so maybe there was something to be said about it.

In a way, I wished that was the deal with Rosie. If that were the case, she'd have to be with me. That idea made me no better than my father. I couldn't force her to want this. That was the only thing I kept going back to. Gabe wasn't wrong. Rosie wasn't wrong. My last name alone made me a target. It was all or nothing with us. They may not have taken blood oaths, but it was an oath just the same.

"Hey, lover boy, cut the shit and tell us why we're here," Rocco snapped. "And why is this asshole here, looking all tan and shit?"

"Tell them what you told me."

Gabe took a breath, knee bouncing. He'd known these guys as long as I had, but he was still nervous around them. Lorenzo cut him off just after he got to the part about Tommy showing up. He still hadn't even said Gio's last name.

"I'll say it," Lorenzo said, then turned to Gio. "We think Joe's alive."

Gio's face was totally blank for three seconds. "How can that be?"

"No clue, but the last name on all of these accounts is definitely Masseria," I said. "He must be trying to buy the club from Tommy and my dad is in on it." I glanced at Loren. "You think Angelo knows?"

Loren shrugged.

"How can that be?" Gio said again before he stood up and started pacing.

The rest of us stayed completely silent as we watched and waited for all of it to sink in. It was bad for all of us, but it was worse for him. Or better. I wasn't sure what I'd feel if I'd been told that the controlling father who I thought was dead was actually alive. Had he faked it all? Had they actually tried to kill him and he'd survived? These were questions I had but couldn't answer. The women walked into the room. This was exactly why they hadn't been allowed in here previously, and the reason I understood the rule. Some women were passive, let men lead, and only spoke when spoken to. Not these women. Not Rosie. It was probably why we never stood a chance.

"What's wrong?" Catalina asked.

"Go to the other room," Gio said, not leaving any room for argument.

Cat looked at her husband, who shot her a look that said she should do as her brother said. She must have sensed the severity of it, because shockingly, she took a huge step back. I watched as Isabel looked at Gio from her place next to Cat. It looked like she was assessing whether or not it was worth going up to him. I wouldn't have. When Gio got like this, the best thing anyone could do was keep their distance. Rocco was the same in that. They were both dormant volcanoes and you just never knew when they were going to blow the fuck up.

Isabel walked over slowly. She stood in the way of his pacing, set a hand on his chest, and whispered something to him. Whatever it was seemed to calm him down. He nodded at her, pulled her into his chest, and held her there for a moment before releasing her. He said something quietly, and whatever it was made her walk away, grab Cat and Petra by the arm, and lead them outside. The door shut loudly behind them. I met Rocco's gaze. We both blinked in surprise. Under any other circumstance, I would've made a joke about Rocco needing someone like that in his life. Under any other circumstance, I probably would've made three jokes by now, but this felt too heavy, too serious, and I didn't feel like laughing.

I knew Joe's loss hit the girls hard. He'd always been the world's greatest asshole to Gio, though, and still, I knew he'd been taken aback by the news of his murder. We'd all been in the car when he got the call and seen the look on his face.

Then again, that news had been followed by news of his evil mother kidnapping his wife, so he had a lot to process that night.

"I'll call my cousin," Gio said after a moment.

"Let's pay him a visit together." Lorenzo stood up. "I doubt Marco knew though."

"I know." Gio stood. "I trust him, but that doesn't mean he's not in trouble if Dad is alive." He took a breath, shaking his head. "It seems improbable."

"But not impossible," Loren said.

"No, not impossible," Gio mused, lost in thought. I could almost see the wheels turning in his head. He looked at my brother. "He's dealing drugs?"

"As far as I can tell. The only people with this kind of money usually deal drugs or . . ."

He let the sentence hang, unable to say it, but we all understood. Shit, up until a few months ago, we were still shipping weapons in and out of the country. That operation was on hold until further notice after an ordeal with the bratva. Still, nothing was as bad as trafficking humans.

"Joe wouldn't do that," Loren said, but he sounded like he didn't believe his own words.

Behind us, the door opened and all of us turned to see Dean walking over. He took in each of our faces and faltered a step before walking into the room.

"Who died?"

"More like who rose from the dead," Gio said, then explained in two seconds what had taken my brother twenty minutes.

"No fucking way." Dean took his usual seat, looking more shocked than I'd ever seen him. "In Colombia?"

"Cartagena," Gabe said.

"Shit." Then, as if he'd just noticed my brother, Dean

turned to look at him. "You're the idiot who left your hot girl-friend unattended."

I glared at him.

"To be fair, she was only my girlfriend for like five months when we were in high school," Gabe said.

I didn't know if he said it because he was finally done taunting me, or if he was afraid to taunt me in this setting. Either way, I appreciated it. Dean shook his head trying not to smile as he reached for a lighter. Rocco's phone rang, not vibrated, rang, loudly on the table. All of us shot him a look. He didn't flinch or apologize. He reached for the phone, hit the side button, and looked at the screen with a frown. From where I sat, I saw his brother's name on the screen before he set it face down on the table again.

"Do you think we can find him?" Loren asked, looking at Dean.

"He'll be nearly impossible to trace in Colombia," Dean said. "If Gabe gives me more information, a specific area, an address, something, I can get a drone out there." He paused. "Emma tried to find him and failed."

"What?" Gio froze, walking up to his chair and setting his hands on the top as if he was trying hard not to throw it.

"She tried to convince Enrique to fly her over, but he went on his own."

"What the fuck." Gio shook his head, letting out a breath. "I swear she has a death wish. It must be a youngest child trait or something."

"Enrique was the one they threatened and he's trying to go back again, so if anything, he's the one with the death wish." Dean kept smoking.

"What does that mean?" I asked. "They threatened him?"

"Did you know this?" Gio looked at Loren.

"Not about Emma trying to go, but I knew armed guards were waiting for Enrique when he landed his plane."

"Jesus." Gio breathed out, pushing off his chair. He looked at Gabe. "Thanks for telling us." Then, he looked at Dean. "Keep me posted." Then, at Lorenzo. "Let's go talk to my cousin."

Rocco's phone vibrated again. He picked it up and turned it over. Mike again.

"You might want to answer that," I said.

Rocco spared me a glance. "Nah. I'll call him when we're done."

"I have an early flight and some of us aren't vampires and need sleep." He stood. I stood with him and returned the tight hug he gave me. "Let me know if you want to join."

"I don't think I will this time." I pulled away and watched him walk out before I turned to Dean. "I need security on him."

"Loren already set it up."

Good.

"I'm going to head out." Dean stood.

"You just got here."

"Yeah, well, I'm tired as fuck. Sandy doesn't feel well."

"The wolf?" Rocco's brows rose.

"Yeah, the wolf. Why do you say it like that?" Dean frowned.

"You're psychotic." Rocco shook his head. "Who the fuck buys three baby wolves?"

"Someone who has two hundred acres of land," I said.

"Someone who's insane," Rocco said.

"They have their own area; it's not like you'll see them when you visit. Unless you want to," Dean said as he walked out.

I shook my head.

Rocco's phone buzzed again. Mike again.

Finally, he sighed and answered it, putting the phone to his ear and waiting. He always waited for the person on the other end of the call to speak first. His brother must have and from the way Rocco's brows lifted, I knew he hadn't started with a friendly hello.

"No." Rocco said, standing up and walking to the other side of the room, where a red punching bag hung from the ceiling.

I looked at my phone. Still nothing from Rosie. I looked up at Rocco and found him staring at me. To anyone else, the expression might have seemed nonchalant and impossible to read, but I'd known him too long. He looked worried and that made my stomach sink. Rocco never worried.

"Dom." He took a step forward.

It was a slow step and it instantly fucked with me. I could always count on my brothers to not pull back on the punches and say it like it was. This wasn't the norm for any of them, especially Rocco. Quickly, I went through the list of people I cared about and their locations. Gabe had just left, we had security on him, and Mike had been calling before that, so it wasn't about him. Rosie was at her dad's having dinner. My sister was still in England, so it could be her. I couldn't figure out who could have died. It was the only reason he'd call. Mike was the one who told us about Frankie, then about Joey. He'd been the bearer of bad news countless times.

"Spit it out," I said, my stomach churning.

Rocco took a breath as if he was bracing himself for something. "Isn't Rosie's dad's house on West 175th?"

"Yeah," I said, dread slowly coursing through me. "Why?" Rocco didn't answer. I walked over and yanked the phone from his hand. "Why, Mikey?"

"Dominic." Mike's voice was calm.

"No. Why the fuck is a homicide detective calling to ask about my girlfriend's dad's house where she's currently having dinner?"

"We got a call from a neighbor who heard gunshots."

He paused for a second. My heart was no longer beating. My grip was so tight on the phone that my hand started to cramp. Even if I had words to say, I wouldn't be able to speak them. I waited. "I don't know exactly what we're working with here, but word is we have a potential hostage situation on our hands. I wanted you to hear it from me. I'll keep you posted."

I let the phone fall to the ground and stormed out.

CHAPTER THIRTY-FIVE

YOU THINK YOU KNOW FEAR UNTIL YOU HAVE A GUN IN FRONT OF you and you're on the other side of the barrel. I brought my knees up and hugged them, heart pounding wildly. It was the only thing I could hear. I'd lost my hearing when they barged in here. They'd taken two shots to scare us and both were next to me. BANG. One ear shut down. BANG. The other ear did the same. One of the guys was gone, but there was still one by the door, holding a huge gun, watching us. He looked no older than my brother. He *looked like* my brother, tall and skinny with dark hair, dark brown skin, and dark eyes. He was Dominican too. If he was from around here, Santi would've known him. He'd have gone to school with him.

All of those truths cut deeply. What kind of world did we live in where a kid his age led the life he did? Where one of our own people, our *compatriota*, would turn against us like this? There had to be a cardinal rule against this. There had to be some kind of standard, where if someone called you to do a job on someone from your fucking island, who may or may not share your blood, you'd have to decline. He didn't look scared, but he also didn't look like a killer. The entire time we'd been sitting against the wall, he hadn't looked in our direction once. I didn't know anything about him, but I knew his mother would be devastated by this.

"You should be ashamed of yourself," I yelled, the words sounding muffled in my ears.

He turned his head away a little more. I swallowed and

rested my forehead on my knees, focusing on breathing. The police would be here soon. They had to be. My brother was sitting next to me in the same position, knees up to his chest, hands tied behind his back, his forehead resting against them as he shook uncontrollably. Through glassy eyes, I could only make out my father's legs from the other side of the kitchen. I didn't even know if he was alive. I hadn't seen him move. A sob racked through me. God, please. Please let him live. It wasn't fair if he died. It just wouldn't be fucking fair.

I started crying openly, loudly, when I looked back at Santi to check on him. He didn't look up, but at least he was still breathing. He hadn't been too badly hurt. They'd punched him and tied him up. I wasn't sure it mattered. Emotional trauma was worse than physical scars. Scars you could cover. Scars you could ignore. After a while, those healed and became a part of you, like tattoos. You could cover emotional trauma with fake smiles and bullshit lies, but even as you did those things, the knife twisted deep in your gut. Santi had been staying at a friend's house when those men barged into our house and killed Mom, but this time it was inescapable, and I knew that even if Dad was alive, the damage was done.

He'd never have the luxury of hearing a loud sound, or even fireworks, without jumping out of his skin. A luxury. That was what it was to be able to walk around without glancing over your shoulder, out of fear of being followed, to sit in a place that was supposed to be a safe haven for you and not worry about someone barging in to try and kill you. I swallowed past the lump in my throat and turned my attention to the guy manning the front door. God, he couldn't have been any older than Santi. I wiped my face as best as I could with the shoulder part of my t-shirt and sniffled. I flinched at the head pressure the simple sniffle caused. I wondered if Santi's hearing was okay. I shut my eyes again. Please, God. The door opened again, and Anthony Costello appeared there. He looked down and said something loud that made Dad stir. I held my breath, anticipating the worst, but he took a step forward and left him alone. When he looked at me, he smiled. A shiver raked through me but I didn't allow myself to cry. I wouldn't. He'd already hurt me in so many ways that it had become our norm. This was too far, though; he had to know that. I wiggled my fingers behind me so they wouldn't fall asleep.

Through the kitchen window, I saw red and blue lights. I hoped they'd be able to end this safely. I wished Anthony would just take me and leave my brother and dad alone. I said that, screamed it, and even though I didn't hear a sound, I saw the way Anthony's eyes lit up at the words and knew he'd heard me. I looked around for Marco and didn't see him, and hoped that didn't mean he was already dead. I shut my eyes tightly. The moment I did, I saw Dominic's face. The way he smiled, the way he laughed, the way he looked when he was pissed off, the way his eyes darkened when he was turned on. My chest shook again. Would I ever get to see those expressions again?

He'd blame himself for this, and the worst part was that maybe it was his fault, but it could've also been my father's. Anthony had issues with both of them. Dad liked to point fingers, but his hands weren't clean either. I couldn't argue that he was completely wrong about Dominic, though. His own brother warned me away from him, and that was after all of the alarm bells had gone off in my head telling me to leave. I knew being with him was dangerous, and yet, I knew that if Anthony hadn't involved my brother and dad, I still would have chosen to stay. I would have chosen to stay because I wanted him, but I couldn't put my family at risk again. Maybe I wouldn't have to. I was sure whatever plans Anthony had for me would end with me six feet under.

Dad's feet moved again and disappeared out of my line of vision. Anthony turned at something he must have said, reached down and picked up the black duffle bag I'd brought Tommy's money in, and said something. I thought I read, "Right thing" on his lips. Anthony took one step toward me and said something to the guy beside him. From the way he kept his eyes on me, I knew he was giving him some type of instruction. Would he kill me? Would he torture me? Rape me? Would they do these things in front of my brother? My lip trembled. I bit the inside of my mouth to keep myself from crying. Suddenly, Anthony walked to the back door and walked out, leaving us there. I started crying, closed my eyes, and then I did something I hadn't done since the night my mom died. I started praying.

CHAPTER THIRTY-SIX

Dominic

W E WERE ON THE ROOF OF THE BUILDING ACROSS THE STREET, and I was going out of my fucking mind. I tried to drive to the front of the street, but everything within a two-block radius was swarming with cops. I didn't even know how we ended up here, but I was sure Mikey had something to do with it. Rocco had been talking to him the entire time we were in the car and again when we got up here. I hadn't even been able to hear what he'd been discussing. I only knew three things: we were on a roof where we had a clear view of Santiago's kitchen window, Rocco brought the case he kept his sniper rifle things in, and I was scared out of my fucking mind. That last one got me. The last time I'd been this afraid was ten years ago. The first time I went on a job with Dad and his men, I was nervous but never afraid, and soon, nerves gave way to excitement. Some people, like my brother, thought that made me a monster. I wasn't going to deny it, though. I thought I'd put that behind me, but whoever was responsible for this would soon find out they fucked with the wrong people.

I looked across the street, where Rosie was inside that house, reliving the same damn nightmare we'd been trying to overcome for ten years. I hoped against all odds that it wasn't the same, that no one had been killed in front of her again, but even if that were the case, it had to feel the same. She had to feel that desperation, the gripping fear that we'd felt when masked men broke into our homes and killed our mothers.

My chest tightened. I'd known something was wrong when Marco didn't answer my phone call. Nico arrived just as the first police officer was pulling up and he was able to take Marco to the hospital.

Now, there were at least a dozen cop cars down there.

"Why the fuck are they outside, congregating like this is a fucking family gathering?"

Rocco was still setting up his gun. When we went to the gun range, he showed up with the weirdest fucking weapons, one being this sniper rifle. I'd made fun of him the entire afternoon, the first time he brought it along and started using little black circles to mark the exact spots he was going to hit. He didn't even entertain my jokes. *"This is part of my training,"* was the only thing he'd said, and it dawned on me that while I'd pictured him in the Marines fucking women in foreign countries, this man was actually doing some real shit. Shit you need sniper rifles for. Right now, I was glad for his rifle, his training, and the little obstacle courses I'd made fun of. He hadn't switched on the red light yet, so I didn't know where the hell he was thinking of aiming. From our vantage point, we couldn't see people in there.

"Where are you pointing it?" I asked. "Can you see through that window?"

He lowered his head and adjusted it slightly, still not saying anything.

I sighed heavily, running a hand over my head. "Can I see?"

He stepped away and let me take his place.

"You're pointing it at the yard." I stood straight. "Mike says they're inside."

"You don't understand, Dom. If they come out—"

"*When,*" I said, voice cracking. "*When* they come out, Roc. Don't say *if.*" For the first time in a long time, I felt tears sting my eyes as I said the words. "*When* they come out."

"When they come out." He set a hand on my shoulder and squeezed. "It'll be through the backdoor. The nearest cop is on the other side of the other house right now, and the one standing there." He lifted his hand off my shoulder and pointed at the officer standing on the sidewalk, waiting. "Will probably get shot."

"Fuck." I looked over and thought about it. If I'd been the one holding someone hostage and wanted to get out, that would be the first person I'd shoot.

"I'm also going to assume whoever walks her out will be wearing a vest."

"So you'd aim for his head?" I asked, and how my voice sounded calm and not as panicked as I felt was a mystery.

"That's the only option." He paused. "It's an FMJ. It won't be messy."

That was what the assassins had used that night to kill our mothers, so I knew it wouldn't be messy. I also knew that any sudden movement and Rosie would be the one taking a bullet to the head. Fuck. It wasn't often we were on this side of things. It wasn't often that we were forced to take a step back and analyze the consequences of our actions. I bounced from foot to foot, my adrenaline still pumping, my nerves making me feel like I was bouncing off the fucking walls. A black truck drove down the street and we looked down to see that it was the SWAT team. We shared a look. Holy shit. I couldn't just stand here and watch. I had to go into that fucking house before they did. We'd done it before. Hell, Rocco was the one who trained me how to fucking do it. As if sensing my dilemma, Rocco pulled his phone out and pressed it to his ear.

"How much time?" he asked. "Fuck." He breathed out, still listening. "How much time would they give me?" He listened some more, breathed out again. "Yeah. If they agree to hold off, I'll do it. Once though. Only once. I want that shit in writing." He paused again. "Fuck you. I have my own lawyer.

Yeah, well, Lorenzo Costello is a good goddamn lawyer and the only one I trust."

I felt a lump form in my throat. He was willing to do time over this, for me, for her. We'd all taken an oath, we'd promised loyalty, our willingness to kill to protect our brotherhood, to die for it, to go to jail for it, but so far, I'd only done the first two and I couldn't bear it if Rocco did that for me. When he hung up with his brother, he slid the phone into his back pocket and faced the gun again.

"I'll let you pull the trigger, but you're not going down for this. If they take anyone in, it'll be me."

"Dom, don't be stupid." He let out a laugh, adjusting the scope. "It won't come to that, but if it does, you'd have to leave Rosie and you'd have done all this for nothing."

"Not for nothing. For her safety, and if not for her safety, to avenge her." My throat clogged again when I said that last bit.

If she didn't make it out of this alive, I'd never forgive myself anyway, so I might as well be dead or in jail. As it was, this only solidified her fears and proved Gabe's warning was valid. I'd make the choice for her and walk away. It would kill me. Fuck, it was already killing me, but I loved her too much to do this to her. My oldest friend stood up from his crouched position so we were at eye level, and just stared at me for a moment. I saw something shift in his eyes, as if he was just now realizing that this wasn't just a childhood crush or someone I'd fuck out of my system. After a few seconds, he gave a nod, took a really deep breath, and got back into position.

"They're giving me a five-minute window," he said. "After that, they'll move in." He looked at his watch and took a long, deep breath before getting in position.

When he set his finger on the trigger, I didn't dare say a word. I tried not to even breathe too loudly. This wasn't the shooting range. This wasn't for fun. On the other side of the red dot, there would be a human being, not a white sheet of paper with little dots to shoot at. It wasn't something I thought about often. I usually just did a job and went on with it, but something about tonight was giving me pause. Maybe it was because I knew Anthony and Tommy had kids barely out of high school doing their dirty work. I'd started when I was in fucking high school, so it shouldn't get to me, but the older I got, the more it did, because a lot of these kids wouldn't have been in this life if it weren't for their persistent recruiting. That made them more like Gabe and less like me.

I'd seen more dead bodies after spending six months with my father than I had the previous seventeen years of my life in real life and movies combined. Maybe it was because I dealt with bigger monsters than the ones in fiction, but at some point, I was able to take my emotions out of it. The way I saw it, it was shoot or get shot at. Right now, all of my emotions were sitting inside that house.

Through the kitchen window, I saw sudden movement. The SWAT team was still coming up with a plan by the stairs. How many minutes had passed? I should've been looking at the time. My heart raced. If they broke down the door, she would die. I knew she would. Rocco tapped the side of his gun slowly with his other pointer finger, as if counting down.

Tap.

Pause.

Tap.

Pause.

Tap.

Pause.

Tap.

Pause.

Tap.

He shifted his shoulders slightly. I stopped looking at him and turned to see a man walking out back holding Rosie's arms, which were tied behind her body. Some of her long dark hair was sticking to the side of her face, her expression anguished. Rocco switched on the red light, and I held my breath again. The person holding her was young, definitely one of Anthony's guys. If this was his message to me, he'd succeeded. Seeing the woman I loved like this was already killing me.

CHAPTER THIRTY-SEVEN

THERE'S A MOMENT DURING CATALYTIC EVENTS WHEN TIME SUSPENDS. Some people say your life flashes before you. Others say you see a white light. Some claim it was nothingness. Peace. Ten years ago, what I felt was grief. Pure and utter grief. The kind that sunk its claws in the middle of your chest and squeezed. The kind that made you bleed out. This time, I felt nothing. I was struggling to get free after the guy who'd been watching us pulled me up and started dragging me out of the house. I struggled to break free, looked back at my brother and father who were tied at the wrist and ankles, and screamed. When I realized that no matter what I did, he'd pull me out of the house, I told them it would be okay. I couldn't hear my own voice, but I hoped they could.

Outside, he dragged me down the steps as I continued to thrash against him, pleading, begging him not to take me to Anthony. That was where he was taking me. I knew it. One minute he was walking me across the yard, the next he was pulling me down to the ground with him. He broke my fall, but somehow when I landed, half of his body shifted over me. Time suspended then. I waited for the panic to set in, for my hearing to come back, for Anthony to walk back here and take me or shoot me between the eyes, the way those men had done to my mother, but nothing happened. No sound, no movement, no bullet between the eyes. I wasn't sure how long I just lay there, underneath the kid. Even without being able to see his face, I knew he was dead, and it did nothing to appease me. I pushed my face onto the lawn to get my hair out of my face. My hands were still tied behind my back, and I wasn't sure how the hell I was going to get out from under him.

In the movies, in the shows, people untied themselves. They found a surface or a tool or pulled hard enough and were able to get free. I couldn't. I used the strength in my legs to kick sideways. It took a while, but I kicked again and finally was able to roll away from him. I used my core strength to bend my knees behind me and stand. My knees were shaky, though, and hit the ground immediately. I looked at the guy who'd been dragging me out of the house and saw the small hole in the middle of his head. I sank back on my heels and stared at him in disbelief. He looked too much like my brother, like family, and somehow looked even younger now. Too young to be doing this. Too young to die. His brown eyes were wide open, mouth parted as if he didn't even have time to react. Faintly, I heard an animalistic sound as sobs raked through me. The sound of grief, the feel of it. Grief was what made my chest heave as I sat there, taking deep gulps of air that I couldn't seem to get enough of. I cried for him, for his family, for the cards we'd been dealt and what he'd chosen to do with his. I hiccupped a shaky breath and wiped my face the best I could with my shoulders.

When I stood up again, I was determined to walk back to the house. Dad and Santi were tied up and left behind, but they'd been tied at the ankles too, so they wouldn't be able to move. I was almost to the stairs when a force stopped me. Strong arms, I realized. They were wrapped around me and holding me back. I screamed, kicking and thrashing. A man wearing a SWAT uniform appeared in front of me. I screamed again, screamed at them to get my brother. The one behind me didn't let me go. I could see their lips moving, but I couldn't hear a thing. Not a thing. I looked at the back door and saw Santi walking down the steps on shaky legs, a SWAT person holding him up. I kept looking at the door. Kept waiting for Dad, but he never came. I started to shake hard again. They untied my hands and let me go slowly, still holding me up, but no longer squeezing. My wrists felt like they'd been set on fire. I walked toward my brother and cried into his chest when he wrapped his skinny arms around me, chest shaking against me so hard, I could feel his ribs. If he was talking to me, I couldn't hear him. The only thing I could think about was how much he looked like the dead boy. The boy who could have been our brother, our cousin, *him*. That made me cry harder. My brother held me tighter.

After a moment, they led us out the side door, the one Dad always used to take out the trash and recycling bins. Once on the sidewalk, my head whipped in every direction as I looked for Marco, but I never found him. Maybe that was a good thing. God, I hoped that was a good thing. They ushered us into the back of an ambulance. I was still shaking from the adrenaline, reeling as if I'd drank an entire bottle of Red Bull. They set me on one bench and tended to me while they did the same to my brother across from me.

"Dad is okay," he mouthed. "Dad is okay."

My heart stopped for a moment and I started crying again. Everything else was a blur. The only thing I knew was that I couldn't stop shaking and I still couldn't hear a thing.

CHAPTER THIRTY-EIGHT

IT WAS MY FIFTH DAY AT THE HOSPITAL. FIVE DAYS OF IVS. FIVE DAYS of probing. Five days of missing work. Five days of nothingness. I glanced at the flowers on the table next to the sink. Everyone sent flowers. I had so many they barely fit on one side of the room, so many I could open up a flower shop right here. Roses from Catalina and Lorenzo, wildflowers from Madam Albert, succulents from Veronica and Patty, daisies from Joshua, peonies from Petra and John, more roses from Rocco, and sunflowers that came with no card but I knew were from *him*. Every time I thought of him, I felt my eyes burn with fresh tears. I felt so incredibly hurt by him. He hadn't come to the hospital once, as far as I knew, and I asked. The only people I hadn't asked were Dad and Santi, and that was because I was afraid they'd flip out on me for caring about the man "responsible for this." I knew that was what they'd say, and for Dad, I had a comeback ready, because this had nothing to do with Dominic. This was Anthony's warning for us not to step out of line.

At the sight of the door opening, my eyes swung from the flowers to Yari, who was walking in with a brown bag in her hand. Every day, she'd visited with food from the outside. That was what she called it, like if I was in prison. She smiled brightly and pointed at her ear, her way of asking whether or not my hearing had returned. I brought a hand up to signal so-so and she smiled brighter as she pulled up the chair to sit next to me and set the bag on the table in front of me.

"Can you hear me now?" she asked. She sounded like she was underwater.

"A little."

She reached into the bag and started taking out food. Today, she brought lox bagels from Russ & Daughters. Normally, I'd be awed and ask her how long she had to wait to get in there, but I couldn't find it in myself to care. I ate in silence as she leaned in close for me to hear and told me all about some guy who hired her to be his date for a wedding in Dubai. A week-long affair, she said. When we were finished, she took our trash and discarded it before coming back and sitting next to me. I kept my eyes on the sunflowers. She set a hand on my fingers, careful not to touch the IV in my hand, and squeezed so I'd look at her. I did.

"He was here," she said. "Your brother asked him to leave, and Ros, you know he had every right to."

I nodded slowly.

"He looked like shit. Like he hadn't slept in days," she said. "I don't know if that gives you peace or not, but I figured you should know."

I looked back at the sunflowers. He'd been here and Santi hadn't mentioned it. Did it even matter?

Something touching my hand startled me awake. I jolted, eyes popping open with a gasp. The room was dark now. The nurse had switched off the lights and promised she'd leave me alone for a few hours, but I didn't need light to tell me Dominic was here. I turned my hand over so that his covered the entirety of my palm and moved it to squeeze his. He hung his head like a defeated man, the sight of it making my throat grip painfully. I squeezed his hand harder and tugged for him to come closer. He pulled the chair behind him, moved the safety rail down, getting as close as he could, the top half of his body flush against mine as he lifted a hand to my hair, my face, my neck, examining me. He'd find nothing. There was nothing on me that would hint at what was wrong with me, only raw skin around my wrists from where I'd tried to tug free. The only reason I was still here was dehydration and high blood pressure. Santi and Dad were let go the next day, Santi with minor scratches, Dad after they cleared him after they cleared him for the concussion he got from getting hit by the butt of a gun. We'd been lucky. That was what the nurses and doctors and police officers kept repeating. We'd been lucky. Maybe we had been.

When he was done with his inspection, Dominic sat down on the chair, his chest still on the bed as he held me, one hand on my waist and the other on my arm. He looked at me for a long moment. We still hadn't spoken, but the agony in his eyes said everything. I blinked and felt tears roll down my face. He reached up and wiped them with a thumb before setting his hand back on my waist. After an eternity, he dropped his head on my chest. Had his shoulders not started to shake lightly, I wouldn't have known he was crying. It made my throat squeeze impossibly tighter. I set a hand on his back and moved it side to side slowly, hoping to somewhat soothe him. It made his shoulders shake harder. We stayed like that for a while until he took a long, deep breath and straightened, wiping his face and bringing his hands to the one closest to him, the one free of the IV.

"I'm so sorry." I could barely hear him, but I read his lips perfectly. "I'm so, so sorry."

I took my hand from beneath his and brought it to his face, running the back of it over his forehead, his closed eyes, the bags under them, his lips, his now full beard. His hair was in a weird stage where it was no longer cut short but wasn't long enough to style. He was gorgeous, but he looked like shit. When I dropped my hand, he lifted it to his lips and kissed it once, twice, three times, before setting it gently on the bed. He stood then and looked down at me, dark eyes full of anguish. His hand moved over my forehead one more time, pushing the hair that had fallen onto my face out of the way, and leaned down to kiss me. His lips were soft against mine, the kiss slow, the grief in it matching our own. When he pulled away, he set his forehead against mine and breathed me in for a moment. He looked at me again, eyes searching my face, and I knew it would be the last.

CHAPTER THIRTY-NINE

Dominic

I LET MY PHONE BUZZ A FEW TIMES BEFORE ANSWERING MY FATHER'S call. I'd been ignoring him all week. Ignoring everyone, really. This morning, I woke up and told myself I was done with the self-pity. I had things to do, and at the top of my list were two people I needed to get rid of. It might start a war. The guys were with me, though. I'd done way too many things for them, no questions asked, for them to not have my back. That didn't mean my father would be okay with it, or Angelo. Getting rid of an entire crime family would surely come with consequences, but I really didn't give a shit anymore. My voice sounded as annoyed as I felt when I finally answered the phone.

"Così rispondi a tuo padre?"

"Ciao, papa." I took a breath. "È bello sentiri."

"Liar." He chuckled into the line. I kept quiet. He sighed. "I hear you're heartbroken."

"I'll live."

"I told you to stay here and find yourself a good Italian girl."

"Says the man who's on his third Italian wife."

He laughed again. "Touché."

"What do you want?"

"I can't call my son to say hello?" he asked. "Your brother is on his way back to America and it occurred to me that we haven't seen each other in a long time."

"I saw you two months ago."

"I meant the three of us. It also made me think about how

proud I am of my boys." He paused. "Gabriel is doing very well for himself."

"I guess the high-end thugs you've sent him pay him well."

Another laugh. "Says the high-end thug."

I took a seat on the corner of my bed. "What do you really want, Pa?"

"I hear we have a common enemy."

I scoffed. "Aren't your enemies mine to inherit? Isn't that what you always said?"

"Yes, but this is different," he said. "Costello."

I gripped the phone tighter. Tommy hadn't even bothered hiding; he was back at Tempt every Tuesday and Friday, business as usual. We all had different opinions as to why he'd be out in the open, but mine always went back to the fact that he thought the big names were backing him. Big names, like my fucking father.

"I heard you were working with him," I said.

"Working with him. Please."

I had it on the tip of my tongue to bring up Joe Masseria, but doing so would incriminate my brother, and he was already too involved for my liking.

"What's your issue with Costello?" I asked instead.

"We had an understanding with Tommaso, but he's overstepped. He's taking our men, stealing from our fleets. We thought letting him think he was part of our circle would make a difference, but it seems he thinks he takes precedence over our own sons and has mistaken our kindness for weakness." He paused. "We're all giving you our blessing to get rid of him."

Their blessings. I bit back a harsh laugh. They were so fucking ancient, these guys, but it was what it was. Technically, Angelo should give us his blessing to get rid of the head of a family. Sometimes I wondered if they still abided by that rule so no one would come for them.

"I'm getting rid of both of them," I said. "All of them."

"All of them?" My father had the nerve to sound both surprised and impressed.

"All of them," I said again.

"Okay. Good." He paused again. "Once they're gone, you'll have no problem taking over their territories."

"We don't need your permission for that part," I said, because I liked to remind him where his reign ended when it came to what happened over here.

We said our goodbyes. He had to know that even if he hadn't called, I would have gotten rid of both of them. I wondered if this was a favor for him or a gift to me. He'd said I was heartbroken, since that was how my brother had been describing me lately. I wasn't heartbroken; I was just broken, and broken men did reckless things. I'd been good for a couple of years now. I hadn't lied to Rosie when she asked about that. I planned to keep it that way until now. As far as I was concerned, I had nothing left to lose. Even though they'd let her live, they'd fucked with her and ultimately, they took her from me. Surely, they'd heard rumors about me and the way I operated. Maybe Tommy's angle was just to get his money back, but Anthony got personal. I'd warned him to stay away from Rosie, and he still went to that grocery store and pushed a cart filled with soda cans into her. I'd warned him to stay away, and he went into her house, waving guns, and tying her up. He'd taken the only woman I'd ever opened up to, the only woman I'd ever loved. He'd learn soon enough. Chaos reigns in the absence of love.

CHAPTER FORTY

I TOOK A DEEP BOW AND SMILED AS THE CROWD CHEERED FOR ME, then bowed again when they cheered for me and Josh together. Two little girls wearing tutus ran to the stage and handed me a bouquet of flowers, and I thought my heart just might explode in that moment. I thanked them and blew them a kiss as I backed up and joined Josh again. This particular ovation hit me hard. Maybe it was because it was my first show back after fifteen days, or the fact that I could hear them clearly. Whatever the case, I'd never been more grateful to be there. Josh squeezed my hand and hugged me to his side as we walked off the stage.

"You did great." He kissed the side of my temple, tilting the crown on my head slightly.

"Thank you." I took a deep breath. Adrenaline was still coursing through me as we walked down the hall. We stopped in front of the changing room, and I smiled at him. "It's like riding a bike."

"Like riding a bike." He dropped his arm. When he turned to me, he was serious. "You know I'm here for you, right?"

"I know." I smiled softly and walked into the room.

Every smile was a performance. That was what these last fifteen days had been, a performance where I was playing the role of a woman who was totally fine, a little injured from a breakup, but otherwise, fine. I played her in front of my brother, my father, in front of Yari, even though we both knew she knew that it was bullshit. Every once in a while, when I noticed Nico following me, I'd laugh extra loudly, so he could go and report back that I was doing well. I wondered if Dominic even asked, even cared. I'd been sad when I left the hospital, then angry, so angry, then sad again. Now I was just in a state of limbo, waiting for the next wave of emotion to hit me and wondering what it would be. Would it ever be real joy? I wasn't sure. I wasn't even sure I wanted to feel that again. If I did, cool; if not, cool. I was doing a great job of playing this girl anyway, what was a few more years of it? I was almost at my new building when my phone buzzed in my hand. I didn't look at it. Even though I knew Nico was watching me, I wouldn't let my guard down until I was safely inside my apartment. The last guy who was supposed to protect me went down before I did. Thankfully, Marco was okay. Broken arm, broken ribs, bruised ego, but otherwise okay. Now the men alternated between Nico and some other guy. I didn't know his name since we never spoke. I just pretended they weren't there. Sometimes, when I was feeling up for it, I nodded a hello. Most of the time, I kept my eyes forward unless I felt a presence at my back.

I thanked the door attendant as I walked into my building and waved to the woman at the front desk. It was that kind of building. Expensive as fuck, but thankfully, Madam Albert pulled some strings and got me my spot as a principal dancer, which meant I made enough money to pay for the luxury of security. Once I got to my apartment, I opened it, switched the lights on while I was still in the hall, looked around quickly before stepping inside, and shut the door and locked it behind me. For a moment, I stood there, back against the door, listening for sounds. My bedroom and bathroom were the only places someone could hide, and I could see both from where I stood.

I grabbed the can of pepper spray in my hand and checked the bathroom thoroughly first before moving onto my bedroom. Once I knew I was safe, I let myself breathe. I rolled my neck as I walked over to the kitchen, grabbed my container of water, and headed to the balcony. I liked stepping out and listening to the buzz of the city one last time before I shut it all out. When Santi came over the first time, he'd laughed and said the balcony was smaller than the bathtub. He wasn't wrong, but I still loved it. Expensive as the rent may be, being that it was in Chelsea, it was still a one-bedroom apartment on the fifth floor of a thirty-five-story building. I was living it up, but I wasn't *living it up*. I liked to remind my brother that one of us lived in a dorm. After having leftover sushi from last night's dinner, I showered and went back to the kitchen to have some fruit. Even the fruit container reminded me of him.

The most annoying thing about this situation may just be that I'd been the one who wanted to break it off with him because I wasn't sure I could handle this life. What happened at my dad's should have solidified that sentiment, but instead, it did the opposite. Instead, it made me remember how things had been before, made me realize how fragile life was, and how fast it passed us by. If I was going to die anyway, I might as well live while I was here. It was that thought that pushed me to call Dominic. I'd called once before, and he never answered. To my surprise, he did this time. Wherever he was, it was loud, and I wondered why he'd answered the phone at all.

"Rosie?"

"Yeah." I cleared my throat. "You haven't called."

"Is everything okay?" He was shouting over loud music. Was he at a club? Seriously? Before I could even ask him that question, I heard a woman ask him if he needed anything else. The way she asked him that, all sugary, near his ear, near mine, made my heart sink into my stomach.

"Not as well as it's going for you apparently," I said. "I guess moving on is easy for you."

"What?"

"Are you seriously at a club right now?" I asked. My ears were hot, but my chest burned hotter.

"It's not like that," he said, and I decided no amount of explaining would make me any less upset. I hung up the phone.

For the millionth time, I cried.

Dominic: it's not like that

Me: You don't call, you don't text, you don't visit, and then you answer the phone while you're out?

Dominic: it's not like that

Me: you know what? I don't care. Have fun. Go fuck the entire universe if that's what you want to do. I'll do the same. Goodnight.

No new texts came from him, and I pressed the side button of my phone before going back to angrily eating my bowl of fruit. It wasn't like he didn't know my every waking move. I was sure his guys, who were watching me twenty-four-seven, reported back everything I did and everyone I spoke to. Thinking about that made me even angrier.

When my phone started buzzing, I froze for a solid minute, heart racing as I picked it up. I'd expected Dominic's name, but Veronica's was the one that was flashing on my screen.

"Hey," she said softly. "How are you feeling?"

"Good. You?"

"Great." She paused. "Listen, I know you said you'd call me when you were ready, and weren't sure whether or not you wanted to keep your job with Oui, but I was wondering if we could talk?"

I shut my eyes. I felt awful leaving Billie high and dry, but I'd told myself it was just a job with no attachment, and anyone could pretend to decipher a painting with her. Maybe she'd find someone who could actually tell the difference between a Monet and a Manet. I was pretty sure I never would. It wasn't like I didn't love the extra money, but I wasn't sure if I could work for a company Dominic owned. It was too weird.

"Sure," I said, sounding a little more cheerful than I felt.

"You live in Chelsea now, right?"

"15th street. Why?"

"I'm at 130 W 15th," she said.

"You're kidding." I let out a laugh. "I'm at 101 W 15th."

"Kismet," she said.

"Maybe so." I smiled wide for a second, then realized maybe she wanted me to invite her over, which was weird, but I couldn't be rude. "Are you . . . do you . . . "

"Oh. No." She laughed. "I'm not inviting myself over. I was wondering, if you're not bone tired, would you want to meet me for a drink?"

"Um . . . sure. Why not?"

"Have you heard of Raines?"

"No." I didn't want to remind her that I'd just moved here. I was sure she'd heard it from someone, either Yari or Dominic or one of his guys.

"You're going to love it. It's on 17th. I'll send you the location. Meet me there in an hour?"

"I'll be there."

❧

It was freezing tonight, but my palms were sweating when I turned the corner and spotted Veronica waiting for me. I returned her smile as I approached, and when she hugged me, I had no choice but to hug her back. She rang a doorbell next to us and the door opened up, a bouncer looking at me, then her.

"Ronnie. Where's Patty?" He held the door open wider.

"She's home. I brought a friend. New customer, guaranteed." She winked at him, and I smiled at him as I followed her inside to the coziest, sleekest bar I'd been to in a minute.

Yari would love this place. We sat down on a long leather couch and ordered drinks. I turned my body to face her, and she did the same. We studied each other for a second before she reached over and set a hand on mine.

"How are you really?"

I opened my mouth, the lie on the tip of my tongue, and shut it. A server brought our drinks at that moment, and I took a sip of mine. I'd ordered one called Victory March. I didn't know what was in it, but I was sold on the name, and thankfully, it was fantastic. I lowered my glass and looked at her again.

"Honestly? Surviving." I shrugged.

"Have you spoken to him at all?"

"Dominic?" I scoffed. "Right before you called, actually."

Her brows rose. "And?"

"And he was at a club. I'm living this monotonous, boring, excruciating life, and he's at a freaking club."

"I'm sure he's not there for fun," she said softly, her eyes genuine.

"It doesn't matter," I said. It really didn't because even if that was the case, he never called me back.

I took a gulp of the drink.

"Dom and Rocco are in the midst of opening a place just like this." She sat back slightly and signaled around the place. "A secret bar."

"It suits them."

"It does." She smiled, then turned serious. "He's a fucking mess, Rosie."

"Didn't sound like that to me." I shrugged like I didn't care, but it hurt to hear that, despite everything.

"Like I said, I don't think he's out clubbing for kicks. That's never been his scene." She took a breath. "So the reason I wanted to speak to you is that I'm wondering if you want to expand your horizons a little at Oui."

"Meaning?"

"Meaning, not only going on museum and bingo dates with Billie and Jack."

I laughed but it was short-lived. "Is this because I'm no longer with Dominic?"

"Yeah." She watched me for a moment, studied me really. She set her glass down on the table in front of us and played with her wedding ring. "Look, despite whatever he may have sounded like when he answered your phone call, he's not doing well. He's miserable, I mean, unbearable and making all of us miserable in the process. I've never seen him like this."

"He can't be that bad," I whispered.

"He's worse." She raised an eyebrow. "Much worse. Not even his brother can stand him."

I looked away. I'd been in touch with Gabe, but only through texts. I couldn't bear seeing him yet. "So you want me to expand my horizons because Dominic is miserable?"

"It may be the only thing that will get him to snap out of this."

My attention snapped back to her. "You want me to do this to make him jealous?"

"Patty seems to think this is a brilliant plan, and who am I to go against her? Happy wife, happy life, and all that." She added, "I completely understand if you can't do this."

I mulled it over for a moment. Did I want Dominic back? Despite all reason, yes, I wanted that. I wouldn't go to him, though. I'd called twice. The ball was in his court now. Did I want to play games and make him jealous, though? I'd never been like that. That was Yari's thing. She loved purposely making guys jealous to get a rise out of them. It didn't really take much to get a rise out of Dominic, though, and if he was already hurting, was this really the route I wanted to take? I thought about the woman I heard when I spoke to him earlier and my blood started to boil all over again.

"You're not going to set me up with Gabriel, are you?" I asked warily. "Because that's a hard pass."

"God, no. It'll be someone completely unknown to him." She laughed. "We actually already have someone in mind."

"Who?"

"Patty's godson. He's a pro athlete. Plays football for the Jets."

"Ew." I scrunched my nose.

"See?" Veronica laughed. "This is brilliant. Dom hates them too."

"Dom is a Patriots fan. He hates everyone."

"We really don't want to push you, especially if you're not interested in getting back together with him." Veronica's smile faltered. "If that's the case, we can continue to drink and not mention him at all."

"Would it only be this one guy?"

"You want to make it two?" She raised an eyebrow. "That can be easily arranged, but I don't think it'll matter if it's one or one hundred."

"Does Patty's godson understand that this isn't a dating service?"

"Not really." She shrugged. "We've explained it to him dozens of times, but, well, funny story, we took a little family trip to see *The Nutcracker*. I pointed you out and he said you were hot. I told him you were one of our girls, and he said he was looking for someone to take to a team event."

"A team event?" I frowned. "Like a Jets event?"

"Yep."

"What kind of event?"

"The kind that club-level owners go to. He doesn't have to take a date, but he's new blood here. He's taking the starting QB position from a well-loved guy, so he's nervous. I figured since you're an athlete, you might know what that feels like."

"Yeah." I licked my lips. It was tough for me when I first moved here, since everyone already had their cliques formed. Most of them had known each other since they were kids. I knew how difficult it was to be a newcomer, and I knew it was much worse when money and fame were involved.

"Look, he just ended things with his long-term girlfriend, and just moved here after a trade, and the event is this weekend, so you see where the dilemma is," she said. "He wants to pay you five grand to attend with him."

I blinked. "Five. Thousand. Dollars?"

"Yep."

"To go to one event?"

"You want to see a picture?"

"He's willing to pay me five thousand dollars for one date. I don't really give a shit what he looks like."

"So, you're in?" She laughed.

"I'm definitely in." I picked up my drink again.

"I'm going to be fully transparent," she said after a beat. "We're going to carbon copy Dominic in the emails we send you, and act like it was a mistake, since he'd been included in the originals."

I felt my eyes go wide.

"I know," she said. "One last thing. The only requirement Jimmy has for this is that you meet him before the event. He wants to make sure you're not an overenthusiastic fan who's going to make a scene there."

"I don't even watch football, but sure." I pulled out my phone and opened up my calendar. I mean, five grand. "When is the event?"

"Saturday night at The Bay Room."

"Fancy." My brows rose. "I'll have to figure out what to wear."

"Oh. He's paying for that too. When he meets you, he'll sort that out."

"I'm starting to think this may not be a good idea. I'm falling in love with this Jimmy guy already."

She laughed. "Hey, if that happens, then tough luck for Dom."

My smile faded. I knew I wouldn't fall for anyone else. Dominic owned me and I was starting to resent him a little bit for it. It wasn't like this plan was foolproof. It might not work at all, but if it didn't, at least I'd be heartbroken with an extra five grand in my bank account.

CHAPTER FORTY-ONE

Dominic

WALKED INTO THE BODEGA WITH ROCCO AND SAW SANTIAGO VEGA standing by the Snickers with a price gun in his hands. He lowered it when he saw us.

"Nope. Get the hell out of my store." He walked toward us pointing a finger at the door. "Now."

"Nope," I said right back.

"Aw, and here I thought we'd get a warm welcome," Rocco said behind me.

Santiago scowled. "It would have been a warm welcome if my house hadn't been invaded the other night."

"And you think that's my fault?" I asked. I thought it was my fault too, but his hands weren't clean by any means.

"I . . ." He shook his head quickly, eyes wide, as if it just occurred to him that we all knew about the debt he owed Tommy. "Look, I know what you did for me when I was locked up, and I'm grateful for it, but I can't have you putting my family at risk."

"I'm here to put an end to the risk."

"An end?" He shot me a look. "The only way you put an end to that is by never seeing my daughter again."

My chest instantly ached. I swallowed and looked around, ignoring what he said. I had left her alone. I'd left her alone and it was fucking me up more than I ever imagined it would.

"I know what they call the two of you," Santiago said. "I've heard the rumors."

"What do they call us?" Rocco asked, opening the fridge on the other side of the store.

"Ghost Assassins." Santiago glared at me.

"Fun," Rocco said. "We should start a band."

"I can't believe I didn't know you owned bodegas here," I said quietly, looking around.

"I'm not surprised. It's not your territory." Santiago said a little forcefully. "Now leave before I call the police."

"It's not my territory, *yet*." I walked a little closer to him.

His brows shot up. "What does that mean?"

"It means what I said."

Rocco walked down the aisle, and it was then that Santiago seemed to really take in our attire, saw our weapons. He took a step back, eyes wide.

I put a hand up. "We're not here for you."

"There are innocent people back there."

"We don't hurt innocent people," Rocco said, walking over. "They should call us the Grace Brothers, since we give grace."

"There's nothing graceful about the things you do." Santiago's mouth flattened.

"Maybe not, but he needs to pay for what he's done to your daughter," I said.

"What he's done to . . ." Santiago's bushy brows furrowed. "I don't understand. We paid them back."

"This isn't about money, Mr. Vega. You've dealt with men like him before. You should know that."

"I told Rosie to stay out of it, but she insisted. I told her not to go to that nightclub." His eyes were welling up as he spoke. "I told her to stay away from guys like that. Guys like you."

"Guys like her father too, then, I assume." My jaw clenched. I didn't like where this was going. "I didn't come here to chit-chat, Santiago. I came to end this. You can either stay out of our way, or you can join the people in the back. Your call."

"And you can't call the cops if you decide to stay up front," Rocco said, grabbing a bag of peanut M&Ms and tearing the wrapper. He reached into his pocket.

"Keep your money," Santiago said.

"You sure?" Rocco's brows rose.

"Positive. When you were a little shit, you stole more M&Ms than I could count; what's one more?"

Rocco laughed.

"I never understood why you stole when you had money in your pocket."

"I just really liked the thrill of stealing." He shrugged, popping an M&M into his mouth. "I left an envelope with cash in your mailbox before we moved out."

Santiago's frown deepened. "That was you?"

"Catching up has been great and all, but we have things to do." I looked at my watch. "Roc."

He gave a nod and went to the back room.

"What will he do to them?" Santiago shot a worried look over his shoulder.

"There's only four back here," Rocco announced from the door.

"They're regulars," Santiago said. "Old men. They don't want trouble."

I kept my eyes on Rocco. "Tie them up."

Rocco disappeared back into the room.

"Dominic," Santiago warned.

"Do I need to tie you up?" I looked him straight in the eyes, this man who'd known me since I was a fucking child, who'd cheered for me when I finally learned to ride a two-wheel bike. Who'd taken me home after I got into a fight at the park and lied to my parents on my behalf. I had so much respect for him back then and it was that sentiment that I was trying to hold onto, because what he did to Santi and Rosie was fucked up. Maybe what happened at his house was my fault, maybe his, but the fact that his hands weren't any cleaner than mine still stood. I sighed. "Look, those men will be fine. We just can't risk them running and telling people what's happening."

"I understand."

"I need you to look me in the eye and promise you won't call the cops or tip Anthony off that we're back there," I said slowly, as if he were a child. "I need confirmation from you. Once I receive that confirmation, I'll take your word for it and go back there. If you betray me, well, then I guess you may just find out why the fuck they gave us that cute little nickname."

He looked terrified by the time I finished my little speech, and I realized he would make it impossible for me to date Rosie. Getting rid of Anthony was my priority right now, though.

"You have my word," he said. "What happens after this?"

"We'll send someone to clean everything up and from now on, one of our guys will be collecting the money."

"Can you just do that?" he asked, sounding nervous.

I felt myself smile. "Who's going to stop me?"

"Be careful, Dominic," he said, suddenly looking concerned. "Costello has a lot of men who are loyal to him around here."

"Are you one of them?"

"What? No. Hell no." He took a step back.

"Okay then." I started walking again.

"You're really trusting my word?" he asked behind me. "You're not going to tie me up?"

I turned around. "Are you telling me your word means nothing?"

"No, that's not what I'm saying at all, I've heard—"

"That we tie everyone up, I know." I sighed, running my fingers through my hair, which was the longest I'd had it in a while. "You have your daughter to thank for that. I may not give a shit about most people's opinions about me, but I care about hers and she'd kill me if I tied you up."

"Don't talk about my daughter."

"That's never going to happen, by the way, if you ever involve Rosie or Santi in your shit again, it won't end well for you."

"You're threatening me?"

"I'm telling you what'll happen."

"It sounds like a threat," he said as I started walking away again.

"If it sounds like a threat, I'd take it as a fucking threat, Mr. Vega." I looked over my shoulder.

The way his face paled gave me a sense of peace as I went into the back room. Maybe I should have tied and gagged him, but I trusted him when I was a kid and I'd trust him again now. I'd stated my piece. If he fucked up, it would be on him. Rocco was stepping back inside, wiping his hands on his black cargos.

"Fucking guy drooled on me."

"You're really gonna complain to me about drool? I had a guy shit on me once."

"Fuck. I remember that." He laughed as he took a seat. "I had a guy shit on me during combat training once. He's a major now and everyone still calls him Turd."

Of course, they did. The military had to be the only organization that used more nicknames than us. I sat back in my chair and looked around. The room was small but had three long folding tables full of cards and dominoes, with three envelopes lined up in a row. From the look of it, and assuming they were filled with ones and fives, there was probably three grand in each bag, give or take.

"All this for some pussy," Rocco mused.

"Fuck you."

"And it's pussy you're no longer even privy to."

"Fuck. You." I grit my teeth.

"It's true though." He set a leg up on the chair across from him. "You've become the guy you've been making fun of for four years."

"What guy?" I took the safety off my gun and set it on the table, eyes on the TV with the camera feed of the front of the bodega.

"Tony. Loren. Gio. Fucking Vinny."

"Fuck Vinny. I'm nothing like him." I scowled.

"So you wouldn't run away with Rosie if she asked you to? You wouldn't pull a Vinny and go down to fucking Florida and start a new life with an alias?"

I thought about it. "If she asked me to, yeah."

"See? Fucking pussy. It's the devil's work."

"I've had pussy all my life. This is different."

He shook his head. "You realize you can't just leave, right? That's not how it works. It is why Vinny pulled a Vinny."

"I would imagine my brothers would understand if I wanted to walk away and not make me pull a Vinny."

"Your brothers might. Giuseppe wouldn't."

I exhaled heavily. He was right. My father would rather kill me, his own son, than let me walk away from all of this, not that I wanted to. I wanted to be with Rosie more than I wanted anything else though. I just needed to find a happy medium.

"After we take care of these guys, I'm done with this kind of shit."

"Done getting your hands dirty?"

I gave a nod.

"Jesus." He shook his head. "All I know is I don't want to drink the fucking Kool-Aid. I'm not even thirty yet."

"Neither am I, asshole." I laughed, but it died the moment I heard the sound of the chime signaling the front door opening. Anthony walked in the front of the bodega, black bag in his hand, ready to collect. I spared a glance at Rocco, setting my foot on the edge of the table in front of us. "Did you bring the boxes?"

"Yep. They only had Cherry Coke." His lips twitched. "I hope twenty twelve-packs are enough for whatever you're planning."

I looked at Anthony, who was still talking to Santiago. If I had to guess, he was probably around one hundred and seventy pounds. I tilted my head side to side. I wasn't sure how I'd manage to tape twenty packs of soda around his body, but we'd figure it out. We always did. His voice rose to a shout as he pointed at Santiago. I couldn't make out what he was saying, but it didn't take a rocket scientist to know it was another threat. Beside me, Rocco made a disapproving grunt as he kicked the chair out of the way and sat up straighter, still chewing his damn M&Ms. I knew what I'd find if I turned my face to look at him. He probably looked casual, like I did, but we felt anything but. There was a reason Lorenzo, Gio, and Dean liked it when we worked together. There was a dance to all of it, a spark of anger that linked us, fueled us. In the position we were in nowadays, we had dozens of foot soldiers who would love to do our dirty work for us, and we let them for the most part, but we'd both agreed that nothing earned people's respect as much as leading by example.

Anthony barged in the room like he owned the place, like he was going to scare everyone in here to pay up more than they owed. I was sure he'd been doing just that for years now. It took him a second to realize what he was seeing, his pale blue eyes sweeping the room and landing on us. Slowly, understanding sunk in, and his commanding demeanor cracked.

"What is this?" he asked, eyes narrowing slightly.

He was still trying to hold onto his bravado, but we all knew it was pointless. Nothing could get him out of this room alive. Next to me, Rocco popped another M&M into his mouth. My boots dropped on the floor with a thump. That was when it fully registered and Anthony moved. It happened quickly. He dropped the black bag in his hand, I picked up my gun and took my first shot, the bullet hitting his knee. He went down immediately. From the bodega, Santiago shouted. Anthony started dragging himself with the right side of his body, trying to stand. I shook my head, walking over.

"Hold still." my foot on his ribcage, stopping his movements. He looked up at me, still glaring, beads of sweat forming between his brows. "You're making a fucking mess."

"Fuck you, De Luca." He spat. It was strong enough to reach

the bottom of my pants. I sighed and pressed the bottom of my shoe harder against his ribs. Anthony groaned. He looked toward Santiago. "You'll pay for this." His gaze shifted to me. "You really think she's worth this? You think she's worth dying for?" He groaned again when I pushed my foot harder. I heard a crack. I could tell he felt it, the way he gasped in a breath.

I looked down at where I'd shot him then looked over at Rocco. "I missed."

"Really?" Rocco walked into the room, shaking his head. "You're losing your touch."

He leaned against the wall, still eating his M&Ms. Santiago hadn't said a word, but from the way he was breathing, I knew he was hiding behind the counter. Probably praying. I hoped he was. We all could use some of those.

"You're never going to get away with this. You have no idea what's coming. You have no idea who's on our side," he said with a groan.

"You mean Joe?" I raised an eyebrow. "You think we don't know about that?"

The shock on his face told me everything I needed to know. He narrowed his eyes and laughed, trying a new tactic. It was like watching a replay of an old movie. I'd done this song and dance too many times already, so I already knew whatever came out of his mouth next was meant to piss me off.

"Did she tell you how I pinned her down? How I made her squirm?" Anthony asked, a smile still on his lips. I wanted to cut his face up, but I wouldn't. Not yet. I pushed my boot even deeper. Another crack. "Fuck."

"Mr. Vega," I called out. "You can go home. We'll clean up this mess, lock up, and wipe the camera footage. You don't have to worry about anything."

He came out from behind the register, and I thought he'd either look scared or disgusted. What I saw was anger. He stopped right beside me and spat on Anthony's face.

"I'd kill you myself if I thought I could do a better job than these guys."

Anthony gasped out a laugh. "You led me right between her legs."

"Mr. Vega," I said as calmly as I could muster. "You may want to leave within ten seconds."

He walked to the door and stood by it, holding it like he was curious enough to stay a bit longer, like he wanted this guy to suffer as much as I did.

"Were you aiming for the femoral?" Rocco asked, finally walking closer. "You missed it by a lot."

"Nah, he'd bleed out too fast." I pushed down on his ribs again, cracked another one. "I was aiming for his dick."

Rocco let out a laugh, walking to the back. "I have a better idea of what you can do to his dick. I'm gonna need to take a can from one of those boxes though."

"You'll die for this, De Luca. For sloppy-second pussy."

My laugh came out forced and without humor as I shook my head, looking down at the stupid motherfucker.

"Hey, Roc," I called out. "Make that three cans. One for each hole."

I heard the door open and close and looked up to see Santiago locking it from the other side. He gave a nod. Of approval? I wasn't sure. It didn't matter. He had to know I played by no one's rules, except maybe his daughter's.

"Where do you want this one?" Rocco walked back into the room, shaking one of the cans.

It was about to be a very long night, because the man under my boot had marked her, bruised her, traumatized her, tied her up, pointed guns at her, and was going to pay for all of it.

CHAPTER FORTY-TWO

OKAY, JIMMY RYAN WAS CUTE AS HELL.

He had the perfect hair, perfect smile, perfect quarterback thing going, and he was such a gentleman, opening doors and holding out seats. I couldn't imagine a man like this staying single unless he wanted to be. He'd picked Masseria's for dinner. I almost told him to change location, but then I remembered this was all Veronica's doing. Still, the possibility of running into one of Dominic's friends here was making me a little uncomfortable.

"You okay?" Jimmy asked across from me.

"I am." I smiled. "I'm assuming Patty filled you in on why I was doing this?"

"She tried, but to be honest, I didn't really pay attention. I saw you on stage and Googled you that night, so I didn't really care what your reasons were." He chuckled and I swear his teeth twinkled like they do in the cartoons. "I'll tell you my reasons for taking you to this event though. My ex will be there with the guy she cheated on me with."

My jaw dropped. "Someone cheated on *you*?"

"Girlfriend of five years. Fiancée of four months." He paused to listen to the waiter and ordered us a bottle of wine to share. When the waiter left, he said, "I hope you like wine."

"I don't really drink wine, but I promise I'll like it."

"Good." He laughed. "I'm well aware this isn't a real date, but since we're here, tell me about yourself."

And I did. We spent the entirety of dinner talking and getting to know each other, and by the time we were almost done with the wine, I was tipsy and genuinely having a good time.

CHAPTER FORTY-THREE

Dominic

"**W**HO THE FUCK IS JIMMY RYAN?"

"The new starting QB for the Jets." Rocco shot me a look from the other side of the counter. "Why?"

"No reason," I muttered as I continued reading the email Veronica sent Rosie.

She must have not realized I was still in this email chain; otherwise, I knew she wouldn't have done it. Every few days, I'd ask her if she'd spoken to Rosie and she never responded, which meant yes. Nico was being annoyingly quiet about anything Rosie-related as well. The only thing he reported back to me was that she was safe. He didn't even tell me the location she was safe at, which was just as well since I had another set of eyes on them who actually did report back. Mostly because Adio, who was Jamaican Mike's cousin and came highly recommended, was new and hadn't gotten comfortable with me yet. Marco was still recovering from his broken arm, so I had him doing other important things right now. If Adio not being comfortable meant he wouldn't withhold information about Rosie like everyone else in my fucking life, I hoped he never got comfortable around me at all.

Gabe had been in contact with her and didn't offer much aside from "she's fine." They all had the same smartass answer when I lost my temper and told them to elaborate. *"Call her. Go see her."* As if I wasn't dying to do all of the above. I couldn't, though. Not yet. Not until I got rid of Tommy and the rest of his little crew for good.

I looked at the email exchange one more time before I set my phone down and focused on flipping the chicken I'd been making. It was one of those ready-to-cook meals Rosie liked. Well, three of them, since Roc was here and Gabe was on his way. I grabbed my phone again and texted Nico.

Me: you still with Rosie?

Nico: yes

Me: is she on a date?

Nico: she's having dinner

Me: with a man?

No response. Of course. He was really testing my fucking patience lately. I set the phone down and took a breath before picking it up and texting Adio.

Me: is Rosie on a date?

Adio Shaw: looks like it

Me: with a man?

Adio Shaw: White male, 6'2, 225lbs

Me: you got that from watching them? Are you that close?

Adio Shaw: I got it from the internet. It's Jimmy Ryan. The guy's a super star

Jesus fucking Christ. I threw my head back with a groan.

Me: you're a Jets fan?

Adio Shaw: guilty

I took another deep breath and dialed Nico, because fuck this. He answered on the first ring.

"She's having dinner with a fucking athlete?"

"Yep," Nico said, and I heard the smile in his voice. He was also a Jets fan and officially a fucking traitor.

"Where are they?"

"Masseria's."

"You're joking." I set my jaw to contain my fuming.

"Nope. I've been watching them for the last two hours."

"Two hours?" I screamed.

"Two and a half."

"What the . . . what kind of . . ." I stopped talking and took a deep breath. "Are they understaffed?"

"Nope. The food was out in thirty minutes, but they're on their second bottle of wine."

I couldn't take it anymore. I hung up and set my phone down, turning back to the chicken.

"So I guess Rosie's dating again?" Rocco said behind me. My hand tightened on the tongs.

"Not dating. It's for Oui."

"Same shit."

"Not the same shit. It's not a dating service." I shot him a look over my shoulder. He looked way too amused for my liking.

"You're right. Some of them sleep with their dates."

"Roselyn is not going to sleep with anyone."

Gabriel chose that exact moment to join us. He went to the fridge and grabbed a beer. "Rosie's fucking someone?"

I turned the stove off, set my hands on the counter, and focused on breathing. I should let these assholes starve for this.

"She's not fucking him *yet*," Rocco said. "She has a date with Jimmy Ryan."

"No shit?" Gabe sounded impressed. Another traitor. "The women in my office are obsessed with that guy. I wonder if she could get me his autograph."

"When they start fucking, she can probably get him to go by your—"

"She's not going to fuck him." I turned around and pounded both fists on the counter between us.

"If you say so." Rocco shrugged.

"I don't understand why you care. You haven't called her back, you haven't gone to see her," Gabe said.

"Because." I slammed my fists against the counter again, took a breath. "I've been trying to take care of things before I go to her."

Gabe looked at me for a solid five seconds before he took another sip of beer.

"What?" I snapped.

"Nothing." He shrugged. Rocco laughed.

I wanted to kill them both. Instead, I made them serve their own food while I stormed over to the guest room that was on this floor and called Veronica. She answered on the second ring, and I pounced.

"What exactly are you playing at?"

"What are you talking about?" she asked, having the nerve to sound confused.

"What is this email about Rosie going out with some douchebag quarterback?"

"Oh crap. Wait, you just saw it?"

"Yes," I seethed. "What the fuck?"

"Well, I obviously didn't mean to send that to you, so please disregard it," she said. "Secondly, that douchebag quarterback is Patty's godson, which makes him family, and he's the furthest thing from a douchebag."

I felt myself frown. "If he's so fucking great, why does he need an escort service to get a date?"

"Okay, clearly you didn't read the entire email, which is good since it wasn't meant for you. This is not a paid date."

"Why did she agree to this?" I asked. "If it's not a paid date, why is she there?"

"Maybe she thinks he's hot, like everyone else in the western hemisphere. Even I think he's hot and he's twenty years younger than me and I'm not into men."

That made me scowl even more. "I don't like it."

"He's taking her to an event this weekend."

My chest squeezed. He was seeing her again this weekend? I was out here slaying dragons for her and she was letting some prince take her out on the town. What the fuck?

She sighed into the line when I didn't say anything. "You had to know she wasn't going to sit around waiting for you to decide to finally give her the time of day."

"Give her the time of day?" I snapped. "She's all I fucking think about all day. How much more time can she possibly demand?" The line went silent. I looked at the screen to make sure she was still there. "She just left the hospital."

At that, she laughed. "Nearly a month ago. She's been performing all week."

"She shouldn't be dating."

"She's totally fine. I saw her myself. She looks amazing."

"Fuck you."

"Dominic."

"No. Fuck you. Why are you doing this to me?" I sat down at the edge of the bed, feeling like my heart might give out.

"If you want her so badly, why don't you go and get her?"

"Because I'm no good for her." I swallowed thickly.

God damn it. I felt like a golf ball had wedged itself in my throat. It was one of the reasons I'd been keeping my distance. Every time I thought about calling her or texting her or visiting her, I remembered her expression when that guy dragged her out of her dad's house, and I couldn't bring myself to do it. Another week, I told myself, just one more. I almost had Tommy, then I'd either go to her or let her go. But knowing she was on a date, drinking too much wine, and laughing with some asshole jock? No. That was not okay. Only over my dead body, and even then, my ghost wouldn't allow it.

"It seems you have your answer, Dom. Just let her go." She paused. "I have to go. Talk to you tomorrow."

The line went silent. I stayed there for what felt like an eternity, staring at the grey wall in front of me, trying not to picture her on this date. *Let her go*, Veronica said. As if it were that easy.

"You done with your pity party for one?" Gabe said when I walked back into the kitchen.

"You need to watch your fucking mouth, Gabriel."

"Or what, you're going to tie me up to a chair and burn my apartment while I sit there?"

I stared at him, then turned to the food.

"Side note, this chicken sucks," Rocco said.

I looked down at his plate. "You ate the whole thing."

"Because I'm starving, not because it's good."

"Today has been a true test of my patience." I cut into my chicken and tried a piece. Yeah, it was dry as fuck. I ate it anyway because I was also starving.

"So," Gabe started.

I pointed my fork at him. "Don't talk about Rosie."

"I wasn't going to." He chuckled. "But good to know you're finally realizing that ship has sailed."

"That ship hasn't sailed." Jesus Christ. How had I not realized that I surround myself with a bunch of assholes? And I was worse. It was like I couldn't help myself and had to engage.

"Once she sets her eyes on Jimmy Ryan, that ship will be in China by the time you even think to call her."

"Fuck you."

"Yeah, I know." He had some of the fettuccine that went with the dry chicken and shook his head. "Mom would be so disappointed."

I looked at my plate, a new sadness filling me. I knew he was talking about the chicken, which Mom would have totally made fun of me for, but she'd also be disappointed about me letting Rosie slip through my fingers like this. Mom loved Rosie. When Gabe started bringing her over, she acted like she'd won the lottery. She kept calling her the daughter she always wanted. I thought about my trip with Rosie to see the bronze statues. So much happened since that trip; it felt like a year ago.

"Your mom's lasagna was the best I've ever had, to this day," Rocco said, snapping me out of my thoughts. "My mom's ziti was the shit though. I have dreams about that ziti."

"Her ziti was pretty fire," I agreed.

"Do you know how to make it?" Gabe asked.

"Nah." Rocco smiled sadly. "She never got a chance to teach me. Mikey makes it though. Not as good, but it's better than mine." He exhaled. "When I find the fucker responsible for that night, I'm going to make him wish he'd killed us all."

Gabe's fork stopped moving. "You're really looking?"

"I'll never stop."

"What makes you think they're still alive?" he asked.

"Hope."

"Hope." I scoffed, taking a sip of water and unlocking my phone again.

"Hope, since it'll mean that I'll get to kill them slowly and make them pay for what they did."

"But you have no idea?" Gabe asked. "Nothing to go on? Can't your brother help?"

"Trust me, Mikey has everything he needs. If anyone can figure out who did this, it's him, and when he does, I'll be ready."

"We'll be ready," I said.

"I thought you weren't getting your hands dirty anymore?" Rocco raised an eyebrow.

"For this, I would."

He chuckled. Gabe sighed heavily.

I checked my email again, hoping Veronica hadn't taken me out of the thread because I was a masochistic asshole and needed to see all of it.

Sender: RONNIE2077@OUI
To: ROSIE13
Subject: UPDATE??

Just checking in! Also, I accidentally included people who weren't supposed to see the previous message. I keep hitting too many buttons! If you want, we can continue this in text

Sender: ROSIE13
To: RONNIE2077
Subject: RE: UPDATE??

Tonight is still going! lol. He is so nice. AND HE GAVE ME HIS CREDIT CARD AND TOLD ME I DIDN'T HAVE A SPENDING LIMIT! WHOOOO DOOOESSS THAAAAATTT? He must not know I'll take him up on it and swipe the hell out of his card LOL JK I'm only going to buy a dress for the event. But still.

Sender: RONNIE2077@OUI
To: ROSIE13
Subject: RE: RE: UPDATE??

LOL he's rich enough to do that. Glad it's going well!

Sender: ROSIE13
To: RONNIE2077
Subject: RE: RE: RE: UPDATE??

Me too. I have to come back to this place. The wine is so good that I'm reconsidering question #5! I think we're going to The Drunken Rabbit next! OKAY FOR REAL FOR REAL TTYT!!

Question five. I ran through the list of questions and felt the blood drain when I remembered what that one was. FUCK NO.

"You okay?" that was Gabe.

"Fantastic." I grit my teeth. "Why?"

"You're holding the wrong end of your knife."

I looked down and saw blood seeping from my hand. "Fuck."

I cleaned up, threw shit away, wiped the counter again, and washed my hands twice. Good thing it was one of the knives that needed to be sharpened. The cut wasn't deep and had already stopped bleeding. They were still at Gio's restaurant, but the asshole was out of town. The one night I needed him here.

"You need to figure this out and get your head in the game," Rocco said. "We still need to get rid of Tommy and friends."

"I know. You think I don't know that?" I ran a hand through my hair. Fuck. "I have everything ready. Rope. Gasoline. Lighters. Fucking gas bombs. I'm ready."

"You can have an entire armory, but as long as your head isn't clear, this won't go well."

I nodded slowly. I needed to resolve this thing with Rosie. I looked at my phone again. "Have you heard of The Drunken Rabbit?"

"Yeah," they both said.

"Is it a fancy bar or something?"

"No," Gabe said. "Is that where Rosie is?"

Rocco looked like he was trying not to laugh.

"What's so funny?"

"Is that really where they are?" Rocco asked to confirm.

Now, they were pissing me off. I looked it up and scrolled through pictures. Was this a sex club? It looked like the perfect place to fuck someone. I started reading reviews. Not a sex club, but from the looks of it, it would be the perfect place for a drunken hookup. If she was going to start going to this place, I'd either have to burn it down or buy it.

"She shouldn't be going there with a fucking jock." I kept scrolling.

Gabe laughed. "You were a jock once."

"Fuck you." I pointed at him, then at Rocco. "And fuck you."

I rushed upstairs to get ready. There was no way I was staying home tonight.

I'd just stay out of sight, but someone needed to watch her to make sure she was okay, and the two men I was paying to do so were traitors.

CHAPTER FORTY-FOUR

Dominic

MY BROTHER WAS STILL IN A FULL SUIT SINCE HE HADN'T GONE home to change. Rocco and I were wearing jeans, t-shirts, and suit jackets. Even dressed like this, I felt like we looked conspicuous. Not that it mattered whether or not Rosie saw us. We were in a public bar, for fuck's sake.

"Are you here for a drink or am I going to have to escort you out?" Nico asked.

"Shouldn't you be watching Rosie?"

He raised an eyebrow. "Rosie's fine."

"Where is she?"

"In one of those little private rooms."

My heart stopped beating. "The ones with the beds?"

"Really? The ones with the beds?" Gabe asked next to me.

One of us sounded amused, the other sounded like he was about to blow a gasket.

"You said you only wanted us to intervene if she was in danger."

"I did."

"She's not in danger," Nico said.

"How would you know if she's in a private room and you're out here, talking to us?"

"I just saw our girl go into one of those rooms with a bed." That was Rocco as he walked back over from the bathroom.

The pressure that was already in my chest, seemed to keep building. I took a breath, took another. I tried, I really tried not to snap, but it was no use. "Where the fuck is this room?"

"Down the hall near the bathroom," Rocco said. "Room number three."

I ground my teeth, willing the anger to subside. It didn't.

"She's going to a team event with him on Saturday," Nico said suddenly. "I heard them talking about it in the car."

"Oh, so you drove him here?" Gabe asked.

My eyes narrowed on Nico. "What were they saying?"

"She was on her phone looking at dresses. He gave her a no-spend limit on his card." Nico grinned. I already knew about the dress and the no-spending limit. If that was what she wanted, I'd have given her my fucking card a month ago. Nico's grin widened. "I think I may be falling in love with the guy myself."

"Fuck. You." I glared. "This is why I don't like Jets fans."

Nico laughed. Rocco laughed. Gabe laughed. I stormed away and headed to room three. The good thing about these rooms was that instead of doors, they had a white drape that moved side-to-side. When I reached room number three, I took a breath and tried to eavesdrop, which was impossible, as loud as this place was. I moved the curtain slightly and saw them. They weren't alone in the room and there was no bed. It looked more like a cigar lounge than anything else. They were sitting on two separate couches, two glasses between them that looked like water but could've been vodka or tequila. If they'd already shared two bottles of wine, I hoped this was water. I spared a glance at my next victim, and I had to admit he had good hair. I really didn't like this guy.

Rosie's cheeks were flushed, and she was smiling at whatever he was saying. The sight of that smile directed at another man felt unbearable. I hadn't seen her this close in weeks, so I let myself look at her. She was wearing black knee-high boots, a short leather skirt, and a pink blouse. Her hair was down and every time she moved, it swung forward, covering her face. I took a step away from the room and made myself walk back to the bar. I was being unfair and selfish. I'd only answered one call and only because I was in a panic when I saw her name and thought she might be in trouble. I'd sent the texts to make sure she knew I wasn't out partying. I was at Tommy's strip club, trying to figure out if I was going to attack there or at Tempt.

I'd really been trying to let her go, but it was obvious that it was never going to happen. What was my end game here? Was I going to let her walk away and be with some good-looking asshole quarterback? I should. I knew I should, but I fucking couldn't. The thought of not having her in my life made me sick. When I got back to the bar, the three stooges were waiting for me. I wasn't going to tell them anything I saw.

I turned my attention to Nico. "I'm giving you a promotion."

"For what?"

"For being outstanding." I reached for the mescal I'd ordered and took a sip.

"I'm sensing a catch," Nico said warily.

I grinned as I turned to him. "You're getting me an invite to this event on Saturday. If you can't make that happen, you'll find out who owns the catering company and I'll wear a goddamn tux and serve food. Get me in the fucking room."

"You don't have to do that." Nico shook his head, amused. "There's an entrance fee."

"How much?"

"Ten-grand a person."

"For a Jets event?" I asked. Nico nodded. Normally, I wouldn't have paid for a one-dollar seat in their damn stadium. "Fuck it. Buy the tickets. We're going."

For once, Rocco, Gabe, and Nico had nothing to say. They just stared at me like I'd lost my mind. As if I hadn't lost it the moment I saw Rosie at Tempt that night.

CHAPTER FORTY-FIVE

Rosie

MY HEAD WAS STILL SWIMMING IN RED WINE WHEN I HEARD THE noise. I opened the drawer and reached for my gun, pointing it at the dark. It wasn't loaded. Dad bought three guns after Mom had been killed that night. Before then, he hated guns. After that night, he decided we needed to protect ourselves, and we agreed. We'd learned how to shoot, we got our gun licenses, and we were responsible for them. I'd never felt the need to bring it out of my closet until Anthony, and then I couldn't sleep unless it was near me. I used to keep it under my pillow until Dominic gave me a half-an-hour speech about how reckless and dangerous that was. Now I kept it unloaded on my nightstand. After losing my hearing and seeing a dead kid, I never wanted to have a loaded gun anywhere near me again, but I figured if an intruder saw me with it, they'd be more likely to flee. Wishful thinking, probably, but it was the best I could do since there was no way I was going to use it on anyone. Dominic once told me that in his line of work sometimes it was "shoot or get shot at" and after what happened at Dad's house, I decided I'd rather get shot at. Maybe it was dumb, but I just couldn't stop seeing that kid dead on the floor. I steadied my hands and pointed at the dark, heart in my throat as I waited.

"Careful, baby. I didn't take the bullets out this time."

My heart stopped beating. "Dominic?"

"Disappointed?"

I reached out and switched on the lamp next to me. I'd been meaning to get a different bulb for it, since this one seemed to be fading, but even in the sucky lighting, the moment I confirmed it was him, I felt the air leave my lungs. It felt like I hadn't seen him in an eternity. His hair was a little longer now, a casually sexy mess that begged for fingers to run through it. His beard had filled out too, though he kept it trim. And those eyes. Ugh. Those eyes. He shoved his hands in his pockets and took a step toward me.

"Are you that certain I won't shoot you?"

"No." His lips tugged into a sad smile. "But I'd rather die by your hand than anyone else's."

"Dominic." My hand shook as I set the gun on the night-stand next to me. I pushed my palms against my eyelids to try to clear my head. "I drank too much for this."

"Ah." He chuckled. He was much closer now. I glanced up, craining my neck to look at his face. "Did you have fun on your date?"

"How'd you . . ." I frowned. I'd almost forgotten about that. "Oh."

"Did you?" His gaze burned into mine.

"I did."

He let his head hang as he nodded slowly, as if trying to process that. Maybe he was coming to terms with the idea of losing me. I wasn't sure, but the urge to stand and touch him, to run my fingers through his hair, to pull his face up to look at him and kiss him was so strong that I had to make my hands into fists.

"What are you doing here?" I whispered.

"I don't know."

"You don't know?" I blinked. "You snuck into my new apart-ment in the middle of the night, came into my room, and you don't know why?"

He brought his head up. He was quiet for a moment, look-ing at me with those piercing, dark eyes that seemed to burn through me. It was so intense that I started to shake a little, but didn't dare look away. When he finally spoke, his voice was low, soft, unsure. The opposite of the man himself.

"Can I sleep here tonight?"

"Wh—what?" My heart skipped. "Like here in my apartment or here in my bed?"

"Both."

"I . . ." My jaw dropped. I didn't know what I was expecting, but it wasn't this. "I haven't seen you in a month."

"Twenty-two days," he said. "I've been counting."

"Twenty-two days," I repeated.

"Almost twenty-three."

"You haven't called, you answered one call, and you were in a freaking club." I scowled. "I should slap you and kick you out."

"You should."

My chest shook. I took a breath and sat up on my knees, but I still wasn't at eye level with him, so I stood on the bed next. Now, I was taller, and he was the one looking up at me. This didn't seem to bother him in the least, but it made me feel like I had somewhat of an advantage.

"Let me get this straight, while I've been recovering and waiting for you to, I don't know, acknowledge my existence, you're out clubbing, then you don't call, don't visit, don't text, and suddenly you want to sleep here?"

"Not suddenly, no." He searched my eyes. "And I wasn't out clubbing, Roselyn. It was work."

"Work. Right." I rolled my eyes. "The kind that involves women getting really close to your ear and seductively asking if you need anything from them."

"I don't even know what you're talking about." He had the nerve to look genuinely perplexed. "I haven't spoken to any woman . . ." He shook his head, taking a breath and I could tell he was done with that portion of the conversation. After a moment, his eyes and voice softened. "Let me stay."

"Fine, but only because I'm bored."

He tried to hide his smile as he turned around, but I saw it. I plopped down on the bed and turned the light off again as he undressed because I couldn't watch him. I wouldn't. As it was, I didn't know why I'd agreed to this. It certainly wasn't because I was bored. I'd spent the majority of the night talking about him to Jimmy. He'd spent the majority of the night telling me about Jessa, his ex, though, so it was fine. We'd commiserated over wine. I wasn't going to pretend I didn't think he was hot, though. Hot and rich and everything a girl like me should probably want, but unfortunately, my heart was an idiot and wanted this infuriating man. The bed dipped and the idiot in my chest went frantic as I felt him get under the covers and scoot closer to me.

"Can I touch you?"

"What?" I yelped, scooting away as far as I could without falling off. "No."

"I'm not asking you to let me play with your pussy," he said, dropping his voice low. I fought a shiver. "Can I hold you?"

I shut my eyes and tried to bury my face deeper into the pillow, but try as I might, I wanted him to hold me. I needed it. I scooted until we met halfway. In an instant, he had my back pulled to his chest, an arm and leg wrapped around me, holding me like he wanted to swallow me whole.

"I missed you so much, baby." His voice sounded pained against my hair. "So fucking much."

Tears pricked my eyes. I squeezed them shut. "If you missed me so much, you would have come to me sooner."

"I couldn't."

"Why?" I wiped my face and moved until he loosened his grip on me and let me face him.

"I was trying to let you go."

My heart dropped. "Why?"

"You don't want this life, Rosie. You said so yourself."

"That was before." I swallowed hard to contain my

emotions. He shot up on the bed. I followed his movement and sat up as well.

"Before what, Roselyn? Before you were *attacked*? Before you had to relive . . ." He stopped talking and swallowed as if he had a boulder in his throat the size of mine. "God. I hate that you had to go through that."

"It wasn't your fault, Dom."

"It was my fault. I should've . . ." His eyes flashed when they met mine. He shook his head, pain clear in his eyes. I tried to finish the sentence for him in my head, but I wasn't sure what he was going to say, that he should've killed Anthony before he had a chance to do that? That he should've been there to protect me?

"It doesn't matter. What's done is done."

"That was what made you decide that you suddenly wanted to be with me?" he asked, looking at me through narrowed eyes. "Are you insane?"

"Maybe," I said. A small smile lifted one corner of his lips, but it's fleeting, immediately covered by a frown. "And I don't *suddenly* want to be with you, Dominic. I just suddenly realized that it didn't matter what my boyfriend did for a living. Danger could find me no matter what."

"That's not true." He frowned, a new wave of sadness clouding his face. "That's not true and you know it."

I sighed. "Is that why you were trying to let me go?"

"It's the right thing to do."

"So why are you here?"

"Because I don't know how to do the right thing." He shut his eyes, taking a breath. "I don't know how to let you go."

I sighed. He was really starting to piss me off, but I knew his dilemma wouldn't be resolved with a simple conversation, so I decided to set it aside for now. Instead, I brought a hand up to his face. He watched me as I ran my fingers over his jaw, his cheek, and shut his eyes when I sank them into his hair. He set a hand on my waist and made a sound in the back of his throat that made my stomach flip. I ran my fingers through his hair again. "It's gotten long."

"You said you liked it long."

"It doesn't matter how I like it. We've already established that we're no longer together."

His eyes popped open, grip tightening on my waist. "Rosie."

"What? You just said you were trying to do the right thing."

"I also said I don't know how to do the right thing."

"Right, well, we both know that the only reason you're here is because you're jealous." I tightened my grip on his hair. "Because you don't want me, but you also don't want anyone else to have me."

"That's not true, Rosie." He sighed. I pulled his hair harder, hoping he'd confess that he was lying. He hissed, eyes darkening. "Careful, baby. We're half naked in bed together and I've been going crazy without your mouth, your body, your pussy. I'll get the wrong idea and pounce."

My heart skipped about three beats. I let go of his hair and got up on my knees again, pulling the oversized Boston Bruins t-shirt I was wearing over my head. Dominic's eyes stayed on mine, as if he was afraid that any move he made would be the wrong one. I wondered if he'd ever felt this way in his life with a woman and concluded that it was highly doubtful. The thought made me smile as I stood up on the bed, still holding his gaze as I brought my hands to my breasts and cupped them. I pulled my nipples between my fingers, and he shifted beneath me, looking up at me through hooded eyes and biting down on his lower lip, as if it was taking everything for him not to reach out to me. It was all the fuel I needed. I ran my hands down my torso, up to my boy shorts. I turned around, facing the bathroom. With the door wide open, I had a clear view of myself, a clear view of him behind me, on the small mirror above the sink. I reached for my boy shorts again, toying with the elastic for a moment before bending slowly. He inhaled sharply behind me.

"God, baby." He sat up on his knees, taking and letting out a ragged breath, eyes burning as he took me in.

"I guess it's safe to say this is turning you on." I smirked over my shoulder, gaze falling on the huge tent in his boxers for a second.

His gaze burned into me. "Everything you do turns me on."

The sight of his hard, thick dick made my knees weaken, but I was determined to continue my strip tease. I brought the boy shorts slowly down my legs, watching him as he gripped himself over his briefs and started stroking slowly as he watched. With my underwear in one hand, I widened my stance and threw it at him as I bent over and brought my hands to the mattress. It hit him in the chest, but he didn't even seem to register it, as entranced with my movements as he was.

"Rosie." His voice was a strained rumble.

I stood up slowly and turned around, taking the three steps necessary to get to him. He was still stroking, still looking up at me like I was the only thing worth looking at, and I was determined to show him that this would be the last time he'd see me like this, if he didn't get his shit together. I set my hands on his broad shoulders and pushed him back gently. He didn't even bother putting up a fight. He fell onto his back. His arms wrapped around me, and he brought me down with him. I sat up quickly, straddling him, and his hands instantly went to my hips.

His eyes flared. "Roselyn."

"What?" I rocked my hips against him, shivering at the feel of him between my folds.

Damn, he felt good. So good. I rubbed myself against him, biting my lip and throwing my head back at the feel of it.

His hands gripped my hips tight as he pushed himself up into a sitting position, so we were face to face. "Don't do anything you'll regret."

"I'm not drunk, Dominic," I whispered against his lips,

though I wouldn't kiss him. "And even if I was, I would never regret you."

"Fuck." He shut his eyes and took a breath, hands tightening again on my hips. When he opened them, I saw lust and agony. "I need your mouth on mine. I need to kiss you."

I shook my head. "I only kiss my boyfriends."

"Roselyn." He groaned as I rocked my hips against him again.

"You don't have boyfriend privileges anymore, Dom." I smiled. I was going for triumphant, but it felt sad, broken.

In an attempt to cover it up, I lifted a leg to get off him and focused on sliding his boxers off, pausing for a moment to admire the way he sprung out of them, jutting up, long, hard, and thick.

"Come here." His voice was a husky low command that made me shiver.

My eyes snapped back to his as he reached for me and pulled me up. I was prepared for him to settle me on top of him so that he could sink into me, but instead, he kept pulling me up until my pussy was on his face. Strong hands gripped my ass as he set his face between my legs. I hissed when he bit the insides of my thighs.

"God, I missed your pussy."

Those were the last words he said before he started licking me, his grip steadying me when I started moving against his mouth, my body working on its own as it tried to find release. I brought my hands between my legs, to his hair, and tugged on it, eliciting a rumbled sound from his mouth that vibrated onto my clit and through my body. Still grabbing me, eating me, he flipped me so that my back fell onto the mattress with an oomph. His mouth left my pussy for one second, long enough for him to glance up and sear me with a burning gaze before he went right back to his attack, his tongue lashing, his mouth sucking.

"Domin . . . oh fuck."

He slid a finger inside me, then another, pumping into me

as he sucked my clit. "This is mine," he growled against me. "Mine, Rosie."

My hips rocked once, twice, and then he did that thing where he hooked a finger inside me at just the right angle and licked my clit in the place I needed it, and a white light exploded in my vision, blinding me as I orgasmed. I felt his mouth as he moved it against my thighs and up my body. His tongue on my nipples made me arch and whimper, but I couldn't yet open my eyes. When I did, I found him resting his hands on either side of me, looking at me like he was trying to memorize every one of my features. I brought my hands up and ran the tips of my fingers over his clavicle, the ridges of his chest, his abdomen, going over his artwork, the large scarab on his chest, the beautifully painted Mona Lisa skeleton on his side, every single one detailed and as beautiful and faceted as the man himself.

"I'm going to kiss you now," he said, voice low above me. My eyes snapped to his.

I shook my head, eyes wide. "I said no."

"You're going to fuck me, but I can't kiss you?" His eyes narrowed.

"Yep." I licked my lips.

He looked at them and groaned deeply, shutting his eyes and taking a breath. When he opened them, he looked determined, and I was certain he'd lean down and kiss me anyway. He could. What was I going to do to stop him? Anyone else would have taken advantage and done it, but not him. He pulled back and flipped me over so that I was on my stomach, reaching under me to set me on my knees. I had one second to adjust before he brought his hand around my throat and impaled me, hard, deep. I screamed, sucked in air as he thrust again, but it was impossible to breathe like this, with his hand around my neck and his dick so deep inside me that I could feel him everywhere.

"Is this how you want me to fuck you?" He took his hand away from my throat and wound my hair around it, pulling as hard as he was fucking me, making tears spring to my eyes, but the pleasure between my legs overrode the pain on my scalp. "You want me to fuck you the way I used to fuck all of the meaningless, faceless women?" I growled with annoyance. He knew that would piss me off. I felt his lips on the side of my neck, licking, biting softly. He unwound his hand from my hair and brought it between my legs. "Is that what you want? You want this to be a one-off, casual fuck?" His fingers moved faster, the pressure building on my already swollen, sensitive clit. I pushed my hips back with a strangled moan.

"I'm gonna come," I gasped. "Dom—"

His climax overlapped mine, my name sounded like a curse spilling out of his mouth. We were both panting when we fell onto the bed. Dominic turned and got out of bed. I heard him in the bathroom. Felt him wiping between my legs. At some point in my haze, I sat up, went to the bathroom, put my shirt and underwear back on, and went back to the room. He was sitting at the edge of the bed, shirtless but wearing his black boxer briefs. Under any other circumstance, I would've joked that he looked like he was planning to take over the world, but this felt serious, heavy. I got in bed, pulled the covers up, and looked at him, waiting.

"Your dad and brother hate me."

I blinked. Not at all what I'd been expecting him to say. "So?"

"So?" He glanced at me over his shoulder. "That's a big deal for you."

"They'll live."

"Rosie." It was a groan as he turned to me and got under the covers. I moved closer, so we were facing each other on our respective pillows. The agony in his eyes sank into me and weighed down on my chest. "You shouldn't want to be with me."

"I know."

"You called me your boyfriend." He smiled softly. "You said I lost my boyfriend privileges."

"Isn't that what you were?"

"I should've been a better boyfriend."

"You were." I reached out and ran my fingers over his jaw. "You were the best boyfriend I've ever had."

"Don't say that." He swallowed thickly. "Please don't say that."

I took my hand back. "Don't tell me what to say and what not to say. You came here. You asked to sleep here. You initiated this, and for what?"

"Because I needed to see you."

"But not because you're going to stay for good," I said, turning onto my side and facing the other way so he wouldn't see the tears in my eyes. "I can't do this."

"I just need time. I need to—"

"Time?" I scoffed. "It's been a month, Dominic."

"I know." He groaned. "Don't you think I've been counting every second of every fucking day that I've been without you?"

"Well, you could've fooled me."

"Jesus, Rosie. You know I'm crazy about you. You know I'm so in love with you that if you told me to leave all of this behind, I fucking would."

My heart leaped. He was in love with me. Wasn't that what I'd been wanting to hear from him? Why did it hurt so much now? I breathed in shakily, wiping my face again, and turned around to face him.

"I'm not asking you to do that," I whispered. "I haven't asked you for anything at all, Dominic. I just want you."

He shut his eyes. "I know."

"But you can't give me that," I said, then corrected myself. "You're not going to give me that."

"I want to. I want to so much, Rosie, but I can't. Not yet." He looked at me again and I saw the same brokenness I felt reflected back onto me. There was no triumph in this, and there would be none because the ball was in his court, and he refused to make a play. The worst part was that somewhere deep inside, I understood him. I understood his fears and his reluctance. I understood that his need to take care of the people he loved exceeded his need to do what made him happy. It didn't make it hurt any less.

"I won't be around forever." I wiped my face.

"I know."

That was the last thing we said to each other before we went to sleep. The next morning, he was gone, the only sign that he'd been there at all was the ache between my legs and the remnants of his smell on the pillow. It hurt like hell.

CHAPTER FORTY-SIX

"**S**O YOU'RE GOING TO PERSONALLY COLLECT PAYMENT FROM NOW on?" Santiago asked from behind the counter. "I thought you had guys doing that for you."

"I do." I walked up to the counter. "I'm not here on business."

"What are you here for?" He raised an eyebrow, expression weary.

"I'm in love with your daughter—"

"Nope. I'm not having this conversation with you." He went back to his task of counting inventory.

"Did she tell you about the football player she went out with?"

His face soured. "The QB for the Jets? Yeah."

"And you're going to just let this happen?" I asked, since I knew if there was a person on this planet who hated them more than me, it was Santiago, the die-hard Miami Dolphins fan. Of course, he hated my Patriots too, but I could set that rivalry aside for now.

"I'm not going to give you my blessing to date my daughter," he said after a moment.

"I don't need it, you know," I said. "She made it clear that she didn't care what you or Santi said about us."

He faltered, pausing on the box of cigarettes in his hands. "So why are you here then?"

"Because she doesn't deserve for the men in her life to be against each other."

He pursed his lips. "I'd rather take my chances with the quarterback."

A wave of anger hit me, but I pushed it out. "That's not gonna happen."

He studied me for a long moment. I had to hand it to him, after what he'd seen me do the other night, and all the things he could probably imagine me doing, I was surprised he could still size me up like this. "Get out of my store, Dominic."

With a heavy sigh, I did, but only because I'd be back tomorrow.

❧

"Mister Mayor, I don't think we've formally met," I said, holding back my amusement at the way William Hamilton's eyes widened as he looked at me.

"No, but I know who you are." To his credit, he held his hand out for me to shake. I took it, shook it, and smiled. "Are you here on behalf of our mutual . . . friend?" he asked begrudgingly, looking away.

"Nope." I chuckled. "He's in Chicago with his wife."

"Hm." He looked over at me again. "I can't imagine you're here to sit on Santa's lap."

"Nah." I looked over at the Santa Claus he was referring to.

His people put this free event together every year. Pictures with Santa, food for their dinner tables, and firefighters from local stations giving away toys. If I didn't have a deep sense of mistrust for politicians in general, I'd probably vote for this guy every election. He was a bit of an asshole to us, but at least he was good to the people that really mattered.

"I'm here to ask for a favor," I said. "More like quid pro quo."

"I'm listening." He kept his eyes on Santa, just as I did.

"I heard that some of your backers want you to take down Tempt so they can swoop in and buy the land."

"How'd you hear that?" He bristled.

"People talk." I shrugged.

"What's the favor?"

"I want you to shut it down this weekend."

"This . . . it's Friday."

"I know, I have a calendar." I held up the firefighter calendar I'd been given when I walked in.

"And you need it shut down the entire weekend?"

"Yes."

"What reason would I have to shut it down?"

"I figured you could come up with one. You seemed to have a million of them at your disposal when you were trying to halt construction on the ballet theatre last year."

He gave a high-pitched laugh. "It would take me hours to find someone to sign off on such a thing on short notice."

"Really?" I shot him a look. "Your father is a judge."

"On the right side of the law."

"That's cute." I tossed the calendar on the table next to us. "I'll tell you what, I'm going to give you my phone number. If you can make this happen by tonight, I'll take care of your little issue with Tommy Costello, and you'll be toasting with your donors by Monday."

His brows furrowed. "And if I can't make this happen?"

"I can't answer that. I don't know what Tommy will do if he finds out you're trying to push him out of his beloved club for your own gain. The only thing I can guarantee is that he's out for blood these days." I grinned, plucked his cell phone out of his hand, shoved it in his face to unlock it, and typed in my number. I pressed it and waited until mine rang before giving it back. "Perfect. I hope to hear from you soon. Pleasure doing business with you, Mr. Mayor."

Nico laughed when I reached him. "I don't know what you said to him, but he looked like he was one second away from pissing himself."

"If he doesn't come through on this, he'll be doing a lot more than pissing himself." I walked out the door and back to my car. It was going to be a long weekend, but once this was over, I'd have Rosie again.

❧

"We meet again." Gio's voice boomed through the space as he walked in.

"Someone's in a good mood," I said, sitting back in my seat when I saw Loren walking in behind him looking equally as happy. "What the fuck is happening?"

"We got drone footage of Joe," Loren explained as they took their usual seats.

"And this is a good thing?" I asked.

"It's great, considering it was what got him on the phone with me," Gio said.

"How'd that conversation go?" Dean asked.

"Well, Catalina led the conversation, so you can imagine how it went," Gio said.

"She ripped him apart," Loren said, laughing.

"She did." Gio chuckled, shaking his head. "But . . ." He drummed his hands on the table. "Guess who we're meeting with, so that he can verbally announce that he no longer has any stake in anything that has the name Masseria tied to it?"

"We?" Rocco asked.

"Obviously your dad," I said.

"And Giuseppe. And Angelo. And we're also meeting with the heads of the Russian, Turkish, and Mexican cartels."

"Oh, so all of Epcot," I said.

Rocco snickered beside me. "Why are we meeting with them?"

"Mostly to make sure that we're keeping the peace, but we're also setting an agreement in place that prohibits anyone from going after our wives and kids."

"Huh." I rocked back in my chair again. "When is this worldly meeting happening?"

"Tonight."

"Tonight?" I sat up straight. "Is Tommaso going to be at this meeting?"

"Do you want him to be?" Gio raised an eyebrow.

"I have other plans for him."

"Care to elaborate?" Loren said.

"I'm going to burn down Tempt," I announced. "With him inside."

"Of course you are." Dean shook his head, pointing between myself, Rocco, and Gio. "You three have a fire kink."

"You have a fucking wolf kink," I said.

Everyone laughed. Dean didn't.

"Is he going or not? Who's handing out invitations for this?"

"Angelo."

I looked at Loren. "Would he tell Tommy?"

"He wants Tommy gone, so no, but Tommy does business with the rest of Epcot, like you say, so they might tell him."

"Fuck." My knee started bouncing. "I won't be able to sit across from him and not slash his throat."

"Then it's a good thing we're in the 2020s and we have virtual meetings," Gio said.

"We're meeting through a computer?" Dean asked, his face scrunching. "Why? What happened to traditions?"

"Stop acting like a senior citizen," Rocco said, then looked back at Gio. "At what time is this meeting?"

"Tonight at midnight."

Midnight. As long as the doofus that was WilAnthony Hamilton texted me by nine, I should be able to get rid of him by then. I'd get rid of him, go to the meeting, celebrate that he was gone, we'd move in on his territory, and then I could go get Rosie.

CHAPTER FORTY-SEVEN

"IF I EVER GET MARRIED, THIS IS WHERE I WANT MY RECEPTION TO be," I said, taking a sip of the wine Jimmy handed me.

Apparently, I was a wine drinker now. We were in The Bay Room, standing by the window that faced the Empire State Building. The venue had a 360° view of the city, and we'd already stood in front of the others, in awe.

"It is a beautiful view," he agreed.

"I've lived here for ten years and I'm still in awe of it," I said. "Then again, I've only seen it from up here twice and never at night."

"Really?" Jimmy smiled but seemed distracted, looking over his shoulder every five seconds. "I'm glad I brought you."

"Can you stop acting so nervous?" I whispered.

"Can I stop?" His eyes widened. "These guys hate me."

"They don't hate you, Jimmy," I said, hoping I sounded more convinced than I felt, because I was pretty sure they hated him. I guessed it made sense, being that Jimmy was here to steal the current QB's job.

"It doesn't help that Jessa's dating him." His mood soured when he said her name. He glanced over his shoulder again. She hadn't arrived yet, and that had him on edge.

"I still think it's wild that she's dating the guy you took the job from." I hid a smile behind my glass. "It's kind of badass on your part, really."

"Well, it's not like I purposely took his job." He shot me a look. "And I thought I was going to marry her. I would've given up the damn job."

I felt my heart clawing up my throat, so I drank another sip of wine. Dominic hadn't even contacted me since he left my apartment the other night, and this guy was willing to give up millions of dollars for a girl who turned out to be the world's biggest asshole.

"You're a good guy, Jimmy Ryan."

"Thanks." He smiled.

"Hanging out with you is so much fun that I don't even want to take your money." I raised a finger from the stem of my wine glass and added. "I don't want to, but I'm going to anyway."

He laughed. "This is exactly how women get sugar daddies."

"I mean, if you're suggesting you'd like to be my sugar daddy, I may be open to it." I smiled as I looked away from him and back to the city.

He stiffened next to me. "Jessa's here."

I looked around as nonchalantly as I could. I knew it was her the moment I saw her. She was blonde and beautiful and looked like someone who would be married to Jimmy, for sure, with her award-winning smile and the way her blue eyes lit up with it. I looked at the man behind her, tall like Jimmy, older but with the same type of athletic body, and a perfect smile. Okay, so Jessa had a type. I faced the city again.

"She's okay." I shrugged. Jimmy laughed. I glanced up at him. "You know you can put your hand on my shoulder, or we can hold hands or whatever, right? I mean, if we're going to do this, we should really do this, right?" I paused. "I'm not sure that kissing is a good idea since I'll probably have to see you at some point in the future because of the Veronica and Patty connection."

"I would never kiss you." His brows rose. "You said you didn't even kiss Dominic the other day, and from what you've told me about him, well, I'd like all of my limbs to remain intact."

I rolled my eyes, transferred the glass to my other hand, and put my hand in Jimmy's. He took a deep breath as if bracing himself for something to happen.

"You realize Dominic isn't going to shoot you just because you're holding my hand, right?" I asked. "Besides, as far as I'm concerned, I can do whatever I want."

"Yeah, because you know he wouldn't hurt *you*." He raised an eyebrow. "He hates the Jets, and his girlfriend is holding the hand of their new QB. I don't even own a gun and I'd shoot me."

At that, I laughed. "Friendly reminder that I'm not his girlfriend."

"Friendly reminder that he probably still sees you as such."

My lips twisted. "Do you see Jessa as yours?"

"No." He scowled.

"What did you do when you found out she was cheating with that unemployed asshole?"

"He's not unemployed." Jimmy smiled. "We got into a fight in the middle of a game."

My brows rose. "I bet ESPN had a field day with that one."

"Try field *month*, and when I was traded and took his job?" He shook his head. "They still haven't stopped talking about it."

"Ah, so the animosity makes sense." I looked around again. "They seem cool though; I bet once they get to know you, it'll be fine."

"Yeah."

"What'd you do to Jessa?"

"Nothing."

"Nothing at all?" I blinked, turning to face him slightly. Our held hands were dangling between our bodies, but we were definitely leaving room for Jesus, as my mom used to say, and I wondered if getting closer would be more convincing.

"I mean, I yelled at her." He took a sip of his wine. "She'd been seeing him for months. What could I do?"

"You could've shoved all of her clothes in a bag and set it

on fire, and then you could've snuck into his house and set that shit on fire while he wasn't home. They'd live, but at least they knew they messed with the wrong guy," I said. Jimmy's expression shifted and I laughed at his sudden change of mood. "I'm kidding. Geez. But yeah, I guess you can't really do that if you're a famous—"

"I guess it's a good thing I would never cheat on you." His voice rumbled from behind me, and my heart instantly dropped into the pit of my stomach as I whipped around.

He was wearing a tux. His dark hair, which had been tousled when I last saw him, was brushed back to perfection, his beard trimmed and perfectly lined up. God, he looked like he could play the role of a tattooed 007. When I finished drinking him in and met his eyes again, they were twinkling and snapped me right out of my reverie.

"What are you doing here?"

He arched an eyebrow. "It's a paid event, open to any Jets fan with a large enough bank account."

"You hate the Jets."

"Hate is a strong word," he said, eyes dancing.

My eyes dropped to the lapel of his jacket. "You're wearing a New England Patriots pin."

That only made him grin, that wolfish, sexy grin he must have known drove me insane.

"Considering that both times I've seen her, I've heard how much you hate the Jets, I'd say hate is the correct word," Jimmy said behind me.

"Go Jets," Nico said, coming up to stand beside him. He was holding a plate full of hors d'oeuvres.

"What the hell, Nico?" I whispered. "You're in on this?"

"Hey, I wasn't going to miss this event."

"Traitor." My eyes narrowed.

"You two are more alike than you think." He chuckled, lifting the tiny fork he'd been using for the clams on his plate and pointed it between me and Dominic. I rolled my eyes. He smiled at Jimmy. "Great to see you again, Ryan."

"Yeah. You too." Jimmy sounded like he couldn't quite understand what was happening.

"I don't know what this is, but I'm here on business," I whisper-shouted to Dominic.

"Are you?" His jaw twitched as he nodded toward my hand, which was holding onto Jimmy's for dear life.

"The handholding was her idea," he said, somehow managing to get his hand out of my grip.

"I told you he wouldn't shoot you for that," I huffed.

Dominic's eyes glittered. "You told him I wouldn't shoot him for holding your hand?"

"Yes."

"You have a lot of faith in me, tiny dancer." His chuckle sounded forced, dangerous. My heart started beating a little faster.

"I do," I said quietly. "Not that it matters anymore."

"It matters."

"Not anymore." I drained the last of my wine, set it on the tray walking by, and picked up another. "You need to leave."

"I paid for these tickets."

"Dominic." I sighed heavily and inched closer to him, so close that I could smell the scent of his cologne and felt like I might just pass out. "It's taking everything in me not to slap you right now."

"Do you want me to leave you alone to your scheming?" He shrugged. "Give me five minutes of your time and I will, as long as it doesn't involve kissing or number five on the questionnaire."

"What's number five on the questionnaire?" Jimmy asked, genuinely curious.

Nico laughed even harder and patted him on the back. "I love this guy."

Dominic swung his glare from me to Nico momentarily.

"Number five on the questionnaire is fair game," I said. "We're both single."

"Roselyn." Dominic's jaw was set.

"I'm going to go—" Jimmy started.

"I'll go with you," Nico said.

They walked away.

"I'm going to kill you for this," I gritted.

"I already told you, dying by your hands—"

"Shut up." I put a hand up. "Just shut up and tell me what you're doing here."

"Five minutes of your time."

I rolled my eyes and took a deep breath, but followed him out of the room, into the hall, and stood quietly next to him as we waited for the elevator to arrive. In the elevator, I kept my distance as he pushed down a button for a random floor. How I managed not to scream as I stood there, I wasn't sure, but I took the time to breathe and rein in my emotions. Still, how dare he show up the other night and then vanish without another word and then show up here, looking like the star of a fucking action movie and expecting me to just, what, crawl back to him? Yeah, right.

"Penny for your thoughts," he said.

"Trust me, you don't want my thoughts right now." I crossed my arms.

He chuckled. It was low and sexy and annoyed me to no end. When the doors opened up on the sixth floor, he let me step out first and followed. The building was smack in the middle of the financial district, and it was Saturday night, so I wasn't surprised to find we were in a huge empty office space with endless cubicles.

"Don't tell me you own this," I said, arms still crossed.

"No." He frowned, looking around. "It's a more private option than the lobby."

"Why do we need privacy? Why are you here?"

He took a deep breath. "Can I kiss you?"

"What?" My voice was so loud, I was pretty sure they heard it upstairs and in the Empire State Building. I tried again. "What? Dominic, do not tell me you paid twenty-thousand dollars to ask me to kiss you."

"I would've paid thirty."

"I can't with you." I rolled my eyes, crossing my arms again as I turned around and took a few steps into the empty lobby. He came up behind me, engulfing me with his long arms and pulling me flush against his chest. I shut my eyes, heart skipping a few beats. "Dominic."

"Do you still want me?" he asked against my hair.

"Dominic." It was a shaky warning.

"You look so goddamn beautiful in that dress." His arms tightened around me.

A shiver rolled through me. "You need to stop doing this."

"Do you want me?" he asked again, lowering his voice.

"We had this conversation already," I said, eyes still closed. "You know I do."

"Marry me."

"What?" My heart fell into my stomach. I pushed away from him and turned around. "What?"

"Marry me," he said. "It's the only way I can guarantee you'd be safe."

"Wh . . . You're asking me one of the most important questions you could ask a person, and it's just to keep me safe?" I blinked, trying to wrap my head around this. Had he seriously paid all that money *and* interrupted my four-thousand-dollar date to ask me this? Like this? "No."

"No?" He took a step back as if I'd hit him.

"You can't just buy expensive tickets to support a team you hate because you're jealous, and take me out of said event to tell me to marry you, and use that lame excuse as the reason." I crossed my arms again and started pacing, feeling like my heart might just explode on this floor. "No."

"Let me start over."

I stopped pacing and looked at him, waiting.

"*Wives* and children are off limits," he said. "We had a meeting. All the families, the whole fucking Epcot, and agreed to get back to abiding by rules that should have never been ignored."

This guy and Epcot. "Because of what happened in Providence?"

"That's a big part of the reason, since all these guys are next generation, my generation, we felt it bore repeating."

I nodded and looked down at the floor.

"Tommy's out."

"*Out?*" I glanced up. "Dead?"

"That umbrella company you heard about? Someone practically rose from the dead and tried to take over; the rest of Epcot didn't like that, and Tommy was their only link to the Italians." He sighed heavily, running a hand through his hair. "We don't have time to discuss all of the details since you have to get back to that." He pointed a finger up and shut his eyes for a second. "I'll explain it later, but right now, I need to know if you want to be with me."

"Because of this agreement?" I let out a humorless laugh. "Do they need my birth certificate too? My fucking social? Why do they need my answer right now?"

"I need it," he growled, taking a step forward and erasing the space between us. "Not because of this agreement, but because I'm losing my mind without you, Roselyn. I need to know if you're all in or not."

"This is a lot," I whispered. "This isn't how I envisioned someone asking me to marry them."

He glanced to the side. "We're right next to the Empire State. People come from all over the country to propose here."

"To propose there." I pointed at the building. "And they usually get down on one knee, and they—"

Before I could finish my sentence, he fell to both knees, reached for my hands, and looked up at me like the fate of the world depended on my answer, like he couldn't survive another moment without it. "Marry me."

"Dominic." I choked back tears. "Stand up."

"Marry me."

"That's not a question." I inhaled shakily, taking one hand from his to catch my tears before they had a chance to fall. "Please stand up."

He stood slowly and leaned in, setting his forehead against mine. "Is it because you don't want me or because your family hates me?"

I shut my eyes. Traditional proposals were practically fossilized these days, but I knew my father expected to be asked for my hand in marriage. I also knew he'd never say yes to Dominic. I made myself open my eyes and look at him.

"I want you," I whispered.

His entire body seemed to sag with relief. He brought his hands to either side of my face and just looked at me for the longest moment. "Can I kiss you now?"

"I mean, I gu—"

His lips were on mine before I could finish the sentence, his low growl setting my insides on fire, his tongue taking my breath away with each stroke against mine. "God, I needed you," he murmured against my mouth before going back in for more. I was breathless when we pulled away, my hands gripping the lapels of his jacket so tight, I was sure they'd need to be dry cleaned before he went back upstairs. He pulled me against his chest, breathing hard as he held me. I kept my eyes on the Empire State Building, wondering how many people were being proposed to right now, with the beautiful fluffy snow twinkling in their pictures. I didn't know how long we stood there before I pulled away and looked up at him again.

"Dom."

He cupped my face. "Yes, baby?"

"Why do you smell like a forest fire?"

The smile that spread over his face screamed danger. "I was solving a problem."

I shook my head, took another breath, and leaned against him for another second. I did not even want to know what kind of problem-solving required a fire, especially since I knew he wasn't burning someone's clothes like I'd been threatening to do theoretically.

CHAPTER FORTY-EIGHT

Dominic

"I T'S A NICE FUCKING SPACE," I SAID PROUDLY.

I was standing with Rocco, Dean, Gio, and Loren in the middle of the space we were in the midst of repairing. It wasn't very big; there was only one bar and enough room for thirty-five people, according to the fire inspector, but it was fucking badass.

"I still think we should've gone with the sex club they were trying to sell us," Gio said.

"Yeah?" Rocco raised an eyebrow. "So your wife could cut your balls off in front of everyone?"

"Fuck you." Gio laughed.

"It's true though." Rocco shrugged.

"You'll need at least four bartenders to take shifts," Loren said. "The bar is beautiful."

I turned to it. "Dad said it was a bar on the actual *Titanic*."

"Yeah right." Rocco scoffed. "More like a Titanic-themed restaurant."

"It's still nice," I said. I looked at my watch.

"You've looked at your watch ten times since we got here. You got somewhere to be?" Loren asked.

"Yes, actually. I have a meeting in twenty minutes."

"A meeting," Dean said. "You mean with Rosie's dad, who you're still trying to convince you're not the piece of shit you actually are?"

"Fuck you." I scowled. "How do you know about that?"

He shot me a look.

"Don't you have wolves to take care of or something?"

"Hilarious, De Luca."

"Right back at you, Russo."

"Is her dad coming around?" Gio asked.

"No." That was Rocco. "Mr. Vega hates our guts."

"Good luck with that." Loren shook his head. "Fathers-in-law are tricky."

"Well, yours is Frankenstein's Monster, so you'd know." I smiled at the look he gave me, and then at the glare Gio shot me. "That's my cue to leave."

"Fuck you, De Luca," Loren shouted as I walked out, laughing.

The past week had been a blur. With the Costellos officially out, we'd had to split territories with the rest of the Epcot bunch. We kept what we wanted, though, and gave them what was rightfully theirs. Joe Masseria agreed to stay out of anything he'd had his hands in before and just keep what his wife left to him by default. According to Gio, their father had promised Catalina and Emma that he'd completely gotten rid of the human trafficking ring their mother had set up. I wasn't sure if I'd trust a man who faked his death, but it wasn't my place to intervene. That left me with the issue of Roselyn. I hadn't seen her in three days and I was dying. She had performances, though, and I kept telling myself that because of that, the distance was fine. It wasn't fine. I wasn't fine with it. Part of me wanted to show up at the ballet, carry her all the way back to my house, and lock her in there, but I was pacing myself. One thing at a time.

CHAPTER FORTY-NINE

Rosie

>Yari: bro why do all the fun things happen when I'm away?

>Me: are you reading the wrong texts? What is fun about that?!

>Yari: you went on a date with a HOT AF guy and your HOT AF boyfriend showed up and asked you to marry you

>Me: told me. He TOLD me to marry him

>Yari: that's fucking hot. Admit it.

>Me: *eye roll emoji*

>Yari: just sayin'. What's up with the hot football player tho? Is he single?

>Me: IDK. I played matchmaker and he left with one of his teammates' sister's number lol

>Yari: soon you'll turn Oui into a dating service and be the CEO

I laughed as I put my phone away and looked out the window. Marco was driving me to my dad's house and had taken the long way since there was an accident on the usual route. It was yet another reason taking the train would probably have been faster, but I didn't want to argue. Besides, it was cold as hell outside and warm in this car. My smile faltered when we neared the street Tempt was on. I hadn't been around here in so long, and even though I knew Tommy and Anthony were no longer able to get to me, the feeling remained. When it came into view, I had to make myself look at it, but what I saw was not what I'd expected. I sat back in my seat and did a triple-take.

"What happened there?"

"There was a fire."

"Oh my God." I set my hand on my chest. "When?"

"Last week."

Last week. I thought about the night Dominic showed up at the event telling me to marry him and smelling like a forest fire. "Were there people inside?" I whispered.

"The club was shut down," Marco said.

"Oh." I breathed out. "So no one died?"

"No innocent people were injured." His eyes met mine in the rearview.

No innocent people. Interesting choice of words, but I wouldn't expect any less from these guys. I didn't say anything else as we approached my dad's neighborhood. What was there to say, though? Is this who I would become? A person who hears about people dying and shrugs it away just because they weren't innocent? When we reached the curb, I was surprised to find the other SUV already there and Adio standing outside.

"Are you switching this early?" I asked.

"Yeah. I have some things to do. Adio will take you home." Marco got out of the car and opened the door for me. He walked me up to the door and waited for my dad to answer.

"Sir," Marco said.

Dad looked at him and gave a terse nod before opening the door a little wider for me. He never greeted them, which was so unlike him. Dad was the kind of guy who walked into an elevator and said hello, walked into a quiet store and said hello, but he never gave these guys that courtesy. Marco waited until I walked inside before walking away. Normally, that bothered me, but tonight I was already upset at Dominic's lack of communication and was just waiting to get into an argument with someone. In this case, it was going to be my father, because these last few weeks, he'd been a complete jerk; not just to those guys, but to Santi as well, and I'd been biding my time until Santi wasn't here and it was just the two of us. so I could really give him a piece of my mind.

"You could say hi, you know," I said. "They've done nothing but protect me."

"So I've heard." Dad shut the door behind me. I turned around and gave him the fastest kiss on the cheek I'd ever given him. "What was that?"

"Nothing." I looked around. "Where's Santi?"

"He just stepped out to get something."

"Good. I've been meaning to talk to you. The way you've been treating him lately is total bullshit."

"Roselyn."

"No. You want to lecture us about our language? Maybe try treating people with respect first." I turned around to take a breath and looked at the table. "Is Vicky coming?"

"Yes," he snapped.

I looked up at him. "What the heck is wrong with you?"

"I'm just a little out of sorts," he said.

"A little out of sorts," I repeated. "What happened?"

"Your boyfriend came by."

Oh God. My heart stopped beating. "What did he want? What did he say?"

"He was talking about marriage."

"What? Oh, God." I set a hand on my stomach and reached for the nearest chair. "I need to sit down."

"He says he's done with the thug life." Dad's lips twisted. His eyes snapped to mine. "What? Why are you shaking your head like that?"

"Because it's Dominic, not Tupac."

Dad scoffed. "Have you seen how many tattoos the guy has?"

I rolled my eyes. "So that's it? He came to tell you he was done with 'the thug life'?"

"He came to ask for your hand in marriage."

Holy shit. He'd actually done it. I was so grateful to be sitting down because I felt like I was about to faint. I buried my face in my hands and breathed. What I wanted to do was cover my ears because I really didn't want to hear the rest of it. I could only imagine how that conversation must have gone down. Had Santi been present? Ugh. I hoped not.

"What did you say?" I asked, muffled.

"I said no."

I dropped my hands. "You said no?"

"Of course I said no." He shrugged and turned to the food on the stove.

"And you think, what, that this is going to keep me from seeing him?"

"I'm your father."

"And?"

"And that's it. Do I need more of a reason?" He raised an eyebrow.

"Actually, yes. I respect that you're my father. I respect *you*." I stood up. "But that doesn't mean you have the right to tell me who I can and can't see. I'm twenty-seven."

"You'll be twenty-seven next week."

"You know what I mean, Papi. You can't . . . I mean . . ." I growled, throwing my hands up as I started pacing. "God, you're as impossible as he is." I stopped pacing and laughed, setting a hand on my hip. "That's the funniest part, you know? You have more in common than you think."

"I can't argue there."

I shook my head slowly. "I can't believe you said no."

"You wanted me to say yes?"

"Obviously." I shot him a look.

"Why?" His face pulled like he was genuinely confused.

"Because I love him," I shouted, throwing my hands up. "Why else, Papi?"

He set down the spoon he'd been using to serve the beans from a platter and turned to me. "You need to think about this, Roselyn. Do you really think he's worth the trouble? You actually trust him to keep you safe?"

"I know he's worth the trouble, and he's the person I trust the most in the whole fucking world to keep me safe and otherwise." I gasped a breath, wiping hot, angry tears away from my face quickly. I buried my face in my hands again and walked away, still crying. "God, I seriously hate this."

Arms wrapped around me, and I stiffened at the width of them, the strength. I held a breath in and let it out shakily, another sob leaving my chest, making me cry harder. He kissed the top of my head.

"I hate you," I mumbled through my hands.

"Really?" Dominic asked, amusement clear in his voice. "I heard you love me."

I couldn't help it. I laughed and dropped my hands. I pulled back to look up at him. He was wearing a suit, his hair brushed back. I frowned. "Where are you going?"

"Nowhere."

I blinked, wiping my face again. "What is happening? I feel like I've stepped into another dimension."

Dominic sank down to one knee and brought out a small ring box. I gasped loudly, my hands coming up to cover my mouth as I felt the tears instantly come back. His eyes crinkled with his smile. "Roselyn Vega, my tiny dancer, my favorite person on the planet, will you be my wife?"

"Jesus Christ, Dominic." I sobbed harder.

"I asked this time. I got down on one knee. I asked for permission." He raised an eyebrow. "Did I miss any steps?"

"No." I shook my head hard and doubled over, hands still over my face as I cried. He moved a little on his knee, leaning in to pick up my hair and throw it around my shoulder, away from my face.

"No?" he asked, his voice almost a husky whisper. I wiped my face, took a breath, and lowered my hands to look at him.

"No, you didn't miss any steps," I said shakily, feeling like any minute, I'd start crying again.

"Oh." He breathed. "Will you marry me?"

I threw my arms around his neck and kissed the side of his face over and over.

"I'm going to take this as a yes." His chuckle rumbled against me.

I pulled away, leaving my hands on his shoulders. "It's a hell yes."

His grin was wider than I'd ever seen it, as he took my hand and slid the ring onto my finger. My eyes widened at the familiar stone.

"Dominic," I whispered. I was full out, chest-heaving crying now. I wiped my nose with the back of my right hand and tried hard to wipe my face, but I couldn't.

"I thought about giving you my mother's ring, but we both have brothers, so the three of us came to an agreement," he said. "Half of your mother's stone and half of mine." He kissed the back of my hand as he stood and cupped my face, wiping my tears with his thumbs. "I love you, baby."

I hiccupped a laugh. "I love you too, you sneaky, devious, tricky, hot, gorgeous, most beautiful man I've ever seen."

He laughed against my lips before he pulled me into a slow, deep kiss that I felt from head to toe. When I pulled back, he took a step to the side and let me see that my brother and Gabe were both standing there, smiles on their faces and phones pointed at us.

I turned to my dad behind us. "So I'm assuming you didn't say no?"

"Oh, I said no." He shrugged. "I said no the entire first

week, but when he showed up a few days ago, I couldn't take it anymore."

"You really are sneaky." I looked up at him. He pulled me to his side and kissed the top of my head.

"Only when I'm surprising you with something good." He pulled me into a kiss again. "By the way, Nico's taking your clothes to my house as we speak."

"What?" I pulled away. "Dominic!"

"I want my wife in my bed."

"Your fiancée," I said, smiling wide.

"Mine." He kissed me one more time before Santi and Gabe rushed over to hug and congratulate us.

We set the table, laughing and talking. When we were about to sit down, Dad held a finger up and walked outside. I leaned over to see what he was doing and saw Adio and Marco wiping their shoes on the rug and brushing the snow off their jackets. Dad gave them plates and told them to pull up whatever chair they could find, and we all sat around the table like that. A family. For the first time in a long time, I felt happy, and free, and loved, and safe.

EPILOGUE

"**Y**OU KNOW ROSIE'S GOING TO KILL YOU, RIGHT?" ROCCO SET the other side of the couch down in my new living room, *our* new living room.

"She might."

I hadn't exactly told her that I bought us a house, so I wasn't sure what her reaction to this surprise was going to be. Cat and Isabel were bringing her over here after their girls' night out. Cat had her pack a bag under the guise that they'd be staying at her and Loren's house. I told her to start sneakily recording Rosie's face when they drove past their house and parked two houses down in our driveway.

"I'm thinking she's going to be upset for two minutes and then freak out because the house is nice as hell," Jimmy said, bringing in a lamp.

I smiled. The guy may be the enemy on the field, but he was actually pretty cool. Besides, Rosie liked hanging out with him and that meant that he was forced to hang out with me. Every time she told me that there was no need for me to be around all the time since they were just friends, I reminded her that his ex-fiancée probably said the same thing about the guy she was with now, and that shut her right up. Even if I hadn't known that fact, there was no way in hell my Rosie was going to hang out alone with the nation's most eligible bachelor. The guy was the spokesperson for a shampoo company, for fuck's sake.

"It's a second home," I said. "We're still going to live in the city."

"I'd live here," Jimmy said, looking around.

"Yeah, well, there are a few houses for sale, one block over," I said. "You and your Pantene hair are not moving in here."

He laughed. Rocco shook his head.

"Brought beer, wine, and water," Gio announced from the door. He looked around. "Damn, this is nice."

"You need more furniture," Lorenzo said walking in behind him. "The echo is annoying."

"The only furniture I bought was this couch, side table, and lamp because Rosie pointed the out at the store. I'm not buying anything else without her."

"Sure, nothing else without her, just a fucking mansion," Rocco said with a shrug. "No biggie."

"Holy fuck." That was Gabe as he walked in. "This is way nicer in person."

"Did you assholes park where I told you?" I shot them all a pointed look.

"All the cars are in Loren's driveway," Gio said, looking at his phone. "Isabel says they're a block away."

I took a deep breath and walked to the window. Marco pulled up, parked in front of the house, and opened the door for the three of them. Rosie was talking to Cat about something, probably ballet-related, since Cat somehow managed to convince her to dance in the opening of her new ballet theatre. The historic theatre Gio purchased for her. And they wanted to tell me this was an exuberant gift. Isabel and Yari were having a separate conversation. When they got close to the door, I rushed over and opened it for them. Cat, Isabel, and Yari stood behind her, holding back a laugh as Rosie looked from me, into the house, and back to me, in confusion.

"Dominic." She eyed me warily.

I grinned. "Yes, baby?"

"Whose house is this and why are you opening the door?" she asked. I grinned wider. She looked like she was about to slap me, but I couldn't stop smiling. "What did you do?"

I laughed at the look on her face. She was so fucking adorable.

"Dominic." She glared at me as she brushed past me and walked into the house. She completely ignored everyone standing there and took it in, shaking her head, jaw on the floor. When she looked at me again, tears shone in her eyes. Her voice softened. "Seriously?"

I walked up and swept her into my arms. "Do you like it?"

"Like it?" she squeaked. I set her down slowly. "I love it. When did you do this?"

I took a deep breath. "This is only the second time I've been here."

"When did you buy it?" she asked again.

"I started negotiating a while back."

"When is a while back?" She narrowed her eyes.

"Monday after Thanksgiving."

"You are . . . I can't believe you." She shook her head. "I mean, I *can*, because it's you, but seriously, Dom? This is insane. It's way too big for us."

"It's way too big for us right now." I kissed her lips. "It won't be way too big for us when we start a family."

"Oh. A family?" She raised an eyebrow.

"What was it that you told me when I said it would be cute to see little Dominican-Italian babies running around?" Rocco asked. I shot him a look. He smiled. "Oh yeah, he said Rosie didn't even want kids."

Rosie laughed.

"It doesn't matter. We can fill it up with dogs for all I care," I said quickly. The minute she turned away, still laughing, I pointed at Rocco and mouthed, "I'm going to murder you."

He laughed louder and went over to the kitchen where everyone else was pouring themselves drinks and ordering pizza.

"I really don't care." I turned to face her. "About the kids thing, I mean."

"Hey, Dom." She was smiling hard as she wrapped her arms around me. "I want kids. With you."

I shut my eyes for a moment to settle my heart because I was pretty sure it was going to explode, and the nearest hospital was fifteen minutes away. When I looked at her again, I kissed her hard once, twice, three times.

"So you're not mad at me?"

She looked around again, a happy sigh leaving her. "Do you know how much furniture we have to buy to fill this place?"

"Yep." I kissed her forehead. "I'll give you my card." I raised my voice as I looked at Jimmy and said, "No spending limit."

Everyone laughed hard, including Rosie, including me.

She looked up at me. "You know how some women are all 'oh my gosh, I could never spend his money?'"

"I don't know anyone who would say that." I frowned but was still smiling. "Where is this going?"

"I'm not one of those women. You definitely need to give me a spending limit."

I wrapped my arms around her again. "Why don't we meet with Lorenzo, and he can go over finances and set a spending limit?"

"I thought you said he was a cheap bastard?" Rosie said.

Lorenzo threw his head back with what sounded like something between a groan and a chuckle. The sound of laughter bounced off the bare walls, and even though I wanted to savor that moment forever, I knew there were many more to come.

ACKNOWLEDGEMENTS

Publishing a book really does take a village. Most of the time, I thank them personally and don't include these since they overwhelm me, but I'm going to try to thank some people here. If I don't thank you, I'M SORRY!

Valentine PR, all of you, but especially Kim Cermak, Kelly Beckham, and of course, Nina Grinstead

People who worked on this book:

Hang Le—I'm so happy we started working together and vibe so well because otherwise I don't know what I'd do with myself when I have a cool idea that I can't execute lol

Stacey Blake (Champagne Book Design)—you are a gem

Liza Trice, Gina Licciardi (whom I've known since MIDDLE SCHOOL!), Ashlee (Ashes & Vellichor), Janett Corona, Rea Loftis, Sarah Sentz, and I KNOW I'm missing people (which is why I hate doing this lol)

Special shout-out to:

Everyone in the Claire's Crew group, everyone who interacts with me on TikTok, IG, and Twitter. Everyone who leaves a review after reading my book and helps another reader make up their mind on whether or not they want to read it.

All of the bloggers, YouTubers, Bookstagrammers, and BookTok reviewers—I don't always respond to everything I'm tagged in, but I do see it and appreciate you more than I can ever express to you. You give me life. You're the reason I was able to come back to this series. I seriously love you all.

My family:

Christian—who built a beautiful desk for me and lets me work in peace (most of the time)

Abe & Moses—my biggest cheerleaders and the reason I work so hard. Thank you letting me disappear into my office for hours, sharing cool story ideas that "I should write", and telling me I'm an awesome author (even though you haven't read my books since you're not allowed to yet lol)

Hendrix—my Frenchie, my "favorite child", who obv can't read, but is my companion and puts up with me talking to myself ALL DAY and I feel like that deserves a shout-out lol

ALSO BY CLAIRE

Read Lorenzo & Catalina's story: BECAUSE YOU'RE MINE

Want more romantic suspense?

Try my secret society series:

HALF TRUTHS (dark academia)

TWISTED CIRCLES (dark academia)

Want contemporary romance?

THE PLAYER (sports romance)

KALEIDOSCOPE HEARTS (brother's best friend, second chance romance)

PAPER HEARTS (second chance)

ELASTIC HEARTS (grumpy, sunshine romance)

THE HEARTBREAKER (College, sports romance)

THE RULEBREAKER (college, sports romance, friends-to-lovers)

THE TROUBLEMAKER (college sports romance)

CATCH ME (music industry romance)

THE TROUBLE WITH LOVE (office romance)

THE CONSEQUENCE OF FALLING (enemies-to-lovers)

THEN THERE WAS YOU (enemies-to-lovers, second chance)

Want royal romance?

THE SINFUL KING

THE NAUGHTY PRINCESS

THE WICKED PRINCE

Want something a little different?

FABLES & OTHER LIES (gothic romance)

Want a quickie?

FAKE LOVE

ClaireContrerasbooks.com

Twitter:
@ClariCon

Insta:
ClaireContreras

Facebook:
www.facebook.com/groups/ClaireContrerasBooks